FORD'S FIGHT

WAGNER BRIGADE

BOOK ONE

ASHLEY A QUINN

TCA PUBLISHING LLC

ISBN is 978-1-959943-19-8
Library of Congress Control Number: 2023914726

ONE

Heels click-clacking on the marble floor, the sound echoing through the cavernous foyer. Brooke McGinty made her way through her fiancé's home, brushing a bead of sweat off her forehead. It might be September, but it was North Carolina, and she'd been rushing. When she left her office forty-five minutes ago, she thought she would be late for their dinner engagement. She got hung up with a demanding bride. The resort event planner, Mia, showed up at Brooke's office at her wit's end with the woman in tow two hours prior. The caterer had promised the bride a specific kind of caviar and could now no longer deliver. Mia had called around, but had little luck tracking down the brand the bride wanted. Brooke did her best to console the woman while she sent out emails to all her contacts, hoping someone had a line on a supply of the stuff for the Saturday wedding.

But all that put her behind, and Johnathan hated when she was late. The world operated on Johnathan Cassidy's time-line, and God forbid if you upset the balance. Once she ushered the slightly mollified bride out of her office, Brooke hightailed it to her house and changed clothes, forgoing a shower in favor of some deodorant and a quick spritz of her favorite perfume, then hopped in her car and hurried across the city to the Cassidy's massive estate. She was sure she'd be late, but the traffic gods smiled on her and she was actually a few minutes early.

Raised male voices carried from the rear of the house. She frowned, changing direction for the study rather than the front living room as she recognized Johnathan's voice. Leaving the marble-tiled entryway, the thick carpet in this part of the house muffled her footfalls. Getting closer, she recognized the second voice. It was his brother, Will.

"Are you sure you've thought this through all the way? I mean, hell, John, we're talking about murder here. If we get caught..."

Brooke froze, feet from the doorway. *Murder? What?*

"We won't get caught. It's not like I plan to bludgeon or shoot the old codger. He's ancient. No one will suspect anything but a heart attack."

Leaning against the wall, she edged closer. This had to be a prank. Johnathan saw her coming on the security monitor and roped Will into playing some sick joke on her. He couldn't be plotting the death of someone for real. Right?

A whisper of unease niggled her mind. Johnathan had a temper. He'd never laid a hand on her, but seeing him angry still terrified her. A stillness overcame him that turned his normally handsome face into a cold, emotionless mask.

"Why is this even necessary? You said you want to make sure you take over, but once you marry Brooke, you're a shoo-in. What's the rush?"

Brooke covered her mouth to hold back the squeal that wanted to break free. They were talking about murdering her grandfather! She shuffled closer. Taking her phone from her purse, she opened the camera app and set it to record video, then aimed the receiver at the door with a shaking hand.

"So, you know that blonde chick I brought to the party at Benton's a couple of weeks ago?"

"The one with legs for days?"

"That's the one. I'm not sleeping with her just for her looks. She works in the records room for the old man's personal attorney. I get all the files pertaining to him that come across her desk. We both have a good roll in bed, and she gets some pretty baubles. It's a win-win."

Anger turned Brooke's blood red-hot. She felt heat warm her cheeks as she clenched her teeth together to hold in the growl. The bastard not only wanted to take out her grandfather, he was sleeping around on her too? She shouldn't be surprised. Her relationship with Johnathan Cassidy wasn't a match made in heaven. It was more—expected. Two young people from two prominent families of marriageable age. And they didn't hate each other. He was good in bed. She hadn't seen any reason not to marry him. Love wasn't really one of her requirements for a happy marriage. She'd seen too many couples claiming to be madly in love, only to divorce a few years later because it wasn't enough. Brooke wanted someone compatible and dependable. Johnathan fit that bill.

Apparently, he wasn't as dependable as she'd thought if he was honing his bedroom skills with other women before coming home to her. She rolled her eyes and leaned closer to hear what else he had to say.

"Anyway, she brought me a copy of the changes he wants to make to his will. Brooke inherits his share of the business, but her dad will still become CEO. The old man stipulated, though, that if she sells within ten years after inheriting, she gets nothing from it. All the money goes to the family foundation."

"What happens if she dies before then?"

Brooke clamped her hand tighter over her mouth as she bit back a gasp. Would they want to murder her too?

"Ownership transfers to the foundation. Then it's theirs to do with as they please."

Will cursed.

"Exactly. Which is why we need to act quickly. Before he signs the papers. This is the perfect time to set something up. He'll be out of town for two more days."

"What about her dad? He's in line to become CEO. Do we take him out too?"

"I guess we'll have to. How else will I become CEO?"

Of all the nerve! Brooke ground her molars together to keep in the angry growl. If he thought she would let him get away with this, he had another think coming. She would record every word he said, then take it straight to the police. Then, once her family was safe, she'd tell her dad and grandpa. They could have the pleasure of firing him. Right after she threw her engagement ring in his face and told him to shove it where the sun didn't shine.

"Okay, so what do you have in mind?" Will asked.

The phone lit up in Brooke's hand, cutting off their conversation. The name of the bride she'd so recently ushered out of her office appeared on the display, and her ringtone echoed off the hallway walls.

"No! Crap!" She silenced it, but the damage was done. Conversation in the office ceased. Not waiting to see if they came out to investigate, she spun on her heel and hurried back the way she came. Confronting them was not part of her plan. Especially without backup.

"Brooke!"

She glanced back, heart pounding. Johnathan barreled down the hallway after her, that cold, emotionless mask on his face. Dread filled her belly, and she let out a short squeal, quickening her pace until she ran down the hall. Rounding the corner, she moved onto the tile floor, sliding a bit as her smooth-soled heels skidded on the slick marble floor. She slammed into the front door in her haste to exit, smacking her shoulder hard. Battling with the lever-action handle, she yanked it open and scurried down the steps, thanking the heavens she wore heels every day. She could run almost as well in them as she could in tennis shoes.

At the bottom of the steps, she turned right, heading for her silver BMW convertible, which gleamed in the bright September sunshine. Reaching the car, she yanked on the door handle and fell inside. A quick glance back showed Johnathan and Will exiting the house. Will pointed at her car, and they ran down the steps.

A sob broke free of her throat as she jammed her foot on the brake and stabbed the start button. The engine roared to life. Brooke didn't bother with her seatbelt. She put the car in drive, and with a squeal of tires, shot around the bend in the circular driveway. The car fishtailed as she straightened the wheel, exiting the curve.

Getting the vehicle under control, she sucked in a breath through her nose. She needed to get it together.

Think, think, think! She needed a plan. After seeing Johnathan's face, she had no doubt he knew she'd heard every word. But who could she go to? She knew she could take the conversation to the police, but would they believe it was real and not some joke? Sure, they'd said they wanted to kill her dad and grandpa, but they hadn't actually gotten around to outlining their plan. And Johnathan was buddy-buddy with the city's highest leadership.

Brooke clenched the steering wheel, then loosened her fingers, thinking. No. She couldn't go to them yet. They wouldn't do anything without more evidence.

There was always her grandfather. But he was in Asia. What could he do half a world away? Right now, she needed someone who could help her.

She hit the button on her steering wheel to place a call.

"Call Dad." The phone rang through the car speakers several times before her father, Elliott McGinty, answered.

"Hi, pumpkin. I'm getting ready to head into a meeting. Can I call you back?"

She bit her lip, making a quick decision. It was better if no one else was involved for now. Until she had time to think. To make a plan. And to get far, far away from Johnathan. "Actually, I just called to ask if I could borrow the jet. I need to do some scouting for a client's destination wedding. Mia's booked solid and asked me to help." She crossed her fingers at the white lie. Telling her dad what she overheard—and without further evidence—would just create a sense of panic. And with what she knew, Johnathan would probably put his plan on hold. He'd want to silence her before he went after her family. Staying silent would keep them safe. She needed a plan to stop him.

"Oh. Well, sure. When do you need it?"

"Today, if possible."

"Today?"

Brooke could almost see the frown form between his eyebrows. She had the wheels turning in his brain. But she didn't want to involve him in this. Not yet. The less her family knew, the better.

"I know it's short notice, but so is her wedding. She's in the family way, so they're wanting to get married as soon as possible." She thanked her lucky stars she was good at thinking on her feet. She just prayed she could remember all these lies.

"Oh, well, that's understandable. I'll call Ezra and have him head to the airport. Where can I tell him you're going?"

She scrambled for an answer, not really sure where she wanted to go, just that she needed to get away. What she needed was time to think and plan; and the only way to do that was to run and hide.

Gulping a breath, she responded. "French Polynesia."

That should get the staff at the airport to put plenty of fuel in the jet. She'd come up with a more specific destination when she got to the hangar. Brooke didn't plan to tell anyone except Ezra where she was really headed, and that was only because he had to fly the plane.

"Okay. I'll let him know."

"Thanks, Daddy." She felt tears threaten and rolled her lips in as her voice fell off on the last word.

"Anytime, pumpkin. Have a safe trip."

She let out a shaky breath, then sucked in another one, forcing a cheery note into her voice. "I will. Talk to you soon." He bade her goodbye, and she hung up.

Turning out of the Johnathan's neighborhood, she headed for the freeway. Her mind raced as fast as her car. She didn't dare go home. That would be the first place he would go. But she needed her passport, and it was in the safe at her house.

Brooke uttered another epithet, grumbling about countries and their laws, and pressed harder on the gas pedal. She'd get there, run in and get it, along with some extra cash, then head to the airport. Clothing and toiletries were easy to buy wherever she went.

Cars flowed down the highway at a steady clip. Rush hour was just ending, thankfully. Brooke wove in and out of traffic, going much faster than the posted speed limit. She prayed for no police and kept an eye out. The sign for her exit loomed, and she breathed a sigh of relief.

Her fingers drummed a nervous beat on the steering wheel as she slowed, queuing with the other cars at the red light. She willed it to change. Once it did, she followed the line through the intersection, then resumed weaving in and out of traffic.

At her house, she didn't bother pulling into the garage. She parked haphazardly in the driveway, then ran in through the front doors, pausing only long enough to fumble with her keys.

Stumbling over the threshold, she threw the locks into place—because even though she practically flew here, she didn't trust that Johnathan wasn't right behind her—then ran into her office to open her safe.

Brooke swung open the painting behind her desk to access the recessed safe and spun the dial on the lock to open it. Her fingers shook, and she missed the second number. When she did it again, she forced herself to take a deep breath and slow down. She needed to stay calm. Letting her emotions rule would only hinder her effectiveness in getting out of town before Johnathan caught up to her.

After her third attempt, the door swung open. She reached inside and withdrew her passport, as well as the bundle of emergency money she kept on hand. Her family was quite wealthy, which meant there were always people out there who disliked them. Her father had always cautioned her to be ready for anything—and that included having cash on hand. If he were here with her now, she'd give him a big kiss. It was saving her ass.

She shut the safe and spun the dial, then put the picture back in place. With the items she came for in her hand, she headed for the door, stuffing them both into her purse as she went. Exiting the house, she ran down the walkway to her car. Her heels clacked on the concrete, keeping pace with her thundering heart.

Pulling open the car door, she dove inside, throwing her purse onto the passenger seat. She buckled up, then started the engine, backing away from the house and onto the road with a quick squeal of her tires. Out of sight of her house, she gunned it, making her trip to the airport a quick one. She hoped Ezra was there and ready to go. The sooner she was in the air, the safer she'd feel.

Thankful for her family's status, Brooke bypassed the main airport entrance and went through the private gate. Her dad had alerted the guards, so when she showed her ID, they waved her through. She pointed the car toward her family's hangar, doing her best to keep her speed slow as she crossed the tarmac. Parking beside the building, she got out and hurried toward the plane, which was sitting just outside the hangar.

The tall man walking around it with a clipboard and pen in his hands glanced at her with a smile. "Hi, Brooke. We'll be ready to go soon. If you bring your luggage over, I'll load it once I finish my pre-flight checks."

"I don't have any luggage. Do you mind if I sit inside the plane to wait?"

He frowned. "No luggage?"

Brooke felt a bit like a bug under a microscope as Ezra's gaze sharpened and he stared at her for a long moment.

"What's wrong?" The alert edge to his low voice reminded her that Ezra had been an elite military pilot in a former life and was trained to pick up on danger signals. No doubt her lack of luggage, cocktail dress, and her wide-eyed, freaked out expression were like a flashing neon sign to him.

She fought to put a blank mask over her face. "What makes you think anything is wrong?"

One dark eyebrow shot up. "Spur of the moment trip, no luggage, deer in the headlights look on your face—I'd say something's wrong."

She'd always liked Ezra Chastain, but right now, she was rethinking that position. She'd been right. He was much too perceptive. "I'm fine."

"Bullshit."

Brooke wrung her hands together and glanced away.

Ezra crossed his arms and arched that eyebrow again. "We can stand here all evening if you'd like."

Anger drew her eyebrows together. "You work for my family. Dad gave me permission to use the jet. Your job is to fly it."

A smile cocked one side of his mouth. "Gee, I think I'm feeling a little too tired to fly. Maybe even a little sick. Might be coming down with something." He took a step toward the hangar. "I'll go call the reserve pilot. You can wait a few hours for him to get here from Albany, right?"

Brooke ground her molars together and shot a hand out to snag his sleeve. "Fine. You win." Her eyes darted around again, and she sighed. "I overheard—something—and I need to get out of town while I figure out what to do."

That sharp gaze pierced her again. "What did you overhear?"

She refused to meet his eyes, knowing if she did, she'd spill her guts. No one else needed to be involved. She didn't want to put anyone else in danger.

"Brooke, tell me what's going on. I can help."

She hesitated. With Ezra's skill set, she didn't doubt his ability to keep her safe, but she wasn't sure it was wise to involve anyone else at this point. And he had a family to think about. She didn't want to put his wife, Amy, and their new daughter, Gretchen, in danger.

"Brooke, you need to tell me what's going on. Whatever it is, I can help."

It was the confidence in his tone that made her tongue loosen a little. She looked at him. "I'm in danger. Can we just leave it at that, please?"

"No. What kind of danger? From whom?"

"The deadly kind. And from Johnathan."

He frowned. "Johnathan? Your fiancé?"

She nodded.

He raked his gaze over her, and a banked anger flared to life in his eyes. "Did he hurt you?"

The steel in his voice warmed her a little. It was nice to know someone wanted to go to bat for her. "No. Not yet. Look, I just need time to figure out what to do. Please. I just want to get on the plane and get out of here."

"To French Polynesia?"

She threw up her hands. "Sure. There or anywhere else out of the country. I don't really care, so long as it's not here."

He studied her for another moment. "Okay. But we're not going to French Polynesia."

Brooke frowned. "Then where are we going?"

"Costa Rica."

Two

Darkness enveloped Brooke as she stepped off the plane just over five hours later. She glanced back, waiting for Ezra to emerge. He'd asked her to hang back while he powered the plane down and completed his log. She was okay with that, because she had no idea where to go or what to do now that she was here. All he told her when she asked why Costa Rica was that he "knew a guy." Whatever the hell that meant.

Emotion threatened to choke her. Tears welled in her eyes, and her breath caught in her throat as despair punched her in the gut. She didn't know what to do. It wasn't a feeling she was accustomed to. She was used to taking care of herself. She'd been raised to be a leader. As the sole heir to the family business, her dad had involved her in the day-to-day runnings from a young age. It fostered her naturally extroverted personality and helped her hone the qualities that would make her successful in the hospitality industry. But right now, she felt like a scared, helpless little girl. She didn't like it.

The soft thump of footsteps on the carpeted plane floor pulled her from her maudlin thoughts. She glanced back to see Ezra's tall form emerge from the doorway. He walked down the stairs to join her on the tarmac, a small duffel in one hand. With the other, he motioned for her to walk toward the terminal.

"Where are we going?"

"To meet a friend."

She blinked at him. "Is this the guy you said you knew?"

He gave a quick nod.

"Okay." She looked away. "So, what makes this man special?"

"He's got a particular set of skills you'll find useful."

"Skills?" She glanced at him again as they entered the terminal.

"Yep. Hang tight here for just a moment. I need to get the keys to the car." He nodded to a door marked "Personnel Only."

Brooke nodded and crossed her arms, fighting the urge to fall apart. Instead, she contemplated what skills his friend could have that she'd find useful. Part of her didn't want to know. Thankfully, her imagination didn't have long to ponder that. Ezra reappeared a few moments later.

"Let's go."

"Don't I need to go through customs?" She glanced around the empty terminal office. On every international flight she'd ever taken, even on the family's jet, she had to go through customs.

"Nope." He ushered her through another door.

Confused, she glanced around as they stepped outside, still seeing no one. What was going on?

They stopped in front of a black Mercedes sedan. When he moved to the back passenger door, she paused. "Can I ride in front?" She didn't feel like sitting alone with her thoughts.

"Sure. You can pick the radio station." He opened the car door for her with a smile. "Just no country."

Brooke tossed a grin up at him as she sank into the seat. "You're based in North Carolina, but you don't like country?"

"Sweetheart, I grew up just outside of New Orleans. What plays on the radio today is not country."

Giving a quick chuckle, she reached for the seatbelt. "Clearly, you need to spend more time with my family. They will tell you differently." Her dad and grandpa loved country music. She liked it, too, but preferred the folksier stuff.

He chuckled and gave a quick shake of his head. "Why do you think I want anything except country? Every car ride I've ever taken with any of them, that's what plays on the radio." Grinning, he stepped back and shut the door.

Smiling, she settled into the seat as she waited for him to get in. Silence enveloped her for a moment, and she took a breath, buoyed by the banter. Ezra always knew how to make her smile. He'd only worked for her family for about eighteen months, but he was by far one of her favorites. He had a good sense of humor and didn't bow to her or the rest of her family like he was somehow less just because he was in their service. She respected him for that and was grateful he took her up on her offer to become their chief pilot.

The driver's door opened, and he slid into the seat. With efficient movements, he buckled up and started the car. In seconds, they were on their way out of the airport, heading south and into a dense jungle.

Brooke stared out the window at the passing scenery. She wished it was light so she could see. Finding the window control, she rolled it down and took a deep breath. The scent of damp earth and foliage assailed her. It was almost as nice as the smell of the sea. A yearning to bury her toes in the sand and feel the water lap at her ankles took hold. She loved the ocean. Her dad always said she should have been born a fish. Swimming was one of her favorite things to do.

Their ride was short. In minutes, he turned off the main

road. Brooke frowned, leaning forward. She couldn't see much. A small hotel to her right. The parking lot they were in gave way to a small marina, lit by a single pole light. "What are we doing here? Does your friend live on a boat?"

"Sort of. He has a house, but Ford's always been more comfortable on the water. This is closer than his home, so I figured we'd start here." Ezra parked the car and turned it off. "Come on." He opened his door.

Brooke fumbled with the seatbelt buckle. It finally gave way, and she shoved the door open and climbed out. Tucking her small purse under her arm, she followed him onto the boardwalk. They passed several vessels before he paused.

"This is it."

Tipping her head, Brooke assessed the boat. It didn't look like much. Nowhere near new, it was still in decent shape, but unremarkable. In the glow from the pole light, she could see the name. *Midnight Hooker* was scrawled over the bow of the boat in flowing blue script. No lights shone in the windows. It appeared deserted. "I don't think he's here."

Ezra frowned. "Maybe. Stay here." He didn't wait for her to respond before hopping onboard the vessel and disappearing inside.

Brooke stared out over the water, tapping her toe on the dock, making a hollow sound that echoed off the fiberglass hull of the boat. The only other sound came from the small waves lapping against the boats and docks nearby. She crossed her arms and paced several steps, leaning forward to peer through the boat's darkened windows. Her mouth twisted, and she sighed. It was too dark to see anything.

A thump on the dock behind her made her shriek. She whirled around.

"Sorry." Ezra motioned her back to the boardwalk. "He's not here." Turning, he headed for the car.

Brooke hurried after him. "So, what now?"

"We check his house."

"Can't you call him?"

He lifted a shoulder. "I doubt he'd answer. Ford doesn't like talking on the phone."

"So, text him."

Ezra glanced back. "Don't need to. Are you coming, or do you want to stay here?"

The distance between them registered, propelling her into motion again. She caught up to him as he reached the car. "Does he know we're coming?"

"No."

"Your plan was to show up unannounced?"

He frowned again. "Yes. It's not a problem."

This must be some friend if he could show up out of the blue to ask for help without calling first.

"If you say so." She opened her door and got in. "I take it you've been to his place before?"

"No."

Brooke's frown deepened. "Then how do you know where it is?"

"I know the address. Looked it up on a map while we were in the air. It's not far." He started the car. "Buckle up."

Snagging the seatbelt with one finger, she clicked it into place as he drove out of the parking lot, hanging a sharp right to take them further south.

Ezra drove them a few minutes down the road. They made another sharp right, passing several homes, before he turned right again onto a road that ran parallel to the beach. He stopped at a white, single-story bungalow. A gray off-road pickup sat in the dirt driveway behind a closed garage door. Parking next to the truck, he turned off the car and opened his door.

Brooke followed him, her heels sinking into the sand as soon as she stepped out of the car. Uttering a soft curse, she yanked off her shoes and ran after him. "You could wait for me, you know."

"It's not like you don't know where I'm going." He glanced back, raising a hand to knock on the door.

She huffed and came to a stop next to him. Annoyed, she stared at the cream-colored door, unsure what to expect if and when Ezra's friend answered.

When no one came to the door, Ezra knocked again. "Ford, it's Ezra. Open up."

After a moment, Brooke heard the lock click. The door swung open, and her breath hitched. The man who stood in the doorway was not what she expected. She wasn't sure what she'd been expecting, but this handsome stranger was not it. His light brown hair, with its sun-bleached highlights, hung in soft waves around his face, tapering back and brushing his collar. Beard stubble dusted his square jaw, setting off the mint-green eyes currently raking over her body.

Brooke returned the favor, letting her eyes drift over his long, muscular frame clothed in a soft olive-green t-shirt and khaki shorts. His feet were bare.

"Who's this?"

His low, whiskey-toned voice skated over her nerve endings, making her shiver.

"Can we come in?" Ezra motioned to the door.

The other man stared at him for a brief moment before stepping back. "Sure. I think I want to hear this story. Because that's not your wife." He raised a hand and tipped a finger toward her.

Brooke's mouth pursed. She wasn't a story. But she followed Ezra inside, having nowhere else to go. Once over the threshold, her gaze darted around the beach house. It surprised her. Though on the small side, the space was light and airy. Bright white walls opened up the space, which was furnished with chestnut leather and glass furniture. The back wall was nothing but windows. Pole lights illuminated a long, rectangular pool. Beyond the yard, she could see the shimmer of the ocean in the moonlight. The entire property was modern, but comfortable.

Ford motioned to the couch and chair grouped around a gray and blue area rug. "Have a seat."

Ezra laid a hand on her shoulder and gestured for her to sit. She perched on the edge of the couch. He sat on the other end. Ford took the chair.

Brooke tried not to feel like a bug under a microscope as Ezra's friend continued to study her. She glanced at Ezra, willing him to tell them both what was going on.

"So, it's been a hot minute, Ez." Ford was the first to speak.

"Yeah." Ezra took a breath. "I'm here to collect on that favor you owe me."

Ford's gaze sharpened, but a smile slashed across his face. "Wasn't I the last one to save you?"

Ezra shrugged, an answering smile tugging at his lips. "You didn't really save me. Just rooted out a problem."

Ford tipped his head in a quick nod. "I guess that's true." He glanced at Brooke for a moment, then turned back to Ezra. "But are you sure now is when you want to collect?"

Ezra nodded. "Yeah. She needs a safe place to hide out. No better place than with you."

Understanding clicked in Brooke's brain. "Wait." She stood up, frowning at Ezra. "You mean to leave me here with him?" No. That was not a good plan. She didn't know this man from Adam. And his stare made her uneasy. Those mint-green eyes pierced right through her. She felt like he could see her soul, and she didn't like it.

Ezra frowned back and shifted in his seat to look up at her. "Well, yeah. What did you think I meant when I said we were going to Costa Rica because I knew a guy?"

"Not that you'd leave me with a stranger!" She crossed her arms and paced to the windows. Honestly, she thought he'd bring her to his friend and the guy could set her up in a hotel under a fake name. Not that he'd dump her on the poor man.

"Brooke."

In the reflection on the window, she saw Ezra stand and walk toward her. She stared stubbornly outside at the darkness.

"Brooke." He laid a hand on her shoulder and turned her.

She kept her eyes on the hollow of his throat.

"Look at me, please."

With a soft harrumph, she glanced up, meeting his bright blue gaze. "What?"

A grin quirked one side of his mouth. "Do you trust me?"

"I thought I did until you decided to dump me on your unsuspecting friend. Why can't he just book me into a hotel under his name? No one would find me, then."

"Why can't you use your own name?" Ford's voice broke into their conversation.

"Her fiancé has money and connections," Ezra said before she could do more than open her mouth.

She snapped it shut and narrowed her eyes at him, not sure she liked that he was so willing to air her dirty laundry.

Ford unfolded himself from his chair, coming to stand next to Ezra. "Why are you running from your fiancé?" He raked his eyes over her again with more intensity than before.

Brooke fought back a shiver. She felt like he'd stripped her naked and was peering into the darkest recesses of her mind with those icy green eyes. She crossed her arms. "None of your business."

"Sweetheart, if I'm going to let you stay here and keep you safe, that makes it my business."

"I never agreed to stay, so I guess it's not."

Ezra growled, any traces of a smile disappearing. "Brooke,

stop being hard-headed and think this through. You fled Asheville with nothing but what you had on because of *something* Johnathan said. If a simple conversation is enough to spook you that much, you need Ford's help." His blue gaze bore into hers.

A touch of shame soured Brooke's stomach. He was right and was only trying to help.

"Tell us what's going on." His voice softened.

She sighed and walked around them to the couch, perching on the edge. Her knees wouldn't hold her, she had a feeling, while she recounted what she'd overheard.

Once the two men sat down with her, she launched into a recap of what happened. "Johnathan and I were supposed to go to a gala downtown tonight. I was a few minutes early, and when I neared his office, I could hear him talking to his brother, Will. I didn't want to interrupt, so I paused outside the door, waiting for them to finish." She sucked in a shaky breath, folding her hands in her lap to keep the tremor in them at bay. "That's when I heard them planning Grandpa's and Dad's murders."

Ezra cursed and stood, pacing to the entertainment center before turning. "You're sure? Why were they planning that?"

"It's a business thing. And yes, I'm sure. I even recorded the conversation once I grasped what was happening."

"You did?" Ezra turned his sharp gaze on her.

She nodded.

"Let's hear it," Ford said.

Digging in her purse, she found her phone and opened her saved videos. She touched the play icon and turned up the volume, setting the phone on the table in front of her. Tears formed in her eyes as she listened. Crossing her legs, she clasped her hands over her knee and stared at the floor.

THREE

The tinny audio from the video playback filled the room, but Ford Wagner's attention wasn't on the screen. His eyes were on the beautiful, dark-haired woman seated on his couch. She had her long, smooth legs crossed. Her perfectly manicured hands rested on her knees. To a casual observer, she looked composed, but he could see the chinks in her armor. She twiddled her thumbs and stress made the line of her pretty mouth straight. Agitation showed in every line of her curvy body, and if he looked close enough, he could see the sheen of tears in her eyes.

His gaze lingered on her creamy, exposed thighs. The dress she wore was meant for a party, not for international travel while on the run. Same with her shoes. She'd dumped them on the floor the moment she sat down, having already taken them off before she came inside. Her bare toes curled into the soft rug beneath her feet. Light pink polish dusted the nails.

The woman was a knockout.

It made him wonder what kind of man could throw away a woman like her for a business deal. Or cheat on her with so little compunction. Listening to her fiancé talk about his affair made Ford's blood boil. It didn't matter that he hadn't met Brooke before tonight; no woman deserved to be cheated on.

He heard her phone ring on the recording, closely followed by her curse, then the video ended.

"Why didn't you go straight to the police with this?" he asked.

She scoffed. "With just that? They'd laugh me out of the station. Tell me it was a joke. Johnathan plays golf with several of the area chiefs, as well as the heads of just about every federal law enforcement agency in Asheville. The only person I would get to take me seriously is my friend's husband, who's the sheriff of the neighboring county. But I'm out of his jurisdiction, so he wouldn't be able to do much. I need more proof."

Ford glanced at Ezra, arching an eyebrow as he sought confirmation.

"She's not wrong. Brooke is technically one of my bosses. Her grandfather is the resort chain CEO. Johnathan works for the company as an executive. He has a lot of connections and a lot of influence." Ezra glanced at her. "I understand better now why you wanted to leave the country. I'm also doubly glad I brought you here."

Mouth flattening, Ford turned to the woman on his couch. It didn't matter now that Ezra was cashing in his favor. He would have taken on her case, anyway. People who threw around their influence to the detriment of others, who used it for evil purposes, sent his ire up like no other. "What's your name?"

Amber eyes that reminded him of a cat's met his. "Brooke McGinty."

"It's nice to meet you. I'm Ford Wagner. I want you to try to relax, okay? You're safe here."

More tears welled in her eyes. "I want to believe you, but

you don't know Johnathan." She leaned back against the couch cushions and folded her arms around her middle.

Ford frowned and stood, glancing at Ezra. With a quick tip of his head, he motioned for his old friend to follow him. At the window out of her earshot, he glanced at Brooke, then at Ezra. "How likely is her fiancé to come after her?"

Ezra's lips flattened. "Highly. You heard the recording. He wants that company. She's his key to getting it. As well as a liability now. And Johnathan Cassidy is a cold, calculating individual when he wants to be." A slight frown marred his face. "After hearing that, and what I've seen of him before, I wouldn't doubt that he's a sociopath."

"How long until he tracks her down?"

"A couple of days at most, probably less. I had to file a flight plan. But I didn't declare her as a passenger. I greased some palms at both airports to sneak her into the country. I also talked to Asher on the way," he said, mentioning one of their mutual friends, who was a hacker-extraordinaire. "He's going to put her in the customs' database, so if she gets stopped by police, she won't get flagged for being here illegally. I doubt it'll take Cassidy long to put it together that I flew out of Asheville with her. He's not stupid, and he'll do some palm greasing of his own to get answers. The one saving grace is he doesn't know about you, which is why I brought her here. Nothing connects her to you. And my past is buried under layers of red tape that I'm not sure even he can unravel."

Ford grunted. He wasn't wrong about that. "You sure this is how you want to cash in that favor?"

A corner of Ezra's mouth tipped up. "Are you sure I am?"

He gave a quick grin. "You think you know me or something?"

Ezra smiled, but it quickly died as he glanced past Ford at the woman still sitting on the couch, looking like she bore the weight of the world on her shoulders. "I don't care if I do cash in my favor. Her family has been wonderful to me and Amy. I can't let anything happen to her."

"What about her grandpa and her dad?"

"Her grandpa is out of town, but her dad is back in Asheville. With Johnathan on Brooke's trail, I think Elliott is safe for now at home. As soon as I leave here, though, I'm rearranging my schedule to be the one to pick up Cyrus and bring him home. Brooke told her dad she wanted to scout a wedding venue in French Polynesia. I'm going to let him believe that until I get him and Cyrus in the same place. Then we'll discuss next steps. I'll keep them safe; don't worry about that."

"Good."

"I'm also going to dig into Johnathan Cassidy. In fact, I already set Asher on the task. She can't go home until something's done about him."

Ford agreed. His eyes went to her again. God, she looked young. But most people his age looked young to him. It came with being a jaded former SEAL. He just hoped she wasn't as innocent as she appeared. She had spunk, so he hoped that meant she wasn't some lily-white social butterfly who never got dirty. His ex-wife was like that, and it was one of the reasons they divorced. Brooke wouldn't last long in his world if she was the same. Or she'd learn to toughen up. He still had a business to run, which meant she was going to work right alongside him for the foreseeable future.

He looked at Ezra. "I'll keep her safe. If you need help, let me know. It's good that Asher is already on this. And if you need more hands up there, one of the others can come up." Ford might no longer be an active Navy SEAL, but he had a cadre of people here who helped him out when something like Brooke's situation fell into his lap. He wasn't in the business of protection, but certain people knew he could be counted on when the need arose. People like Ezra Chastain.

"I'll keep that in mind. I might talk to Asher before I head out. He still on the south side of the island?"

Ford nodded.

"Okay. I'll head over there in the morning. I need to sleep before I can fly again, anyway."

"Sounds good. Asher likes to run on the beach at dawn."

"Good to know." A corner of Ezra's mouth raised before he glanced at Brooke again, and his tiny smile faded away. "You're sure you're willing to take her on?"

Ford let his gaze rove over the dark-haired beauty sitting balled up on his couch, doing her damnedest to keep herself together. "Yeah, I'm sure." He looked at his friend. "Don't worry about her. I'll keep her safe."

"I know. I'm more worried about you."

"Me?" He arched an eyebrow. "There something about her you're not telling me?" Ford prayed the woman's normal personality wasn't one of a spoiled rich girl. He could handle a lot, but a snobby princess might make him toss her overboard.

Ezra's smile returned, as did a twinkle in his blue eyes. "She's just feisty, is all. And used to being in charge."

Ford grinned. "I like feisty women."

A seriousness washed over Ezra's face. "Don't mess with her, man. She's not the type to have a fling with."

A scowl descended over Ford's face. "I don't sleep around; you know that."

"I know, but I'm just saying—tread lightly. She might be my boss, but she's like a kid sister to me. I just don't want to see her hurt. Or you."

It was Ford's turn to snort. "Yeah, okay." He shook his head. It would be a cold day in hell before he let a woman get close enough to hurt him again. Once was enough, thanks.

Ezra gave him a rueful grin and shook his head. "It could happen." He took a couple of steps back, turning toward

Brooke. Ford hung back as the other man squatted in front of his new houseguest.

"I'm going to head out now, Brooke." He laid a hand on her knee. "You're in good hands; I promise."

Her lower lip wobbled, but she sucked in a breath and made it quit, leaving Ford impressed with her ability to control her emotions. Maybe she wasn't as fragile as he feared.

"I hope you're right. You'll keep my grandpa and my dad safe, right?" She laid her hand over his.

He nodded. "Don't worry about them. I won't let anything happen to them. You have my word."

That lip trembled again, but she nodded. "Okay. Thank you, Ezra. I'm still a little apprehensive about staying here, but I do trust your judgment. And I appreciate your willingness to help me. It means a lòt."

Ezra turned his hand over in hers and squeezed it. "You're welcome." He stood, glancing at Ford. "Call me if you need anything." He reached into the inside breast pocket of his suit jacket and held out a business card.

Ford took it, then held up a finger. "Guess I need to start answering my phone now, huh? And maybe find my phone." With a frown, he walked across the room to the kitchen and opened a drawer, rifling through it until he pulled out a black smartphone. He held it up with a grin. "I can't promise I'll answer right away, but I can promise to check my messages at least once a day."

"Good enough for me. Thanks again, Ford."

"Anytime. Now get out of here so we can all get some sleep."

With a nod and a quick wave at Brooke, he left. Ford followed him and locked the door, arming the alarm system he rarely used. When he returned to the living room, Brooke had pulled herself into an even tighter ball.

He reached out and lightly took her wrist, urging her to get up. "Come on."

She frowned at him. "What? Where are we going?"

"To bed."

Her eyes widened.

He rolled his. "I'm not an ogre. I have a guest room."

Red tinged her cheeks. "Sorry. I'm not normally so quick to jump to the wrong conclusion."

"You're fine. It's been a rough evening, and you don't know me." He tugged on her arm again, then let go and led her from the room and down a short hallway. Stopping in front of a door, he opened it and flipped on the light. "You can sleep in here. Let me go grab you something to sleep in and a toothbrush." He retreated to fetch the items. When he returned, he found her standing at the window, staring out. "You'll have a great view in the morning."

She glanced back, a startled and confused look on her face as though she hadn't considered what was on the other side of the glass. "Oh." She looked at the window again, then back to him. "Okay, that sounds nice."

He gave a short nod and laid the items he brought her on top of the bureau to his left. "Bathroom's through there." He pointed to a door in the left corner. "There are fresh towels under the sink, along with some shampoo and soap. Help yourself."

She echoed his short nod. "Okay. Thank you."

"Yep. Get some sleep. Tomorrow, we'll worry about the plan to keep you safe long-term."

Her jaw worked, but she nodded and glanced away again. Ford backed out of the room and blew out a breath. He hoped she took his advice and got some rest. He planned to do the same. As soon as he made a few phone calls.

FOUR

A beam of sunlight pierced Brooke's eyes behind her closed eyelids. She winced and turned away with a groan.

"Rise and shine, cupcake."

Brooke bolted upright at the husky female voice. Near the window, a red-headed woman stood, chuckling.

"Sorry. Didn't mean to scare you."

"Who are you?" Brooke's gaze darted around the room. "How did you get in here?" Fear skated up her spine. Ezra said she'd be safe here.

"My name's Edie. I'm a friend of Ford's. He asked me to come give you a makeover."

"A what? Why do I need a makeover? And from you?" Brooke frowned and looked the woman over. Her hair hung halfway down her back in a thick braid. Bright blue eyes blinked back at her from a heart-shaped face. An aqua-colored tank top and khaki shorts covered her petite but muscular frame.

Edie's mouth flattened. "I know I'm not fashion-forward,

but even I know how to match colors. And I'm not here to help you pick out clothes. You need to change your look." She held up a box of hair color and gave it a quick shake.

Brooke's eyes widened. "What?" Her hand went to her long dark locks. "No."

"Yes." Edie walked over to the bed. "Get up. We've got work to do." She yanked the sheet away, leaving Brooke sitting on the mattress in nothing but Ford's t-shirt.

Her eyebrows slammed down. "I am not coloring my hair. Why does he think that'll help? I doubt he'll let me leave this house."

Edie rolled her eyes. "Oh, you're leaving the house, all right." She puffed out a breath. "I hope he knows what he's doing," she muttered to herself.

"What? What are you talking about?" Why did everyone insist on only giving her part of the picture at a time? First Ezra, then Ford with his "Sleep, then we'll figure out long-term." Now this woman with her cryptic comment about leaving the house. Where was she going?

"Ford can explain everything. I'm just here to do your hair."

Brooke scrambled off the bed, fully awake. "You're not coming near me with that stuff." She eyed the woman and backed toward the door before spinning on her heel and exiting the room. "Ford!"

She spotted him at the island, munching on a slice of bacon. He glanced up with a frown.

"What's wrong?"

Huffing and glaring daggers, Brooke pointed behind her at Edie. "That woman says she's here to dye my hair."

He nodded once. "And cut it."

"No."

"Yes."

"No."

Ford sighed and put down his bacon. "Yes. Anyone your fiancé sends to find you will be looking for a woman with long dark hair. Light brown isn't far enough from your natural color, so you're going blonde. And don't worry; she's not shaving your head. It'll still be long enough for you to pull back."

That sense Brooke had last night of being out of control slid through her again. Her hands shook. She balled them into fists at her side. "Why?" She didn't understand why she couldn't just hide out here. No one would find her if she never left the premises.

"You can't stay cooped up in this house twenty-four-seven. I have a business to run, which means so long as you're under my protection, you're coming with me. You can't look like you outside of this house, so blonde and shorter hair it is."

"Come with you? Where? What is it you do, exactly? Ezra told me very little about you before he dumped me here."

"How about you get dressed and eat something before we talk? I think you'll be much more open to hearing me out once you're decent and have something in your stomach. I'm guessing you declined any food on your way here, yes?"

Brooke's mouth flattened again. How did he know that? "Fine." She gave Edie and her box of hair dye one more glance, then stomped toward the bedroom.

"I left a bag with some clothes for you on the chair," Edie called after her.

A slight hitch in her step was the only indication Brooke gave that she heard the other woman. She breezed into the bedroom and shut the door.

Huffing, she crossed her arms and glared at the walls, mind racing. So much had changed in the last eighteen hours, and she struggled to process it all. Mostly, she wanted to go home. But until she was safe from Johnathan, that wasn't an option.

Her gaze landed on the duffel bag on the overstuffed chair by the window. She let her arms fall and stalked over to it. One thing was certain; standing here fuming wouldn't help her figure out how to get her life back.

Brooke unzipped the bag, rifling through its contents. A variety of sundresses and two-piece swimsuits stared back at her. "Couldn't she have at least packed some underwear and a pair of shorts?" Sighing, she found a modest gray bikini and a lavender sundress with tiny white flowers all over it. This would have to do for now.

Retreating to the bathroom, she changed her clothes and brushed her teeth. As respectable and decent as she was going to get, Brooke left the suite.

Edie was now seated at the island with Ford. She had a cup of coffee and a plate of fruit and bacon in front of her. The woman glanced up and smiled as Brooke entered.

"I'm glad you found something in that bag that worked. Ford guessed at your size when he called me."

That explained the lack of undergarments.

"We'll run to a store later and get you some proper clothes," Ford said. He stood to pick up a plate from the counter. "What all do you want to eat?"

Brooke's stomach grumbled. Her mouth watered as she glanced at Edie's plate. "What Edie has is fine. And maybe some toast or yogurt."

Edie stood. "You want some coffee?"

"Yes, please."

In moments, Brooke had a plate of food and a steaming mug of black coffee in front of her. She picked up a slice of bacon and took a bite. Flavor exploded over her tongue as she crunched the crispy meat. Her stomach thanked her for the food and demanded more. It only took her a few minutes to polish off half her plate.

Hunger satiated, she glanced up to see Ford and Edie

watching her. Edie looked amused, but Ford eyed her with a careful curiosity. She could tell he had questions. That was fine. So did she.

She speared a piece of papaya with her fork. "Okay, I'm dressed and fed. Tell me the plan." She paused with the fruit near her mouth, staring at Ford. "And what you do for a living." Brooke ate the fruit.

He brushed a hand through his hair. The papaya lodged in Brooke's throat, and she swallowed hard, glancing away. Why couldn't Ezra have left her with an older, more distinguished military friend? One who didn't make her insides quiver every time she looked at him.

"I own a fishing and charter boat."

"The *Midnight Hooker*." Her head bobbed, and she picked up another piece of fruit. That made sense.

Surprise flashed in his eyes before his expression cleared. "You stopped at the marina first," he stated.

She nodded. "So, you want me to accompany you when you go out on these excursions?"

"Yes."

"Why can't I stay here? Or with Edie? She obviously knows what's going on or she wouldn't still be here."

More surprise flickered in his eyes. Brooke fought back a smile. *Yeah, I'm not a doormat, buddy.*

Edie waved her arms. "Nope. I'm not a babysitter. And I have my own business to run. One that would put you much more up close and personal with the public."

Brooke frowned in question.

"Edie owns a surf shop. You can't stay with her. You'll be too visible."

"But being trapped on a boat with your clients will make me less memorable?"

"To fewer people, yes."

She took a sip of her coffee as she contemplated that. "Something tells me this won't be a pleasure trip."

A wicked grin slashed his face. "That depends."

Brooke narrowed her eyes, and he laughed.

"Don't worry. Your virtue is safe. But you have a choice in how we handle your presence. You can either play the part of my significant other, or you can be a deckhand."

Her hand paused on the way to her mouth with her last bite of fruit, and she wrinkled her nose. "Does that involve handling fish?"

He nodded, a devilish smile quirking one side of his mouth.

A tingle shot through her. Damn, he was sexy.

She frowned and looked away. Thoughts like those shouldn't be ones she entertained. She was an engaged woman.

Brooke bit back a snort. She hadn't formally broken things off with Johnathan, but it was pretty clear that relationship was going nowhere. She'd taken off her ring during the flight and stowed it in her purse. Looking at it just made her more upset. And angry.

She met his gaze again. "Why can't I just hide out down below? No one, not even you, will know I'm there."

"You'll get bored. And more seasick than if you're on the deck. I don't want my stateroom smelling like vomit."

She wrinkled her nose again, setting down her fork.

"So, which is it? Are you my girlfriend or my new deckhand?"

Preferring neither, she glanced away, thinking. When she saw Ezra again, he would get a piece of her mind. Briefly, she considered telling Ford she'd be fine on her own and then leaving.

But she knew she was just fooling herself. She was alone in

a foreign country, with her sociopathic ex-fiancé hot on her heels. Going it alone would all but ensure she ended up back in his grasp.

Brooke heaved a sigh and looked at Ford and Edie. "Fine. I'll be your deckhand. But do I really have to dye my hair?"

FIVE

Climbing out of Edie's blue truck, Brooke closed her eyes, savoring the sound of the waves crashing and the feel of the sharp, salty breeze buffeting her face beneath the floppy hat Edie handed her when they got in the truck to go shopping. They'd decided to wait to dye her hair, unsure how long it would take to bleach and color it. Brooke didn't want to end up without underwear for another day, so she talked Ford into letting them shop first. He'd made her wind her hair into a bun and told Edie to find her a hat. Thankfully, Edie had one in her truck.

Brooke glanced around, taking note again of the yellow surfboard taking up most of the truck bed, along with diving gear nestled in one corner. She itched to climb into a wetsuit and shoulder the oxygen tank so she could sink beneath the waves and lose herself amongst the fish. All she wanted was to forget.

The slam of Edie's car door pulled Brooke from her thoughts. She closed her door and followed the other woman into the small store. Golfito wasn't a tiny town, but San José it was not. Edie told her there was a large duty-free mall near the airport, but she'd need a pass from customs and immigration to shop there, so she'd opted for some smaller, local shops. Which was fine with Brooke. She preferred the local boutiques. She always found such unique and interesting things at them. And this area of town was strung out along the coast around the small gulf. She got to smell the ocean while she shopped. What could be better?

"Where do you want to start first? Clothes or shoes? And keep in mind, I'm operating on limited funds. Ford will freak if I spend too much on you."

"Underwear. And I have cash."

Edie turned right. "Save it. Once this is all over, you can pay Ford back. It's safer if we use his credit card."

"Why? Cash doesn't leave a trail."

"People will remember someone spending large amounts of cash. Plus, we'd need to convert your money first. And tourists use credit cards." She paused outside a women's boutique. "Does this work?"

Brooke glanced inside. "Considering I don't have anything besides what I flew in wearing and the clothes you brought me, yes." She'd find something suitable, she was certain.

Edie gave a quick nod and ushered her into the store. "Make it quick. We have other places to go still."

Brooke wandered off, heading for the racks of silk, satin, and lace lingerie toward the rear of the store. She made a few quick selections based on practicality, then browsed through the clothing. She found a pair of capri pants and a blousy shirt, then headed for the register. Edie reappeared at her side.

"Get what you needed?"

"I think so."

"Good."

Brooke put her items on the counter and smiled at the

clerk, who quickly rang her up. Edie paid for her purchases and they left.

"Tell me something?" Brooke looped the bag over her wrist as they wandered down the street to the next store.

"What?"

"How do you know Ford? And why does he trust you to watch out for me?" Brooke hadn't failed to notice that he had no qualms about letting Edie take her into a public place to shop. For a man who wanted to put her on a boat to keep her safe, it seemed odd.

"What do you know about Ezra?"

"Ezra?" She frowned. "What does this have to do with him?"

"Quite a bit." Edie's eyes tracked over the patrons walking by. "Ford was part of a covert task force a while back. Ford saved Ezra's life." She looked at Brooke. "And mine."

Brooke's eyes grew wide. "What? So, you're former military?"

Edie nodded. "I worked as a liaison of sorts. I was an MP in the Navy, but I have a knack for languages, so I often traveled with my unit commander." Her gaze bounced over the people walking down the street. "Ezra was our pilot."

They walked several moments in silence. Brooke's curiosity got the better of her. "And?"

"And we crashed, and it was Ford's team that rescued us." Edie's open expression had closed off.

Brooke wanted to know more, but knew better than to pry. It was none of her business what happened while Ezra and Edie awaited rescue. One thing confused her, though. "Why does Ford owe Ezra a favor if Ford's the one who saved him?"

"That's not my place to say. You'll have to ask Ford—or Ezra—that question." Edie took a deep breath. "Anyway, that's how I know Ford and why he trusts me. Trusts Ezra."

She halted. "This is a good place for you to find some decent clothes."

It took Brooke a moment for her mind to switch gears. Her brain was too busy conjuring up what could have happened. She blinked and turned to look at the store. A myriad of athletic and outdoor clothes met her gaze. "Oh. Yes." She walked inside, making a beeline for a display of shorts. She cast a glance at Edie and her attire. The woman looked comfortable. And like she'd be able to move easily on a boat.

Brooke looked at the half a dozen styles of shorts laid out before her and picked up a pair similar to Edie's.

"So, how did you end up in Costa Rica?" Brooke picked up another pair of shorts and tried to not look too curious, even though she was. It was in her nature to want to know all the details of the lives of the people around her. Paying attention, learning everything she could about others, were the things that made her good at her job. It was hard to turn that off.

Edie glanced at her. "I needed a job when I left the Navy. Ford gave me one."

"Oh." Again, Brooke sensed a story, but didn't pry. Instead, she turned the subject to something that interested her far more. "So, what about Ford? How did he end up here?"

The other woman scanned the store. "You'll also have to ask him that. It isn't my story to tell, either." She glanced at Brooke and smiled. "I know I'm not a fount of information. I can tell you, Ford's a good guy. He's a little rough around the edges and a lot sarcastic, but you can trust him."

"I keep hearing that." She moved on from the shorts to look at shirts.

"Because it's true." Edie picked up a tank top and handed it to Brooke. "Try this one."

Brooke took it. They spent the next half hour buying clothes and shoes. She might not have learned what brought Ford here or why he was indebted to Ezra, but she did learn that Edie had a wicked sense of humor. It helped relax Brooke. And while she couldn't forget why she was shopping for a new wardrobe, it helped make it bearable.

SIX

For what felt like the millionth time, Ford glanced at his watch and knocked on the bedroom door. "Edie, for God's sake. How long does it take to color hair? I need to go." He'd gotten one of his employees to take out the morning and afternoon fishing charters, but he had a sunset cruise he couldn't get anyone to cover. He'd tried. Even gone to the office to use the radio to call the man he sent out on the charters to see if he'd take the night job too. No dice. He was stuck. Thankfully, he got one of his other employees to restock the boat, which saved him an hour.

The door finally opened. He glanced down at Edie.

She rolled her eyes. "It's not so simple as dumping a bottle of hair color on her head, Ford. I had to bleach it first." She stepped around him, leaving the door open.

His stomach dropped to his toes, then bounced back when he caught a glimpse of Brooke. She stood by the bed, fiddling with the ends of her now blonde and shorter hair. If possible, she looked even younger than last night. A different kind of vulnerability shone on her face, though. Last night, she'd looked scared and alone. Today, she looked unsure and a little lost.

He swallowed. "You look nice."

A frown overtook her face, and some of the vulnerability receded, a hardness replacing it. "If you say so." She dropped her hand. "Can we go?" She walked toward him.

Ford frowned. "I'm sorry. I know this is a lot of change all at once."

She waved a hand, halting anything else he wanted to say. "It is what it is. If changing my hair and doing fish things on your boat keeps me alive, well, then, I guess I can live with that. I'd still prefer to hide out in some hotel room, but I've had a chance to think and have realized you're right. I'll just get bored, which will make me careless." She gestured to the living room beyond him. "So, let's get on with this."

Staring at her, Ford couldn't help but feel both impressed by her determination and also a little peeved at Ezra for dropping this feisty woman in his lap. He might have said he liked feisty women, but he'd really been trying to make a serious situation lighter. The man might owe him after this. Favor be damned.

He stepped back and made a sweeping motion with his arm, bowing low. "As you wish."

Brooke rolled her eyes, but he caught the tiny smile quirking the corner of her full lips. She breezed past him.

"Did you buy a jacket while you were out shopping?" He studied her attire. The khaki Bermuda shorts and quick-dry gray tank top were appropriate for a day on the water. As was the fuchsia sports bra he could see peeking out from underneath.

"Jacket, sweatshirts, pants—you name it, Edie bought it. I just went along for the ride."

Edie chuckled. "You did not. There were plenty of things you shot down."

Brooke smiled, tilting her head. "Don't tell him that. He needs to think I hate everything about being here."

Ford frowned and shook his head. "I'm not sure I like that the two of you are buddy-buddy. "

"Tough titties, boss man." Edie walked up and patted him on the shoulder as she passed. "I like her. Don't scare her off."

He frowned harder. "She's a job, Edith. I'm not doing this to make friends."

She arched a brow at him, and some steel appeared in her bright blue eyes. Ford knew he'd pay for using her full name. She hated it.

"Regardless, be nice." She reached the door. "Brooke, I'll see you soon, I hope. If he gives you crap, smack him."

Ford groaned softly as Brooke gave Edie a thumbs up and a wide smile. The other woman left, leaving them alone.

"Go get your jacket and an extra shirt. And a pair of pants. You might need it all before the day's over." He glanced at her. Steel shone in her eyes too. And that hard edge was back. This time, it told him she didn't appreciate being reminded why she was here.

With a short nod, she walked back into the bedroom. Ford blew out a breath and moved to the couch to pick up his backpack. It had a change of clothes as well as other gear he never left home without.

"I'm ready." Brooke breezed back into the room, carrying the items he asked her to fetch.

"Good. Let's go." He headed for the door. Outside, he did a quick scan of the area before he let her step out. He wasn't expecting her fiancé to figure out where she went and arrive here for at least another day, but he didn't survive combat by being complacent.

When he was sure no one was lurking nearby, he ushered her to the truck, then climbed in beside her.

"So, what all do you expect me to do? I'll give you fair warning. I've fished, but I've always left the gutting part up to someone else."

Ford glanced at her, surprised she knew her way around a fishing pole. He turned onto the main road to take them to the marina. "That's fine. You're going to be my runner. Do you know how to drive a boat?"

"A sailboat, yes. And smaller fishing boats. My family owns a riverfront house, and we take a boat out on the river and fish. Or pull a tube."

"Close enough. I'll give you a crash course before we cast off." Maybe having a greenhorn on the boat wouldn't be so bad. She wasn't as green as he feared.

The drive was a short one, and he soon turned into the marina. Parking as near to his slip as he could, he shut off the engine and got out. He led her down the dock to his boat and helped her aboard.

"You can stow your gear below in one of the staterooms. I keep them locked when clients are onboard unless they've booked an overnight charter. This is just an evening." He led her inside. At the rear of the main cabin and off to one side was a small kitchen, and beyond that, a short hallway with a set of steep stairs. Ford motioned her into the tight space and followed her down into another equally small hallway, though this one was longer.

"This is the bathroom." He opened a door to her right. "That's the spare room." He pointed across the hall, then continued down the hall to the door at the end. "This is the main bedroom." Ford opened it and stepped inside. Brooke followed him in and laid her things next to his bag on the bed. He unzipped his bag and took out his sunscreen and a gun.

Brooke let out a little gasp. "You're armed?"

He glanced up. "Of course. There's a shotgun in here"—

he pointed to the armoire—"and one locked in the cabinet in the pilothouse."

Her mouth flattened. "Is that really necessary?"

"Yes. Your fiancé isn't the only danger out here."

"Ex-fiancé," she muttered. "And what other dangers are there? Sharks?"

He chuckled and turned, heading up the stairs and toward the door. "I wish. No, some of my clients can get a little rowdy, especially if they've been drinking. We get an odd pirate or cartel boat out here too."

"Pirates? Are you kidding?"

"No. With the local economy in Latin America, people turn to all sorts of things to make money."

"Great. That's just great. Totally fantastic. Pirates. Ezra said I'd be safe here and there are fricking pirates." She sighed and rolled her eyes heavenward.

A smile bloomed over his face as he led her topside, finding her mutterings amusing. "Relax. We probably won't encounter any. The weapons are just precautionary."

"Still doesn't make me feel any better."

Ford shook his head, sighing, and climbed the ladder to the pilothouse. He stowed his pistol in the cabinet beside the shotgun, then showed Brooke how to run the boat. She asked a few questions, and he was happy to see she seemed to understand. The true test would come when he asked her to actually drive.

Once the boating lesson was over, he led her back down to the deck to show her what he needed her to do with dinner. She'd be responsible for helping him serve the food and bringing their guests refreshments throughout the cruise.

Standing in the middle of the small galley kitchen, she wrinkled her nose. "I've never worked as a waiter. Directed plenty of them around, but I've never actually been the one serving. I hope this goes well."

So did Ford. The clients on tonight's cruise were on a corporate retreat, and those types of guests tended to be big tippers. His business wasn't hurting, but he'd never turn down extra cash. He had his eye on a couple of deep-sea rods that would allow his clients to catch bigger fish.

"I'm sure you'll do fine. Let's get set up."

SEVEN

Wide-eyed, Brooke stared at the small oven in the galley. He'd left her in charge of the dinner. She didn't cook much. Roasting sausage and vegetables and putting a pre-made meal in the oven was about the extent of her culinary ability. Her stovetop only ever got turned on so she could heat the teakettle.

She glanced at Ford, but he was already retreating to the deck. *Well, hell.* Blowing out a breath, she moved to the fridge. There better be instructions on how to reheat the food. Opening the door, she took out the containers, separating them by entrée and dessert. The dessert was cheesecake and fruit, so she put it back in the fridge.

"Okay, now what do I do?" She lifted one of the foil-covered containers and looked at the bottom. No instructions. "Great." And she didn't have her phone to google it, because Ford confiscated it last night after she showed him the video.

"Um." She scrunched her nose and closed her eyes. She always roasted her sausage and veggies at four-twenty-five. With a shrug, she reached for the oven controls and set the temperature. If it was too hot, well, it would just reheat faster. She found some baking sheets and loaded the pans onto them, then opened the oven door and put all five entrées on the racks.

"There." She dusted her hands together. "That wasn't so hard." With the food reheating, she could move on to gathering the tableware. She set about stacking plates and finding silverware, then carried the flatware outside. Ford had a round table out, secured to the deck through a hole in the floor. He was lifting a large umbrella to put through the hole in the tabletop when she emerged.

"How's the food?"

"Reheating." She raised the silverware in her hands. "I brought the place settings."

He made sure the umbrella was stable in its hole, then stepped back. "Good. Go ahead and set the table. I'm going to get the chairs."

Brooke nodded and went about doing as he asked. This was a task she could do in her sleep. While she was technically the human resources director for her family's resort chain, she was actually a bit of a jack of all trades. She would pitch in whenever and wherever she was needed. Like with the bride whose ill-timed phone call outed her to Johnathan.

In minutes, she had things arranged perfectly.

"Are you done with that?" Ford returned, arms loaded with padded folding chairs.

She nodded.

"Help me with these." He passed her a chair.

She took it. Together, they arranged three chairs around half of the table. The other side had a bench built into the boat. Ford removed the cushions from the closet, and Brooke helped him tie them to the bench.

"What now?"

"We just need the food and our guests. The latter should be here any minute. Dinner's heating, so that leaves drinks. Can you get the ice from the freezer while I make sure the cooler's clean?"

"Yep." She turned around and went back inside. On her way to the freezer, she peeked through the little window in the oven. She could feel the heat and smell the food, so hopefully, it would be hot soon. It hadn't been completely cool when she put it in the oven.

Opening the freezer, she found the two bags of ice and took them out, using her foot to close the door. She trudged back outside, banging into the doorway on her way out. "You know, a gentleman would offer to carry the heavy stuff." She glanced at Ford, who was near a cooler strapped to the wall, wiping it out.

He grinned. "You mean like this?" He pointed to the boxes of beer and soda at his feet, then picked up the beer.

Brooke grunted and set the ice down beside him. "Yeah."

Ford put down his rag and reached for the ice. He tore the plastic and dumped it in the cooler. Brooke bent over and tore open the beer carton, handing him cans until they were all nestled in the ice, then moved on to the soda. Once it was fully loaded, Ford added the last bag of ice and shut the lid.

"I better go check on that food again. It should be warm enough now." Brooke walked away and stepped inside the cabin. Her eyes widened as she stepped over the threshold, and the smell of something burning hit her.

"No, no, no, no." She hurried forward and yanked open the oven door. Smoke billowed out, making her cough. "Shit." She waved a hand in front of her face, clearing the smoke. Blackened food boxes and leaking sauce met her gaze.

The smoke detector shrieked. Brooke let out a startled yelp. Heavy footsteps crossed the deck, and Ford appeared in the doorway.

"What the hell?" He ran forward to look in the oven. "What—" He growled, then grabbed the hot pads from a drawer next to the stove and yanked the pans out of the oven. The metal clattered on the stovetop as he threw them down.

Brooke rung her hands as he turned his eyes on her. Anger and some disbelief colored his handsome face and made his mint-green eyes flinty.

"Why didn't you take the food out of the containers and heat it up on the plates? You can't put cardboard in the oven. It burns."

"Well, I didn't know it wasn't oven safe. Parchment paper can go in the oven. You just said reheat the food." She crossed her arms. "I don't know how to cook any more than I know how to wait tables."

Ford sighed and raised a hand to his face, rubbing his eyebrows. "Christ. Why didn't you say something? If you'd asked, I would have shown you what to do."

"You'd already walked away, and I didn't want to bother you. I didn't think it would be that hard to reheat a few meals." Apparently, she was wrong. "I'm sorry, okay?"

She watched him clench and unclench his jaw several times before he nodded.

"Help me salvage what we can." He yanked open another drawer and withdrew a pair of tongs and a large slotted spoon.

Without a word, Brooke moved forward and picked up a plate, holding it out to him. She felt like a complete and utter imbecile. Who didn't know that cardboard takeout boxes couldn't go in the oven? She'd assumed they were coated with something that made them oven safe. Next time, she'd make sure before she did something so stupid again. She could have done more than burn a few meals; Ford's boat could have been a casualty of her carelessness.

Tears gathered in her eyes. Brooke fought them back. She would not cry. Not over something so dumb. Sniffing, she set the first full plate on the counter and picked up another. Voices outside drew her attention.

"That's probably my clients. Can you finish this?"

Brooke nodded and took the tongs and spoon from him, keeping her eyes down so he wouldn't see the waterworks she was trying to keep at bay. "I'll be fine."

She felt him staring at her, but refused to look up. Finally, he left her alone. A single tear tracked down her face. Wiping it on her shoulder, Brooke took a deep breath and stuffed her emotions back into their box. She pulled her determination to do better around herself like a cloak. Dammit, she might not want to be here, but she refused to make a fool of herself again.

She felt the boat shift under her feet as she worked on the food and knew that Ford had cast off. The engine revved slightly as he steered them out of the marina and into the bay. She hoped he kept the speed to a minimum until she finished her task. Otherwise, his clients might be forced to fish for their supper.

Thankfully, he kept their speed slow, and five minutes later, she had all the salvageable food on the plates. They didn't look the best, but she did what she could to make them presentable. To make sure Ford was ready for the food, she wandered out of the cabin. The five men were settled around the table, beers in hand as they looked out over the water.

Brooke offered them a smile and rounded the corner to climb the steps to the pilothouse. Ford glanced at her as she moved in beside him.

"The food is ready. Are they?" She nodded her head at the men on the deck below.

He nodded. "Go ahead and serve them. We'll be out in open water soon. It might be better if you're not carrying plates when I speed up."

"Agreed." She whirled on her heel. "Okay." Not waiting for anything further, she went back downstairs and ducked into the cabin. Two at a time, she carried the plates out, not trusting herself to carry more. Dumping food on the men would be terrible.

"Hey, thanks, pretty lady." One of the men eyed her like he wished she was on the menu. "Are you joining us?"

Holding back the grimace, Brooke stepped out of his reach. She had plenty of experience with men like him. Her wealthy status didn't change that. Men in every walk of life had hands that liked to wander to places they shouldn't. "No. I'll be up in the pilothouse with Ford. If you need anything just wave." Disgust soured her stomach as he continued to rake her over with his eyes. She couldn't hold back the small shudder as she walked away. Pervy men never got any easier to take, and they all grossed her out.

She ascended the stairs again, then sank into the co-pilot's seat.

"Everything okay down there?"

"Yes. Can I stay up here and drive and you go take care of anything they need?"

He frowned, glancing at her. "Why?"

"I have a feeling the more they drink, the more their hands will wander."

"Did one of them touch you?" A hard edge entered his voice.

Brooke shook her head. "No. But one of them looked at me like a starving man looks at a steak. I figure once he gets a few beers into him, my ass becomes fair game."

"Not if he knows what's good for him. Feel free to punch him if he lays a hand on you. Then I'll come down and make sure he understands. I'd let you drive, but you don't know these waters. I'd rather we not get lost."

Wrinkling her nose, she sighed. While she agreed, it didn't make her happy. She would prefer not to go downstairs again. Her shoulders straightened and her back stiffened. And, really, why should she? She wasn't his employee. She didn't even want to be on the damn boat. With a slight nod of her head to herself, she crossed her arms. "I'm not going back down there. You gave me driving lessons, let me use them. Plus, you have GPS." She pointed at a screen on the dash.

"Brooke—"

"Don't 'Brooke' me. How were you planning to run this cruise before I showed up? By yourself, I'm guessing. So, you can just continue to do it that way. I'm not getting groped just to play a part."

Ford growled and opened his mouth to say something, but she cut him off again.

"I will lock myself in the stateroom until we dock. So, you either let me drive when you need to go downstairs, or you let the boat drift."

"My plan was to anchor us off shore."

"Sounds good." She pulled her feet up and tucked them under her butt, getting comfortable.

"You're really going to pull the 'I'm not an employee' card? What happened to being so gung-ho to help earlier?"

"The corporate sleazeballs downstairs. I've had enough stress in the last twenty-four hours. I don't need more."

Ford sighed and stared out to sea. They spent several moments in silence, both watching the water, before he spoke again.

"I'm sorry for their behavior. I know it seems odd that I'm asking you to pretend to be an employee, but you really will be less memorable if they think you work for me than if you're just a woman on the boat. They won't speculate about who you are or why you're here."

Brooke huffed and sat up. "I understand that." She sighed.

"Look, how about I only go down there if the boat is moving and there's a turn or obstacle coming up, like a reef? Otherwise, you deal with them and I man the wheel."

In the growing shadows, she saw his mouth tilt up from one corner. "Deal."

Eight

Fatigue made Ford's eyes scratchy as he pulled into port several hours later. After not getting much sleep last night, and his busy day today, he was ready to crash. He still had to clean and prep the boat for tomorrow's charter, though. He hoped he could get the princess to help. True to her word, she'd stayed in the pilothouse unless circumstances warranted him driving. Ford didn't blame her, though. He didn't like getting groped by strange women when he went to the bar for a drink.

"Brooke, one of us needs to go down and tie us off." He glanced her direction.

"Oh." She bit her bottom lip as she looked toward the dock that was fast approaching, then at him. "I'll run down and do it. I'd rather you park us."

He grinned. "Good call. Just don't fall in when you jump off." Rescuing her wasn't on his agenda. Plus, there was the very real possibility he could crush her between the boat and the dock.

She gave him a quick, two-finger salute, then descended the ladder. He kept an eye on her as she crossed the deck.

Raised male voices followed her as his clients tried to get her attention. Ford clenched his teeth as choruses of, "Hey, baby," reached his ears. Bringing her on board a charter full of men hadn't been his most brilliant idea ever. He hoped they behaved. He didn't want to get into it with anyone.

Ignoring them all, she picked up the coiled rope used to tie the boat down and opened the gate on the stern. She stepped onto the low deck, holding on to one of the ladder rungs as he turned the boat around and backed it into his slip. As the hull kissed the buoys meant to provide a buffer, she leaped from the boat onto the dock as gracefully as any ballerina.

Ford shut the engine down and left the helm to help her tie up the boat. On the deck, he hurried forward as one of his passengers tried to descend the ladder onto the dock. The man listed forward dangerously when the boat bumped the dock.

"Whoa, there." He pulled the man back from the brink. "Let us get it tied off, then we'll help you ashore."

The man nodded.

"Have a seat." He motioned to the chairs.

"That sounds like a good idea."

"Come on, Mitch." One of the man's friends took his arm and led him to a seat.

Mitch grabbed his head as he sank into the cushion. "Oh, why did you let me have that last shot?"

Ford bit back a snort, not surprised that the men brought a bottle of liquor with them. He provided beer, but never hard liquor. They could get wasted on that stuff on their own dime. And many of his passengers chose to do just that, which he didn't understand. Why would you come to an island paradise on vacation and then drink so much you couldn't remember it?

Walking around to the bow, Ford jumped down with a rope in his hands and tied off the front of the boat. Once the line was secure, he went to check on Brooke. She was winding her line around the cleat on the stern.

"You need help?"

She shook her head. "No. Just taking out the slack."

"Okay, good. I'm going to help our passengers off."

She nodded, and he left her be.

"Gentlemen, we're secure if you'd like to step down now." Ford stood on the dock as close to the boat's exit as he could get. The two more sober members of the group came forward to assist their drunk friends ashore.

"Should I call them a cab?" Brooke asked, coming up beside him.

"I arranged one before we left. It should be waiting in the parking lot."

"Oh. I take it this happens often?"

He nodded as he held out a hand to help one of the men onto the dock. "All the time." His other hand shot out to grab the man's forearm as he slipped.

"Shit! Don't let me fall!"

"I've got you, don't worry."

Laughing, the man got his feet under him and stumbled onto the dock. One of the more sober ones, Jim, jumped down to keep his friend from falling into the water. He glanced at Ford. "Thanks, man."

"Not a problem."

The other two tipsy passengers disembarked with the help of the remaining less drunk man. He leaped onto the dock, and Jim turned to Ford again.

"Thanks again. We had a great time." He pulled a wad of cash from his pocket and held it out to Ford.

"I'm glad. You're welcome." He lifted his hand to take the money, but at the last second, Jim pulled his hand up. Ford frowned.

"Wait." Jim's eyes narrowed, and he focused on Brooke. "Don't I know you?"

Ford's heart flip-flopped in his chest, and his senses went on red-alert.

"No," Brooke was quick to respond. She turned, taking her face out of the light.

Jim stared at her for another long moment. "Yeah. Yeah, I do. You're Cassidy's woman. Brooke, right?" He frowned. "Why'd you color your hair? I liked the brown. And what are you doing here? Where's John?"

Hell. Ford glanced at Brooke, willing her to keep her cool. A slight widening of her eyes was her only tell.

"I'm sorry, sir. You must have me confused with someone else. My name is Meg."

The man's frown deepened. "No, I—"

"She must just have one of those faces." Ford cut him off, and held out an arm as he started walking, urging the men off the dock. "Meg's worked for me for years."

Jim craned his neck, looking at Brooke. Uncertainty now colored his face. Ford wanted to keep it that way. He walked faster and didn't stop until they reached the parking lot and the taxi van waiting for his passengers.

"Thanks for cruising with us. I'm glad you all had a good time." He opened the van's rear door. The three drunk friends stumbled inside, clearly ready to go back to their hotel and pass out for the night. Their other sober friend followed at a more normal pace. Jim still hesitated.

Ford smiled and put his body between Brooke and the man. "Enjoy the rest of your stay in Costa Rica."

Jim met his gaze. Ford maintained his smile and fought to keep his posture relaxed.

Finally, the man nodded. He passed Ford the cash tip. "Yeah. Thanks." He got in the taxi.

Pocketing the money, Ford shut the door, then waved at the driver and stepped away. He didn't relax until the vehicle exited the parking lot. Then he turned to Brooke. "Who was that?"

"I don't know."

"He knew you, so who was that?"

"I told you, I don't know."

He stalked closer, the calm, but deadly serious soldier mask slipping into place. "That's bullshit, Brooke. He obviously runs in your circle if he knows you. Think. His name is Jim. Who is he?" He knew he was being a little harsh, but she needed to think harder. The knowledge had to be locked away in her brain somewhere.

She huffed and glanced away. That bottom lip slid between her teeth, and she chewed on it as she thought. Huffing again, she met his gaze. "He looks familiar, but I can't tell you any more about him than that. He probably has dealings with Johnathan in some capacity. I go to a lot of events and little mixers, which is probably how he knows me. Johnathan and I split up at those things, because we each have our own business interests we want to foster."

Ford ran a hand through his hair and growled. This was not good. If that man said something to Cassidy about seeing a woman who looked like Brooke, it would lead her fiancé right to her.

He grabbed her hand, towing her toward his truck. "Come on."

"What? Where are we going? I thought we needed to clean the boat."

"Change of plans, princess." He unlocked his vehicle and yanked open the passenger door, ushering her inside.

"Huh? And don't call me that."

He'd laugh at the fierce kitten look on her pretty face if the situation wasn't so serious. Instead, he ignored her and closed her door before running around the truck to get in.

"Ford, tell me what's going on. What are we doing?" She squeaked as he tore out of the parking lot, taking the turn too quickly and dumping her into the door. "Geez. Are you trying to tip us over?"

"Tell me what you can about the men your fiancé deals with on a daily basis. Men like Jim. Do they talk often? Is it mostly shop-talk, or do they get personal? How likely would a colleague be to call your fiancé and mention he saw you—or someone who looked a lot like you—in Costa Rica?"

"Ex-fiancé," she grumbled. "And I don't really know. Johnathan is the company's chief financial officer. He's got a whole host of people under him I've only ever met with during the hiring process. Plus investors he's roped in over the years. The only one of those I can name off the top of my head is Jackson Tipton. He used to work for us until he took a position as a CFO for a small marketing firm. He and Johnathan stayed friends. He's a jerk, though, so I try to steer clear of him."

Ford let out a snort. "Why am I not surprised he's not a good guy?" He took the turn onto the main road and pressed down on the accelerator. Shaking his head, he pushed the button on his steering wheel to make a call. "Call Max Carson."

"Who's that? Why are you calling him?" Brooke asked over the ringing that filled the cab.

Loud music and a deep voice took the place of the ring. "Dude. You killed my mojo. I had this fine honey—"

"I need your help." Ford cut him off. He had little time to listen to Max's latest attempt to snag a pretty tourist for a night of fun between the sheets.

The music in the background faded. "Okay, I'm listening."

"I need you to take out my charter tomorrow morning, but you have to use your boat."

"What? Wags, your yuppies can't deep-sea fish from my speedboat."

"Tell them I'll give them a discount, and you can take them fishing for red snapper. Something's come up, Max. I need my boat, and I need to disappear for a while."

"Disappear?" Brooke's voice ended two octaves higher than it started.

"Why is there a woman with you?" Max groaned. "You took on another protection case, didn't you? Seriously? I told you the last time—"

"Yeah, yeah. I'm well aware of what you told me. Doesn't change anything." And it didn't. He knew after the last case that taking on another could be detrimental to his business. He'd nearly lost the third boat in his fleet the last time because he didn't have anyone to man it, and therefore no income to pay the payments. He'd hustled his ass off to keep it and was finally well into the black again. That might all change, now, though. "So, can you take out my charter or not? She's here, and we need to disappear."

Max sighed. "Yes. What am I supposed to tell your group?"

"Whatever you want, so long as you don't mention what's really going on. We're going back to my place now to get some gear. I plan to be out of sight of the island before dawn breaks."

"What? You can't be serious." Brooke groaned.

Max's chuckle filled the cab. "Have fun, my man. And miss?" He paused for a moment. "Don't you worry. Ford will keep you safe."

"So I keep hearing." She groaned again and slumped in her seat.

"Thanks, Max. I appreciate it."

"Yep. I assume you also want me to coordinate with your other crews and work out the new kinks in the schedule?

"If you wouldn't mind."

"You owe me."

"Add it to my tab."

"Oh, I will. Let me know if there's anything else I can do."

"Will do. Thanks, Max." He pushed the button to disconnect the call.

"Can you please explain your plan?"

Ford glanced across the darkened cab. In the dash lights, he could see the pissed off set to Brooke's face. "We need to vanish. I can't take the chance Jim won't say anything to Johnathan about you being here. With me. It's better if we're someplace no one knows about. I'll have some friends keep their ears to the ground. If anyone shows up, poking around my house or the marina, we'll know about it."

"So? How does knowing about it help?"

"Because I have other friends who can find out who they are and hopefully tie them to your fiancé."

"Ex-fiancé."

Ford rolled his hand. "Whatever. My point is, whatever my people gather can be added to what Ezra digs up in relation to what you overheard."

"So, what? We're just going to hide out on your boat? For how long?"

"As long as it takes." He shifted in his seat. Hopefully, his business wouldn't go under in that timeframe. He had two other boats in his fleet. In his absence, Max would shuffle the charters around between them and his speedboat. But if he went too long without some deep-sea tours with the *Midnight Hooker*, he could be in real trouble. Bigger trouble than just losing a boat. He could lose it all. The *Hooker* was his true moneymaker.

He bit back a groan. Max was right. He needed to stop taking on these cases. One day, it would catch up to him.

"Do I not get any say in this?"

"Sure." Her defiance grated on his nerves. He didn't think she realized just how much danger she was in. "You always have a choice. Right now, your choice is to either come with me and live, or stay here and possibly get us both killed."

Those amber eyes of hers shone steely in the low light of the dash as she glared at him. "*Maybe* I'll just leave and go someplace where *no one* knows where I am." She crossed her arms.

Ford rolled his eyes. "We're back to this now?" He shook his head, done with her bullheadedness. "Have you ever had to hide your identity? Your whereabouts? There's more to it than just going somewhere no one knows you."

"I know that. I'm not an idiot. I have cash."

"Mmm-hmm. And a day ago, you were bawling all over your pilot because you didn't know what to do or where to go. What changed, princess?"

"I told you to stop calling me that. And what changed is that I've had a chance to think. To calm down and make a plan."

"Really?" He arched an eyebrow and glanced at her.

"Yes." She narrowed her eyes.

"Enlighten me. What's your plan?"

Silence met his command. He glanced her way again. That pretty mouth worked side to side, and she wouldn't look at him.

"Well?"

She lifted her hand and chewed on her thumbnail, eyes still locked on the darkness outside.

"Let me guess. Your plan is to go—somewhere—and hide out in a hotel until this blows over, right?"

"Shut up. Just shut up." The anger in her voice gave way to a hint of despair, and her words ended on a harsh whisper.

Ford sighed. He reached over and laid a hand on her bare thigh. Heat shot up his arm, and he pulled back. Clearing his throat, he shifted in his seat, a little unnerved by his sudden reaction to her. He needed to keep his mind in the game. This was not the time, the place, or the girl for that sort of thing. Slamming the door on his emotions, he glanced out the window, then turned to her again. "Look, I'm not trying to belittle you or anything. I just want you to realize you need help. That you don't have the skills to do this by yourself. That's why Ezra brought you here."

She sniffed and a single tear fell down her face.

"I need you to trust me, Brooke. I know what I'm doing."

Finally, she looked at him. But Ford wished she hadn't. The baleful vulnerability in her eyes sucker-punched him, and that door he'd slammed shut in his mind creaked open. A fierce protectiveness slid out. Even if she tried to leave, he'd follow her, just to be sure she was safe.

"I'm trying," she whispered.

"That's a start." He patted her knee, then focused on the road.

NINE

Brooke stiffened her muscles to keep from sliding into the door again as Ford took the turn into his driveway. Honestly, she was glad the ride was over. He'd driven like a bat out of hell on the way back from the marina. But she had another ride to look forward to when they went back to the boat. Maybe he'd calm down some between now and then and drive at a more normal pace. It wasn't like Johnathan could get here in the short amount of time it would take them to pack up and go back.

Ford shut off the engine. "Let's go, princess."

Brooke bit back a groan and grabbed her door handle. "Why do you insist on calling me that?"

He shrugged. "If it fits…"

"But it doesn't. I'm not a princess. Nor am I spoiled. I grew up knowing the value of hard work."

He glanced at her as they rounded the hood. "But you don't know your way around a stove?"

"Because I had no interest in cooking. Ever. And my parents never forced me to learn."

"Right. But normal people would have to learn or starve.

At least how to do the basics. We can't eat takeout for break-fast, lunch, and dinner." They reached the front door, and he thrust his key into the lock.

Brooke rolled her eyes. "I don't." Usually. Her breakfast normally consisted of a fruit smoothie and some yogurt. If she was running late, she'd put in an order for a breakfast burrito from a local diner she liked and have it delivered to her office. Lunch was either a pre-made salad she got at the grocery or she ordered out.

A frown darkened her face. Maybe she was a tad spoiled. But she still wasn't a princess.

Ford let out a soft snort as he crossed the threshold. He glanced back. "Sure you don't. I'm not arguing with you about it, though. We don't have the time. I need you to go get all your stuff. Everything, including the fancy dress and shoes you showed up in. If someone breaks in, I don't want any trace of you here. No point in giving them confirmation you're with me."

Brooke nodded, following him deeper into the house.

"There's a small suitcase in your closet. Use that and the duffel Edie brought over. You have five minutes, so don't dawdle." Ford headed for his bedroom, tossing that last bit over his shoulder as he walked away from her.

She scurried into the guest room. Five minutes was plenty of time. It wasn't like she had much to pack.

In her room, she opened the closet door and found the black suitcase Ford mentioned. Opening it up on the bed, she grabbed the clothes she bought with Edie earlier that day and tossed them all into the case, not bothering to fold them. Her party dress and shoes went in the duffel with the few items Edie brought over. A quick trip through the bath-room for her toiletries, and she had everything packed in just a couple of minutes. Zipping the bags closed, she picked them up and went out to the living room. An olive-green duffel sat on the floor by the couch, but Ford was nowhere to be seen.

"Get a reusable grocery bag from the pantry and start filling it."

Brooke jumped at the sound of his voice from down the hall. She laid a hand over her racing heart and glanced that way. Where was he? That hadn't come from his room.

"You can grab stuff from the fridge, but not too much. The *Hooker's* mini-fridge isn't that big."

Pursing her lips, Brooke went into the kitchen and opened the large double doors that housed the pantry. On a middle shelf was a stash of canvas bags. She took several out and set them on the counter, then started pulling items from the shelves. She didn't know what all he wanted, so she grabbed mostly snacks and a few canned goods. He knew she wasn't a cook, so if he wanted things he had to combine with other things to make a meal, he'd have to pack that himself.

Footsteps drew her attention. She glanced up to see Ford emerge from the hallway, another olive-green duffel over his shoulder. This one looked heavy, and whatever was in it stuck out at odd angles. Brooke swallowed hard. Knowing what she knew about him and their situation, she had a feeling that bag was all weaponry. It frightened her to think he might need it, but she was happy he had it.

"What have you got so far?" He set the bag on the couch and walked toward her.

She nudged the sack toward him. "Snacks and stuff. I don't know what all you plan to cook on board, so I wasn't sure what to grab."

He peered inside, then glanced at the open pantry before picking up another sack. "I've got this. Why don't you get some things from the fridge for us?"

Brooke nodded and picked up another bag, then opened

the fridge. She grabbed the yogurt and a pack of cheese sticks, then filled the rest of the sack with fresh fruits and vegetables.

Ford glanced in her bag and nodded. "That looks good. Grab some salad dressing and sandwich condiments."

She added the items to her bag and shut the door.

"Did you get all your things from the bedroom?"

"Yes."

"All right. Leave your purse on the counter. I called Edie while I packed. She's going to come get it and put it in her safe with your phone. Let's go." He motioned to the grocery sacks. "Grab those."

Brooke took her handbag out of her suitcase and left it on the counter, then picked up the grocery bags. Ford grabbed his duffels and the two bags she'd packed, then she followed him out the front door. He tossed everything in the bed of his truck, and they were quickly on their way.

The drive back to the marina wasn't any better than the drive home. She clutched the bar above her door and sent him a dirty look. "Do you always drive like a maniac?"

His teeth flashed white in the truck's darkened interior. "Is there any other way?"

"Yes. Like a normal person. I don't squeal my tires every time I go around a corner."

His low chuckle filled the cab. "Then you aren't doing it right."

"Men," she muttered under her breath.

He just laughed louder.

By the time they reached the marina, her knuckles were white. Brooke uncurled her fingers from the bar and got out. At least on the boat, he couldn't take such sharp corners. She hoped.

Bags in hand, she followed him down the dock to his boat. He led her inside.

"I'll put your bags in your stateroom. Why don't you unpack the groceries, and I'll get us underway?"

She nodded. He continued past her, disappearing downstairs for a moment before reemerging and leaving her alone in the galley.

Brooke let out a breath, taking in the moment of silence. It was the first she'd had since Jim recognized her. Her hand shook as she reached for the grocery sacks. She curled her fingers into a fist and clenched her teeth. She would not fall apart. Ford already thought she was some spoiled rich girl, and she would not turn into a blubbering mess, incapable of anything, and prove him right. She was tough. Always had been. And she would get through this just like anything else—with grace and dignity. Johnathan Cassidy wouldn't win. She had to make it through this and prove he was a sociopathic monster, so she could save her family and their business.

Resolve in place, she snatched the bags off the floor, the tremble in her hands gone, and unpacked. The boat moved beneath her feet as Ford shoved off, but she just locked her knees and went about her business.

Once the groceries were stowed, she went outside, climbing the stairs to the pilothouse. Ford stood at the helm, staring out into the darkness. He glanced back as she approached.

"Hey." She wandered closer, her gaze on the blackness beyond the windows. Clouds scuttled across the sky, obscuring the moonlight. "The groceries are stowed." She stopped at the edge of the helm, still looking out the windows. Looking at Ford did something to her insides. Especially with the fierce concentration on his face. It brought out the warrior in him, and she liked it. Too much. "So, where are we headed?"

"Into the gulf for now."

"For now?"

He nodded. "I'd like to say we'll stay in the gulf; it's safer. But if your fiancé comes after you, we might have to head for deeper water."

She huffed. "Ex-fiancé. Can we agree on that, please?"

He lifted a shoulder. "Sure."

"Thank you." Brooke shifted her weight and squinted at the darkness. "I don't know why you bother even looking outside. With the cloud cover, the water is barely visible."

"It's visible enough. I'm mostly using the nav system to guide us out, but it can't spot other boats or rogue waves."

"Rogue waves? The water is calm." And it was. They had the perfect weather for night sailing.

"For now, yes. But there's a system off shore. It can push waves in even when the weather here is clear. It's not common, but it can happen." He kept his eyes on the water as he talked.

Brooke crossed her arms and stared outside. Now she was paranoid. What happened if one hit and he didn't see it? Would it roll them? The *Midnight Hooker* was a decent-size, but it could still capsize under the right conditions. How big did these waves get?

Ford's low chuckle drew her attention. "Relax, Brooke. We'll be fine. I'm more worried about boat traffic. I've lived here several years and have never seen a rogue wave outside of a storm."

Her eyebrows drew down, and she glared at him. "Then why would you bring it up?"

He shrugged. "Because I do watch for them. Every mariner does."

She rolled her eyes and pushed away from the helm. He was teasing her. She wasn't in the mood. "I'm going to bed. Wake me if we get hit by one of your imaginary waves."

He flashed her that charming smile again. She clenched her fists. Why did Ezra have to dump her with someone so good looking? Why couldn't he have a potbelly and be missing teeth? Or have a giant face tattoo?

"If you hit the deck in your sleep, you'll know."

With another roll of her eyes, she spun on her heel. "Goodnight."

"Night, princess."

Brooke ground her molars together at the nickname, but kept walking. Maybe if she ignored it, he'd quit.

Sure. Keep telling yourself that.

She shook her head at herself as she descended the pilot-house ladder. She doubted anything she did would make him stop. Brooke had the sneaking suspicion Ford Wagner did whatever he wanted.

TEN

A cool breeze blew over Brooke's face. She snuggled deeper into the blanket she'd hauled out onto the forward deck with her and watched the first shades of gold lighten the eastern horizon. She'd tried to go to sleep in the stateroom, but her mind wouldn't shut off. Eventually, she'd gotten up and come out here, hoping the open space, salty breeze, and endless stars would help.

It hadn't, but it had been far better than staring at the cabin's paneled walls.

Soft thumps alerted her to Ford's presence shortly before a cup of coffee appeared in front of her. The rich scent wafted to her nose. She shook the blanket free from her hands and accepted the steaming mug. "Thank you."

"You're welcome." He sank into the chaise beside hers.

Brooke sipped her coffee and tried not to stare at him. That golden brown hair of his was mussed in thick waves that fell around his face. Matching stubble dusted his square jaw.

"Did you get any sleep?"

"Not really, no." She took another sip. "This is good."

"Savor it. I only brought one bag. Once it's gone, we're drinking the instant stuff."

She wrinkled her nose. "So long as there's creamer." She'd seen that in the cabinet when she put everything away last night. It was the powdered stuff, which wasn't the best, but it was better than nothing.

He chuckled. "You surprise me."

The cup paused on the way to her mouth. "How so?"

"You have spoiled rich girl written all over you. Perfect nails, high-end dress and shoes, that five-hundred-dollar haircut." He motioned to her now shorter hair, then shook his head. "You balked at running from a man who wants to kill you, but instant coffee you can handle."

She held up a finger. "Only if there's creamer." A smile quirked her lips before she smothered it by taking another drink.

Ford chuckled again. The sound warmed something deep inside Brooke. It also left her feeling—bewildered? Something, some strange feeling, swirled through her mind, but she couldn't put a finger on it. Ford sparked something—an attraction—but it wasn't just that. Whatever it was left her perplexed and a bit off-kilter.

Brooke rolled her eyes at herself. It was probably just sleep-deprivation. She took another sip of her coffee and settled back into her chair to enjoy the sunrise. "Do you ever get tired of seeing this?"

He sighed and sat back, extending his long legs and crossing them at the ankles. "No. Every morning is different, and they're all gorgeous."

She could imagine. Today's was shaping up to be just that. "So, tell me about yourself. Since we're going to be stuck together—alone—for the foreseeable future, I'd like to know my shipmate."

"Not much to tell. I was in the Navy for about twelve

years. A SEAL for the last eight. Now I run a fishing charter business."

"Why did you leave the Navy?"

"An injury. It sidelined me from the SEALs and would have made me a desk jockey." He glanced at her. "I lost part of my left lung to a bullet."

Brooke knew her eyes looked like saucers, but she couldn't help it. "Oh my goodness! That's terrible."

His head bobbed once. "Yeah." He took a sip of his coffee. "I couldn't pass the fitness standards for the SEAL teams. They wanted to make me an instructor." Giving a quick shake of his head, he raised his mug again. "I wasn't a good fit for that job, so I left with a medical discharge."

"Was this during the mission to save Ezra and Edie?"

Ford visibly started. "What? How do you—? Edie." He closed his eyes and shook his head. "What did she tell you?"

"Don't worry. She didn't reveal any deep, dark secrets. I asked why you trusted her to help me. Why she was so willing. That was her answer. That you saved her life, and Ezra's."

He was silent for several long moments. "Yeah. Yeah, that was the mission that ended my career."

"What happened?"

"Things went FUBAR. But no one died—at least, not during the rescue mission—so there's that."

It was Brooke's turn to be silent. She didn't know what to say to that, and she didn't want to pry. So, she changed the subject. "Why Costa Rica?"

He shrugged, taking another drink. "I like the tropics, but the summer weather in other sunny locations can be a bit wild. Hurricanes, you know? Costa Rica doesn't get many."

"How long have you lived here?"

"Three years."

"Do you have any family back in the States?"

"My mom. She lives in Florida at a retirement community,

where she is loving life. My dad passed away about ten years ago. I'm an only child."

"Why didn't you start your fishing business in Florida so you could be close to her?"

Ford blew out a breath. "Anyone ever tell you you're nosy?"

Brooke grinned. "I'm a human resources director and an event planner. It pays to know things about people."

He let out a soft grunt.

She chuckled. "So? Are you going to answer my question?"

He eyed her for a moment before continuing. "I wasn't in the best place, mentally, when I left the Navy. I needed space. Plus, my ex-wife decided to make Florida her home. Chancing a run-in with her wasn't on my agenda."

"Oh. You were married?"

Ford nodded. "Six years."

"Florida's a big state. Who's to say you'd have run into her?"

"Because that's my luck." A corner of his mouth quirked.

Brooke's mouth twisted. "It can't be any worse than mine. Did your wife try to kill you?"

"No. But she has a way of making me feel like dirt beneath her expensive shoes."

Why did women do that? Brooke didn't understand it. She scoffed at herself. Who was she to talk? She'd let Johnathan dictate her life. Convinced herself he knew what was best for her. All because she liked the idea of stability and having a family of her own.

"I finally got tired of the guilt-trips about being away all the time, and she got tired of being by herself so much. The divorce was a mutual decision, but it doesn't mean I have any desire to see her again."

"So, she got the entire state of Florida in the divorce?"

He chuckled. "Something like that. I go home to visit my mom several times a year."

"That's good. So, how did you end up with a rag-tag group here? I met Edie, and you called some guy named Max—who you obviously trust to take care of your business. Are there others?"

"A few. I met Max on a joint op with the Air Force."

"Air Force?"

Ford nodded. "He was a PJ—a pararescueman. Anyway, he's a little older than me and was ready to retire not long after I left the Navy. He thought a life in the tropics sounded good, so when he retired, he came down here. Bought himself a small house and a speedboat. Now, thanks to some wise investments, he's upgraded his house and spends his days doing whatever he wants."

Lucky man. Few people could do that. Brooke didn't take it for granted that she was one of them, even if she chose not to be. "And the others? How did you get them here?"

"Edie needed a place to heal. So did some other friends." He shrugged. "I just offered them a place to stay and sort out their heads. They stayed beyond that because they wanted to."

Brooke stared at Ford, wondering what it was about this man that made people flock to him. To put their unwavering trust in him. She'd so far glimpsed someone who seemed steadfast. But he was aloof. This was the most they'd talked since she arrived.

"What?" He frowned at her.

She shook her head and looked away, lifting her coffee cup to her lips. "Nothing."

He grunted again, casting another confused glance at her, before turning back to the sunrise.

The first stirrings of peace settled into Brooke's heart. Since this all began, this was the first time she felt like things might turn out okay. Maybe. "So, what's the plan? Do we just float around out here and wait for word that Johnathan's in jail and I can go home?"

"Generally speaking, yes. But we're not just going to float around. I'm going to take this time to scout some fishing locations. I've been considering doing weekend trips, not just day trips."

Brooke looked around. "Where would everyone sleep? There are only two staterooms."

"Right, but the room I'm in is large enough I could retrofit it with two sets of bunk beds."

She frowned. "And you'd take the room I'm in?"

He nodded. "That or sleep in the common room on the couch. Which, honestly, is what I normally do. Or I sleep on deck. The stateroom beds are short, so they're not super comfortable for me."

She could see that. Ford was tall. "Do they make longer beds?"

"For bigger boats, yes. One day, I'd like to have a larger cruiser. More of a yacht. I'll get there."

By the look of determination on his face, Brooke had no doubt. She'd be willing to help him achieve that dream if he kept her alive and helped lock up her crazy ex.

Brooke shifted in her seat, nestling deeper into her blanket. She sipped her coffee and watched the sun rise over the horizon, enjoying the peaceful silence. The ombre blue sky gave way to purples and teals before shafts of gold shot overhead and the bright sun crested the horizon.

Warmth touched Brooke's face, and she closed her eyes. Waves lapped the hull, creating a steady beat to accompany the rocking ship. Lulled by the sun and waves, she drifted off. The last thing she noticed before she slipped into a deep sleep was Ford lifting the coffee cup from her hands.

Eleven

Ford tucked into the coastline near Osa Peninsula and dropped anchor. They'd spent all of yesterday and today cruising around the gulf. Last night, he'd anchored well offshore. They'd endured some rain, but the wind was light. Tonight, though, the forecast was for stronger winds and more rain. The monsoon season was settling in, and he wanted to be closer to shore, just to be safe. The weather they had when Brooke arrived was an anomaly. What was coming was more common. He hoped Brooke didn't get seasick easily. The next few days would test her sea legs.

Shutting down the engine, he left the pilothouse. Exhaustion weighed on his shoulders. He planned to sleep for a few hours before the weather woke him.

After making sure the deck was secure, he headed down to his stateroom. Brooke's door was closed and the light was off, for which he was glad. He'd done his best to stay away from her the last two days. That talk they had the other night left him feeling raw and exposed. He didn't like talking about his past. Some memories were just too painful. Others, he just didn't care to think about. Like his ex-wife. She was in the past, and he wanted her to stay there. Marrying Gina had been a mistake. He'd wanted the stability of having a home to come back to after a deployment, and she wanted to stick it to her parents by marrying someone "beneath her station." Ford should have listened to the voice in his head that said it was a dumb idea. It would have saved him a lot of trouble.

But he'd learned from it. He was choosier about his relationships now—with everyone, not just women. He took his time and watched people now. The only good thing to come out of his disastrous marriage was that the experience made him a better soldier because he was now a better judge of character.

Ford glanced at Brooke's door once more. She reminded him of Gina, with her fancy clothes and ritzy background. It made him want to steer clear. But something still pulled at him. Yes, she was rich, like his ex, but she didn't act anything like her. The dichotomy had his emotions all tangled—hence the reason he'd been avoiding her. He was attempting the out of sight, out of mind approach to things.

Too tired to even try to sort out his feelings, he turned away from her cabin and opened his door. He had another task to do before he could get some sleep.

Inside his room, he flipped on the light and shut the door. Opening the nightstand drawer, he took out his satellite phone and powered it up. He needed to check in with his team and see what, if anything, they'd uncovered before he bedded down.

He let out a snort as the phone powered up. Calling the band of former military friends his team was a stretch. This was not their job. It wasn't even his job. But somehow, they'd formed an unofficial group that took on security and protection cases. Edie even gave them a name. Started calling them the Wagner Brigade. He'd just rolled his eyes at her the first time she said it in front of him. Maybe he should have discouraged her, because the name stuck.

The phone screen lit up, and he input Asher's number. It rang through as he lifted it to his ear.

"Why don't you keep your phone on? Any phone, not just the sat phone? Someday, it'll be an emergency, and none of us will be able to get a hold of you." Asher's irritated tone rang over the line.

"It's nice to hear your voice too." Ford rolled his eyes and sat on the edge of the bed. "I take it you tried to call me?"

"Yes. Multiple times."

"Why didn't you use the radio?" It was always on, and Max had access to several. Asher could have asked him to call.

"Because we didn't want to take the chance Cassidy's goons would hear. Word's reached him that Brooke's here. Ezra said his wife called. She heard through the grapevine that Cassidy took some unexpected time off work. I've had Dean sitting on the airport here, and he reported a man matching Cassidy's description get off a plane with several other men. And they were, and I quote, 'beefy bouncer types.'"

Despite the situation, Ford chuckled. Leave it to Dean to use colorful adjectives to describe people. "Okay. Did he tail them?"

"He did. They ended up at a house not far from yours, actually. A rental property. After a brief stop, they left again, and he followed them to a boat dock. He lost them when they got on the water."

Ford let out a soft curse. "We've been out in the middle of the gulf, but now we're anchored near Puerto Jiménez. I figured we'd be harder to spot at night where there are other boats. I'm not running dark unless it's absolutely necessary." His boat, like most others, had lights that came on at dusk to alert other mariners to his presence. It was a safety feature he didn't want to go without. It made them vulnerable to a collision if the lights were off.

"Fair enough. You need to put some distance between you and this crew, though. Dean took pictures of the boat they were on. It was more of a yacht, really. And I'm betting it had all the bells and whistles. Cassidy isn't playing games. He wants Brooke and is willing to pay for it."

Ford cursed again, getting up to pace to the small window in the cabin wall. He peered out at the blackness, seeing the lights onshore in the distance. "You get a name on that ship?"

"*Estrella Brillante*. It's a hundred and fifty to a hundred and seventy-five feet and is white with a gold stripe running about midway along the hull all the way to the stern. Three decks and a pilothouse."

That was a decent-sized boat. "Okay. I'll keep an eye out for it. We'll probably head out to sea tomorrow morning. I'll chance a run into town here for supplies, then we'll make our way around the peninsula and stay offshore."

"Sounds good. Can you keep the sat phone on, though?"

"I'd like to say yes, but the battery dies too fast. I'll check in every night. If there's an emergency, use the radio. We can use a code phrase so I know to get on the sat phone."

Asher let out a snort. "I thought I was done with all the cloak and dagger stuff."

A quick grin flashed over Ford's face. "You picked the wrong man to attach yourself to if you really wanted out of the game." Ford didn't advertise his protection services; it wasn't really a job he wanted full-time. But if there was someone in need of help, he'd never turn them away. His friends here knew that. They also knew they could opt out. He'd never ask anything of anyone who wasn't willing.

"Yeah, yeah." Humor colored Asher's voice. "Fine. So what's our code phrase?"

"Mention the brigade. Just don't use my name."

"Like, 'Anyone from the brigade listening?'"

"That works. Just coordinate with the others so the call doesn't go unanswered. No need to make anyone suspicious."

"Will do. Watch yourself. Call if you need anything. Unlike some people, I keep my phone on."

Again, Ford chuckled. "Normally, it isn't a problem."

"I'm buying you a better sat phone. Stay safe." Without waiting for a reply, Asher hung up.

Ford pulled the phone away from his ear and stared at it for a moment before powering it down. His amusement faded as the reality of what Asher told him sank in. They were in for some trouble.

Twelve

"Brooke."

Brooked turned to look at the man slowly walking toward her on the sunny beach. With his shirt hanging open, she could see the thin trail of dark hair disappearing beneath the waistband of his navy-blue swim trunks.

She smiled and sighed. It might suck having to hide out and put her life on hold, but having eye candy like Ford Wagner helped make up for it. She could stare at him for days.

"Brooke."

Warmth skimmed her arm, like a lover's caress. She glanced down and frowned, seeing nothing.

"Brooke."

The ground shook. Eyes widening, she glanced up. The sunny beach gave way to a dark room.

Confusion colored her mind, so it took her a moment to realize she'd been dreaming and was now awake. Ford was real, though.

"Hey. You awake?"

The whiskey tones of his voice chased away the confusion. She rubbed her palm over her face and nodded. "Yeah. What's going on? Why are you in here? It's early yet." She squinted at the small window. It was still dark outside.

"There have been some developments. Get dressed and come up to the main cabin. We need to talk."

Brooke groaned and flopped back onto her pillow. "Okay."

"Five minutes, Brooke. I mean it. Don't make me come fetch you."

Anger surged at his tone. He acted like she didn't understand the urgency of her situation. He was the one who'd never had to deal with Johnathan Cassidy's moods. His quiet anger had always scared her. Now she understood why. She'd been engaged to a psychopath.

Reaching beneath her head, she grabbed the pillow and flung it at Ford. "Then get out."

"No need to be hostile." He retreated toward the door, his teeth gleaming in the low light as he tossed her what she imagined was a wicked smile. It was too dark for her to really tell.

Glaring at him, she waited until he crossed the threshold and closed the door before she got up. No need to flash the man. The humidity here was something else. The boat had air-conditioning, but it struggled to combat the moisture, and she'd felt sticky last night. So, she'd stripped down to her bra and panties for bed. Both of which left little to the imagination.

She crossed the tiny room to the dresser bolted to the wall and took out a pair of shorts and a t-shirt, slipping them on over her undergarments. Opening her door, she went across the hall to the bathroom and used the facilities before brushing her teeth and hair. Finished with the necessities, she joined Ford in the main cabin.

"You took six minutes." He held out a mug of steaming coffee.

"Thank you for not barging into the bathroom." She took the mug. "And thank you for the coffee."

"You're welcome." He nodded toward the table. "Have a seat."

Brooke slid onto the bench seat and put her mug down, wrapping her hands around it. She needed the anchor. Whatever he needed to tell her couldn't be good. Not when he had to wake her up before dawn to do it. She just prayed her family was all right.

Ford sat down on the end of the bench. "I talked to Asher last night—my tech guy?"

She nodded, a frown furrowing her forehead. "Is my family okay?"

"They're fine. But Johnathan's here."

Her eyes widened, and she clutched her mug. "Crap. That was fast."

"Yeah. It seems our fears that my charter would tip him off weren't unfounded." His mouth twisted. "For that, I'm sorry."

"You couldn't have known." She swallowed hard. Up until now, she'd felt safe. The world was a big place. But Costa Rica wasn't. And Johnathan had the money to put resources into finding her. People would talk. All he had to do was flash some cash around, and he could get pretty much whatever information he wanted. "So, what's the plan?"

"We're staying on the boat. I woke you up early, because we need to go into port here and get some supplies. Enough for a week or two."

"A week or two? On the water?"

He nodded. "Once we're stocked, we're going out to sea. I can anchor well offshore, and we can just sit there. So long as the weather holds. If not, well, we'll meander around closer to land. But we can't stay in the gulf."

"So, just hang out, is what you're saying? Until Johnathan gets tired of looking for me? Newsflash—he won't."

"It won't come to that. Asher's working to gather evidence of his plan to murder your dad and grandpa."

"How?" She highly doubted Johnathan wrote any of it down.

"Your fiancé isn't the only person involved."

"Ex-fiancé," she growled. "And you're talking about his brother, Will?"

Ford nodded. "Asher will work his magic and find the evidence, trust me."

Brooke raised an eyebrow, still skeptical. "You sure have a lot of faith in him."

"I do in all of my team. My job is to keep you safe. Theirs is to help me do that. And if that means rooting out evidence, that's what they'll do."

"Okay, but I'm still confused about how he'll find evidence of something I doubt either Johnathan or Will wrote down."

"I've learned it's best not to ask questions about how Asher does things. I just say thank you when he gets me what I need."

She stared at him for several beats and blinked. "If you say so."

He flashed her that wicked smile again. That fine tremor she felt in her dream came back, but this time it was all too real.

"I do." He slid out of his seat. "Finish your coffee. I'm going to start the engine and head for shore."

Brooked glanced down at the still full mug clutched in her fingers. Why was this happening to her? Johnathan was supposed to be safe. She'd wanted vanilla and thought she had it. How did he hide that pungent black licorice side of his personality behind that boring façade?

"Hey."

She looked up.

"It'll be okay. Give me and my team some time—and some trust—and I promise, it will all work out fine."

"I'm trying, but considering how I am apparently a very poor judge of character, I'm questioning everything right now."

His mouth flattened, and he nodded, understanding in his light green eyes. Giving her a soft smile, he left the room.

Brooke blew out a breath and sat back. This wasn't supposed to happen to her. She had a plan for her life. And up until a few days ago, it was going swimmingly. She'd made all the right choices, aligned herself with all the right people. She had the perfect life—a great family, an awesome career, a man she thought she could raise children with. How did she get it so wrong?

Thirteen

Ford's gaze swept the damp street as he and Brooke searched for an open store. Puerto Jiménez was just waking up, so there were few people out, for which he was grateful. Seeing two tourists—alone—this early was an anomaly. They would be remembered.

Luckily, he'd been here often enough he knew of a few places that opened early for the fishing boats, and they weren't far from where many of the fishermen launched, which worked in their favor. There were locals around who were willing to help the captains—for a price. He needed fuel, but didn't want to take the time to get it himself, so after hiring someone to fill his tanks and extra cans, they'd set off for town.

He led Brooke past several closed businesses before stopping in front of what amounted to a convenience store. Grasping the door handle, he let them inside.

A man behind the counter looked up. Ford raised a hand in greeting. "*Buenos días, señor. Necesitamos suministros para un viaje de pesca de una semana en alta mar. ¿Puedes ayudarnos?*" He walked toward the man, asking if he could supply them for a long trip.

"Sí. Reúna lo que necesita. Te conseguiré algunas cajas."

Ford nodded, then turned to Brooke. "He said to gather what we need while he finds us some boxes to carry things."

"I know." She turned away, heading down an aisle.

He blinked, staring after her. She spoke Spanish?

Rolling his eyes, he followed. It shouldn't surprise him. Lots of people did. And in her line of work, it probably paid to know several languages. "Try to pick things that we'll use all of when we open it, or things that don't need refrigeration."

She gave him a thumbs up, already gathering things into her arms.

Ford's mouth flattened. She was a joy this morning. He wasn't sure if it was from their predicament or the fact she'd only had one cup of coffee. He'd noticed she drank several each morning, one after the other.

Eyeing the shelves, he spotted the tins of coffee and grabbed two. One would probably be enough, but he didn't want to chance that they'd run out. He didn't do well uncaffeinated, either.

They made quick work of picking out what they needed, each taking several armloads to the register. The clerk rang items up and boxed them as they dropped them off, so checking out only took a minute.

Ford counted out the bills to cover the cost of the supplies, then added a little extra, making sure the clerk saw. *"Nunca estuvimos aquí."* He couldn't be certain the clerk wouldn't mention them to someone, but tipping him put the odds in Ford's favor.

The clerk winked as he took the money. *"Sí, sí."*

With a nod, Ford lifted the heaviest box, then looked at Brooke. "Can you carry the other one?"

She stepped forward and wrapped her arms around it—barely. Ford was glad the man packed everything in two large boxes—fewer trips—but Brooke was just able to get her arms around it.

"Don't walk too fast." She eyed him over the top of her box.

"I won't. Holler if you need to stop." He turned and headed for the door.

The clerk came around and held it open for them, wishing them a good trip. Ford thanked him, then took off down the street. He was glad the rain had stopped for the time being. Soggy cardboard was not stable cardboard.

But the lull meant more people taking their breakfast outside. They needed to get out of town before too many saw them.

"Ford, you said you wouldn't walk fast."

He glanced back to see Brooke lagging several feet behind and slowed. "Sorry. We need to get back to the boat. Too many people."

Her gaze tracked to the side, lighting on a woman staring at them. She picked up her pace.

Pushing her as fast as he dared, they made it back to the boat in just a couple of minutes. He hopped onboard and set his box down in time to hear Brooke groan from the dock. Glancing up, he saw her straighten from putting down her box. She shook out her arms.

Ford jumped onto the dock. "Hop on. I'll get the box."

She flexed her fingers. "Thanks."

He eyed her as she grasped the rail and pulled herself aboard. Once he was sure she was safe on deck, he picked up her box and hopped on behind her.

"Drag that toward the door, would you?" He nodded to the box he set down as he walked past her. The sound of cardboard dragging over the deck followed him as he entered the living quarters. He headed for the galley and set his load on the table, then returned to get the other box.

"Can you put all of this away?" He looked at Brooke, who'd followed him down. "I want to get us out of port. Now's a good time, because all the fishermen are heading out. We can blend in."

"Sure. But don't blame me when nothing is where you want it."

He flashed her a quick grin. "It's a small kitchen. I'm sure I'll find it eventually." Turning, he lifted a hand. "Thanks." Not waiting for a reply, he hurried through the cabin and out the door to the deck, where he cast off the lines. Taking the steps to the pilothouse two at a time, he sat down at the helm and started the engine.

Ford maneuvered the boat out of its slip and into the small harbor, blending in with several other boats heading out. He'd stay with the crowd until they were a little further out, then he'd slide around the point and head south.

Urgency had him tapping his fingers on the helm as he followed the other boats. Knowing Cassidy was out there looking for them had him on edge. The gulf wasn't large, and while his boat was small, they were still too closed in for comfort. He'd feel a lot better when they were out on the open ocean.

Eyes on the water, he stayed close to shore, putting other boats between him and the main body of the gulf. Near the point, something in the distance caught his eye. He reached for the binoculars on the helm and trained them ahead and to the left.

A yacht came into view. He couldn't see the name, but everything else about it looked like the one Asher described. The gold stripe gleamed in the early morning sunshine.

"Dammit." He lowered the binoculars and opened the throttle. They needed to get out of sight before it got any closer. Once he turned to go around the point, the name of his boat would be visible until they made it to the other side.

Thankfully, they were far enough out he could put on a little speed.

Footsteps on the ladder alerted him to Brooke's presence.

"Sit down on the floor."

"What?"

He glanced back to see her stopped at the top of the stairs.

"Get down," he barked.

Fire flashed in her eyes. "Excuse me?"

"Bad guys ahead." He pointed into the distance. "Sit down."

Her eyes widened a fraction as her gaze darted in the direction he indicated. She walked forward and sat down, her back against the wall. "You're sure it's them?"

"Not a hundred percent, but the boat matches the description I got."

"Okay. What's the plan?"

"We're going to round the point, then hightail it for open ocean."

"And if they see us?"

"Same plan."

She groaned. "Can we outrun them?"

"Maybe. I can do twenty knots, max. The boat they're on —" He lifted a shoulder. "It probably does about the same. So long as we stay ahead of them, we should be okay." He peered up at the sky through the window. "Once the rain moves back in, it will reduce visibility, which will help."

"You hope. We could turn right into their path and not even know it."

"Honey, I don't intend to turn. Once we pass the peninsula, we're burning fuel until we're well offshore, then anchoring. They'll have to find us in the vast Pacific."

"Oh."

Ford focused on driving. The point loomed ahead. As they neared, he sped up. He wanted to get around it quickly, but he also didn't want to draw attention to them, so he kept it lower than he'd have liked. Grabbing the binoculars, he turned, finding the yacht. It had turned and was coming toward Puerto Jiménez.

With a curse, he lowered the glasses and opened the throttle.

Brooke let out a squeak as the boat lurched forward. "Crap. Did they see us?"

"Not sure, but they turned this way. Could be they're just checking out all the fishing vessels, hoping to find us hiding in plain sight." He glanced at the thinning crowd. A few others had come up this far, but most were heading more north, into the gulf.

He sped ahead of the few remaining boats and rounded the point, not backing off on their speed. He hadn't been kidding when he said they were going to burn fuel. When they docked, he'd paid a local to fill up his tanks and all his extra fuel cans. They had enough to take them well away from land and still get back with room to spare.

Fourteen

Brooke tried to meld into the floor as Ford sped away from land. How did Johnathan find her already? It didn't seem possible they could be so unlucky that he would stumble over them so soon. They were across the gulf from where they started. It was a small gulf, but it was long. Why would they come to Puerto Jiménez first? She didn't have an answer, but she hoped Ford could lose them.

They bumped over the waves, which grew as they headed south. Rain slapped the windows again, reducing visibility and forcing Ford to slow down. Brooke's stomach turned. She clenched her teeth, trying not to puke. The bow tipped skyward, then pitched low.

Oh, that did it.

She scrambled to her feet, heading for the stairs.

"What are you doing? Stay down."

Ford's tone brooked no argument, but she ignored him and just kept scrabbling toward the ladder. The boat pitched again, sending her crashing into the wall. She dropped to her knees and slid, holding her breath. If she breathed, she'd throw up.

"Brooke?" Ford called her name, then cursed.

She made it to the ladder and gripped the rails, descending as fast as she could with the boat rolling in the waves. Her singular focus was on reaching the bathroom.

Reaching the bottom tread, the boat pitched up, and she slammed into the deck as she stepped off. Knees throbbing and palms stinging, she pushed to her feet, sliding on the wet deck, and hurried around to the door leading into the cabin. Stumbling inside, she ran through the main cabin and down the steep stairs, into the bathroom. In the same move, she threw open the toilet lid and landed on her knees. Her stomach heaved, rejecting the yogurt and coffee she had earlier.

As the boat rolled and swayed, Brooke hugged the toilet, praying for the storm to end. She had nothing left to give to the porcelain god, but the dry heaves were relentless.

The rolling slowly ebbed, taking her heaving with it. Clammy and her muscles aching, she slid to the floor and laid on her side in the small area around the toilet. She'd get up in a minute. Once she had some energy back.

"Brooke?" Ford's voice carried down the hall a moment before he appeared in the bathroom doorway. "Jesus." He took two hurried steps toward her and crouched at her side. "Are you all right?"

"Just peachy, captain." She mustered the effort to roll her eyes, then closed them.

"Come on. Let's get you to your room."

Hands slid under her body, and she rolled toward him. Brooke opened her eyes. "What are you doing?"

"I just told you." He stood, taking her with him.

She looped an arm over his shoulder to steady herself. Muscles shifted beneath her fingers. A tingle of awareness shot through her, edging out some of the fatigue that had taken hold. She bit her lip, trying to hold it at bay. Ford was an attractive man, but letting her attraction grow would be a colossal mistake. He was here to help her. She didn't need *another* man complicating her life.

In a few long strides, they were out of the bathroom and in her stateroom. Ford set her against the pillows on her unmade bed, then straightened, turning on the bedside lamp. "Can I get you anything? Do you want some water?"

Brooke laid a hand over her stomach and bit back a groan at the thought of putting anything in it. "I'm good for now." She'd live with the sour taste in her mouth until things were more settled.

"Okay. I have some sea sickness patches in the med kit. I'll bring you one. We need to use them sparingly, though. There are only a few." He backed toward the door.

She nodded. "Sounds good. Thank you." She closed her eyes as he turned and left. Her stomach still churned, the motion of the boat keeping the feeling alive, but it was better than before. She'd be glad to slap one of those patches on, though. Never in her life had she been bothered so much by the ocean. But she'd always been on bigger boats. Ford's boat wasn't small, but compared to the yachts and cruise ships she'd been on, it was dinky.

Footsteps in the hall made her open her eyes. Ford turned the corner into the room. He flipped on the overhead light, making her wince.

"Sorry. Do you want me to turn it off?" He paused and motioned to the light switch.

"No. It's fine." She pushed against the pillows and sat up.

Ford walked closer and sat on the edge of the bed. Opening the med kit in his hands, he rummaged through it, then pulled out a small package. Paper ripped as he opened it. "Okay, pull your hair back. This goes behind your ear."

She swept her hair to the side and turned her head, exposing her left ear. His fingers skimmed the sensitive skin on her neck. A tingle of awareness zipped down her spine, despite her unsettled stomach. She clenched her teeth and willed him to hurry.

"This can stay on up to three days. I have some tablet medications, too, if the patch doesn't work." He pressed on the bony area behind her ear, then rubbed in a small circle before removing his hand. "You should probably come up on deck. The roll isn't as bad, and you'll be able to see the water. Both will help with the seasickness."

"Is it safe?" She wasn't talking about the weather. On deck, she'd be exposed, where anyone could see her.

He nodded. "I lost them in the storm. We'll tuck you into a corner just to be safe, but you should be fine."

"Okay." Swinging her legs around, she grimaced as her stomach rolled.

"Do you want me to carry you?"

Brooke shot him a dirty look. "I'm not an invalid. It's just a little seasickness."

His lips twitched, and a twinkle danced in his eyes. "I'll follow you, then. Make sure you're steady on your feet."

She wasn't about to argue with that. The last thing she needed was a tumble down the steep stairs. Sliding forward, she found the floor and stood. She swayed and shot a hand out, clutching Ford's shoulder.

"Easy. I've got you." He stood, wrapping a hand around her forearm.

Taking a deep breath, Brooke uncurled her fingers from his t-shirt and headed for the door, using the furniture and walls to support her unsteady legs. With Ford behind her, she made it up to the main cabin and outside.

Wind whipped her in the face, bringing the scent of rain and sea with it. The air was damp, but the rain had moved on, and the sun was trying to peek through the clouds.

"Where are we?" She glanced around and saw nothing but ocean.

"About seven miles out. I wanted to clear the weather. Thankfully, it was just a squall."

"That was some squall."

"They can be, especially over the water. The storms feed on the warmth and moisture." He urged her toward the bench built into the wall to the side of the door they just came through. "Have a seat."

Brooke shuffled over and sat down. The vinyl seat was already dry. "Is there more weather coming?"

"Always at this time of year. If it looks too bad, I'll try to steer us away from it, but a lot of it we'll just have to ride out. I don't have the fuel to dodge them all."

She wrinkled her nose. "Great." She made a mental note to find the cleaning supplies once she felt better and go down and scrub the bathroom. If she was going to spend a lot of time hugging the porcelain throne, she wanted it to be squeaky clean.

"Can I get you anything?"

"No. I'm fine. Thank you."

His head bobbed once. "I'm going to go straighten up and put away anything that came loose during the storm. Holler if you need me."

The boat rolled with a wave. Brooke closed her eyes and held back the moan that started in her throat. She swallowed hard. "Yep."

After a long moment, she heard the soft slap of his shoes on the deck as he turned away and went inside. Once she was sure he was out of earshot, she let the moan loose. The patch needed to kick in quick. This was dumb.

FIFTEEN

Glancing around the cabin, Ford propped his hands on his hips. He finally had things where they belonged. That squall had been worse than he anticipated.

His stomach rumbled, reminding him he'd eaten little today. He eyed the cabinets now stocked with everything he just put away again. Hauling things back out held little appeal. And fresh fish sounded amazing. This area was a good place for snapper and mahi-mahi. Either one would be fine with him.

Mind made up, he headed outside. Emerging from the cabin, he looked to his left, where he'd left Brooke. She had wedged herself into the corner, feet propped on the seat, and was sound asleep.

Good. That meant the patch was working. Her body needed the rest. He'd catch them some lunch, then wake her.

As quietly as he could, he crossed the deck and opened the cabinet where he kept his lures. Choosing an appropriate one, he unlatched a pole from the rail and tied on the lure, then cast over the side.

The slow tick of his reel accompanied the sound of the

water lapping against the hull and the snap of the flag flying above the pilothouse. Ford closed his eyes and took a deep breath, letting the peacefulness wash over him. He let the adrenaline of the last couple of hours go and felt his shoulders relax. For now, they were safe.

A soft groan cut through the sound of the ocean. He glanced back to see Brooke sit up and stretch. Her breasts pressed against her t-shirt with the move. Ford quickly glanced away, clenching his teeth. He did not need to be attracted to this woman. It could never amount to anything, and she wasn't the type for a fling. If he wanted to scratch that itch, there was always a willing woman at Sam's bar.

He chanced a glance at Brooke again. She ran a hand through her hair.

But, damn, she was pretty. He looked away.

"What are you doing?"

Ford kept his eyes on the water. "Catching lunch."

"Oh. Can I try?"

He felt, more than saw, her presence as she came up beside him. "You know how to fish?"

"Of course I do."

Her indignant tone brought his head up, and he looked her way. "Don't get your panties in a wad. You don't exactly look like the type who spends her time handling slimy things." Her manicured nails and soft hands said she didn't exactly spend her days getting dirty.

"Yeah, well, you should stop assuming you know me. Rich girl doesn't mean helpless girl." She crossed her arms and pinned him with her amber-eyed stare.

"Fine." He stepped back and held out his pole. "Have at it." Letting her have a go would be preferable to her standing there—within touching distance—while he tried to fish. She wrecked his concentration when she was so close.

She took the rod. "What am I trying to catch, anyway?"

"Snapper or mahi-mahi," he said over his shoulder on the way to get another lure. Opening the cabinet, he selected another lure and closed the door. He turned back in time to see her wrinkle her nose.

"Mahi-mahi are fast, aren't they?"

"Yes. They'll put up a fight. If you need help, just holler."

A determined glint entered her eyes. He bit back a smile. She wouldn't ask for help until the fish pulled her overboard. Even then, she'd probably swim to the ladder in the rear and pull herself back on board.

Tying on the lure, Ford cast it over the side, then slowly reeled it in.

"So, you really fish all day for a living?"

"No, I help others fish."

She shook her head. "I have a hard time picturing you doing that." She sent him a quick look. "You're not the most —peopley person I've ever met."

Ford chuckled. "You should stop assuming you know me."

A smile tilted her mouth. "Touché." Her reel ticked as she wound the line back in. "You know, maybe we should get to know each other a bit." She cast him a quick look. "Since we're stuck together."

His light mood darkened. He didn't want to get to know her. It would just make him care more. "That's not a good idea; and you learned enough the other day. This is temporary."

"So? We'll be quite bored if we don't talk the entire time we're out here."

"We can talk. Just not about anything personal." He had no desire to clue her in to what made him tick. She could just keep wondering.

"Oh, yeah, sure. That'll work." She rolled her eyes. "So, you said you're from Florida, right?"

Ford huffed, getting the sense she'd pull every bit of information out of him she could. Short of yelling at her to leave him alone or locking himself in his stateroom, he didn't know how to stop her. The silent treatment would only work so long. "You don't give up, do you?"

"Nope." She brought her rod back and cast the line out again. "Answer my question. You can tell me that much."

He pressed his lips together and brought his line up, casting it out again. *Dammit.* "Yes."

"Really? Well, the water thing makes a little more sense now. Did you live on the coast?"

"Yeah."

"And your ex-wife is really the reason you didn't go back there when you left the Navy?"

He kept his eyes on the water. "Yep." She wasn't the only reason, but she was the only one he was willing to talk about.

"She must be a piece of work."

"She is." His words came out clipped and curt.

Her gaze darted toward him. She opened her mouth, but her line jerked before she could say anything.

Ford blew out a breath of relief. He didn't want to alienate her—she was right; they were stuck together—but his personal life was none of her business.

"Do you need help?" Muscles popped in her arms as she pulled back on the rod and reeled in the line. She had her feet braced against the wall and leaned back.

"No." She spun the reel again.

Ford reeled in his line and propped his rod in the holder. He wanted to be ready if she needed help. For now, she was doing great. He was actually a little impressed. She seemed to know what she was doing.

Standing back, he watched as she brought the fish in. It was a nice size mahi-mahi. Enough to easily feed them both.

A bright smile on her face, she grasped the line and turned

to him. "So, you're doing the gross part, right? Since I caught it?"

Ford let out a short laugh. "Sure, princess."

Sixteen

Brooke glared at the rain from her seat beside the door to the main cabin. She hugged her legs tighter to her chest and rested her chin on her knees. Why couldn't she be in Costa Rica during the dry season? The sunshine they had at lunch didn't last long. Ford got the fish clean and grilled on his little propane grill just as the first droplets smacked into her face. They'd retreated to the cabin to eat. Brooke tried going back to her room, but the motion of the boat threatened to bring her lunch up, so she moved back to the bench. At least there was an overhang, so she stayed dry.

She sighed. She should have grabbed a book. What she really wanted was her phone. She probably had a million emails.

A harsh laugh burst from her chest. It wouldn't matter if she had her phone. She'd never get a signal way out here.

Tears welled in her eyes. How did this happen? Where did she go wrong that she got engaged to a psycho? That she now had to hide out on a boat with a stranger in the middle of the Pacific? Things like this only happened in books and movies. Not in her life. She was boring. Despite her wealth, Brooke didn't lead an exciting life. The most excitement she saw was a live band at the local bar with her friends. Most trips she took were for work. Maybe once a year she took a decent vacation. This year, she went to her family's lodge and shut off her phone. It was bliss.

She turned her head to rest her cheek on her knees. She just wanted to go home.

Staring out at the rain, she didn't really see it. Her mind swirled, trying to process the craziness of the last few days. She was so lost in her thoughts, it took her a moment to recognize that something had changed.

She lifted her head and stared. The wind blew, shifting the curtain of rain, and a light appeared in the distance.

"Shit!" Brooke scrambled to her feet. They were miles out to sea. In bad weather. There shouldn't be any other lights. She grasped the ladder leading up to the pilothouse and Ford. Unless he was turned around, watching their stern, he wouldn't see the light.

"Ford!" Her head crested the landing. He glanced back. She pointed as she entered. "I saw lights."

His eyebrows slammed together. "You're sure?"

"Absolutely." Breathing hard, she reached his side.

"How far?"

"I don't know. Far enough it wasn't that bright, but close enough I couldn't mistake it for anything else." She stared at the rain behind them, willing it to die down and make the light visible again. At least then he'd be able to plot a course away.

"Where was it?"

She gestured in the general direction of where she'd seen them. "Off that way."

The engine revved as Ford pushed the throttle higher. "Damn this weather. I can't go as fast as I want. Even this is pushing it. Sit down. It's going to get rough."

Brooke sank to the floor and clutched the bottom of the captain's chair. She'd sit in the co-pilot's seat, but was afraid she'd fall off. No, the floor was definitely safer.

The boat shook as they rammed a wave. Brooke clenched her teeth to keep them from jarring together. They hit another one, then another. Her muscles shook as she held on.

"Where are we going?" she yelled.

"Away."

She rolled her eyes. Well, duh.

The rough ride continued until Ford finally slowed the boat fifteen minutes later. Brooke relaxed her grip on the chair and flexed her fingers.

"Are we safe now?"

His eyes scanned the ocean. "Maybe. I went west. We're a little closer to land than I'd like, but I'm hoping they continue out to sea. It would be nice to be between them and land. It gives us more options."

"The jungle gives us options?"

"Of course. Places to hide. Food. And a way to get help if we need it."

Brooke scrunched her nose and looked away. He had a point. "I thought you wanted to be on the open ocean, though."

"That was before."

"Before what? They were already on our trail when you said that."

He cast a glance at her. "How's your stomach?"

"Huh? My stomach?" Her expression cleared, then turned incredulous. "You're altering our plan because I'm seasick? Ford, I can handle being nauseous. I can't handle being dead."

"We'll be fine. And I do like the idea of having land as an option. You didn't answer my question. How's your stomach? Is the patch working?"

Her mouth flattened, and she blinked twice before answering. "It's all right. The rough waves made me nauseous, but not like before. The patch is doing its job."

"Good." He pushed the throttle higher. "Time to put some more distance between us and them. Let me know if you see any more lights."

Her stomach flew up into her throat as they hit a wave and the boat dipped. She laid a hand over her belly. He expected her to focus at this speed? And what happened to being concerned about her stomach? Apparently, he also agreed that being dead was bad.

She clenched her teeth and tried not to think about how she felt. He couldn't drive the boat and keep watch. And she definitely didn't want Johnathan catching up.

The further west they went, the more the weather cleared. With the ride smoothing out, Brooke decided it was time to move around. Her legs were asleep. Unfurling from her cramped position, she hauled herself to her feet. She bit back a groan as the muscles in her back and hips protested.

"You okay?"

Brooke looked at Ford. "I'm fine. Why?"

"Your face scrunched, like you were in pain."

"Oh." She waved a hand, pressing the other one to the small of her back as she tried to stretch out the kinks. "My back just aches. I'm fine, though."

"You're too young for back problems."

She held up a finger. "First of all, I don't have back problems. I sat on a hard floor too long and my muscles cramped. Second, I'm older than I look." She hated when people said she was too young. Which was usually in the midst of a business deal. She was twenty-nine. That wasn't young. Besides, age didn't trump experience. She'd grown up in her family business, and people seemed to forget that.

Ford mumbled something under his breath that sounded

like thank God. Brooke squinted at him, but he kept talking before she could ask what he said, and she let it go.

"Why don't you go walk around? Stretch out your muscles. Take advantage of this weather." He motioned to the sun peeking through the clouds. "It won't last."

Giving him a long look, wondering about the abrupt change in subject, she finally nodded. "I'll make us some sandwiches for dinner too." She didn't know about him, but she was suddenly famished.

"Sounds good."

Back still stiff, she headed for the stairs, hoping she looked graceful and not like some little old lady who really should use a cane. She really was older than she looked.

Hanging on to the railing, she made it to the main deck. Rounding the ladder, she headed for the door into the cabin when a noise, like a loud puff of air, caught her attention. She looked up in time to see a whale breach the surface and come crashing back down.

"Holy crap!" She put a hand on the wall and stared a moment before edging closer to the railing to watch.

Another whale broke the glassy surface, blowing air through its blowhole. It disappeared beneath the waves with a flick of its tail and a quick spray of water.

Transfixed, she watched the pod cruise past. They continued to breach, sending waves and fat droplets of water at the boat. Brooke gripped the rail and watched them as the vessel bobbed.

"It's amazing, isn't it?"

She jumped at the sound of Ford's voice, then glanced at him, a wide smile on her face. "Yes. We don't get things like this in North Carolina. I see a lot of dolphins and a few sharks when I stay at my parents' beach house, but nothing like this. What kind are they?"

"Humpback. It's migration season. They come here for

the warmer waters. This group is here from down around Antarctica."

She sent him a quizzical look. "How do you know that?"

He shrugged a shoulder. "Just knowledge I've picked up living here the last few years. We're a hot spot for wintering humpbacks. The northern group comes in December and stays until March or April. The southern group comes in July and stays until November."

"Really? That's neat." She looked out at the water as another whale broke the surface, then crashed back down, sending water spraying. Droplets pelted her. "This is so cool."

The angst and worry of the last few days faded away as she stood there and watched. Whale after whale broke the surface, putting on a spectacular show. From large to small, young to old, they surfaced. She could even hear them talking to each other; their whistles and clicks filled the air.

Eventually, they moved on, but the wonder at what she witnessed didn't fade and left her more relaxed than she'd been in days. It almost made her forget why she was out here. Almost.

SEVENTEEN

Silence enveloped Ford as he cut the engine. With calm seas—for now—and the anchor down, he could relax and get some rest. It had been a long day—in fact, it was a new day. But he still needed to talk to Asher. See if there was anything new on the investigation.

Digging into the small satchel he'd brought up with him, he removed the satellite phone and powered it on. Once it was booted up and connected, he dialed Asher's number.

"Hey, man. You all safe?"

"Yeah. We're holed up near Punta Salsipuedes. It's shallow here. Should keep Cassidy's bigger boat further out to sea." He'd brought them in closer to shore when he realized where they were. He could maneuver here, and the larger yacht couldn't.

"Have you seen it?"

"Maybe. I'm pretty sure we saw it near Puerto Jiménez this morning. We got into some weather and lost them, but later in the day, we saw lights through the storm. I didn't stick around to see who emerged from the rain. Haven't seen anyone in a while now."

"Okay. Be careful out that way. Help is a long way off."

"I know. Have you heard anymore from Ezra? What's going on back in the States?" He didn't need a lecture on the dangers of being at sea with the bad guys chasing him. He'd lived it and survived.

"Ezra's apprised Brooke's family of what's going on. He's got some friend of his who's an ATF agent looking into things off the books. I guess he also found Will Cassidy, Johnathan's brother, and is trying to get some dirt to get him to roll."

"Damn. He's been busy today."

"Yeah, well, Brooke's his friend."

Ford's mind wandered to the woman sleeping below deck. It seemed improbable that his little socialite passenger could inspire such loyalty in his friend. Sure, she was resilient, but the pampered princess side of her had shown its face a few times since she'd been with him. Apparently, she showed a side of herself to Ezra he'd yet to see. Though, to be honest, he hadn't really tried to get to know her. He didn't want to get attached; he didn't need another friend.

He cleared his throat. "So, what about you? Have you uncovered anything?"

"Actually, there are some skeletons in Cassidy's closet I don't think Brooke knows about."

"Oh?"

"So, when Johnathan and Will were in high school, their parents sent them to some out-of-state boarding school in Virginia. When Johnathan was a senior and Will a sophomore, one of their classmates died. A girl in Johnathan's class. Wendy Swenson."

"How did she die?"

"Car accident."

"Teenagers die in car accidents all the time, Asher. What makes Ms. Swenson special?"

"If you'd give me a minute, I was getting to that." A note of exasperation colored Asher's voice.

Ford grinned. He loved messing with the man. He was quick to rise to the bait. Especially when he couldn't see Ford's face. "My apologies. Do continue."

"Thanks." Sarcasm dripped from the word. "Anyway, what makes her special is she was Johnathan's girlfriend."

Any trace of amusement fled. Ford straightened. "Why didn't you lead with that?"

"'Cause it's fun to screw with you."

Ford rolled his eyes. It seemed Asher was on to him and was turning the tables. "Was Johnathan involved in the accident?"

"No. But Will was. He wasn't in the car, but he told investigators she showed up at one of their local hangouts looking for Johnathan. He said he told her his brother was at his dorm, studying. Said she left, and that was the last he heard from her. She crashed on the way there."

"Why didn't she check his dorm room first? Why the hangout spot?"

"I don't know. But there's more. I got ahold of the case report. The detective spoke with some of Wendy's friends. She and Johnathan were on the outs. I guess he dumped her, but she wouldn't tell her friends why."

"What? That doesn't make sense. Teenage girls tell each other those things."

"Yep. Which is why I dug deeper. Wendy Swenson's autopsy revealed she was pregnant."

"Holy shit."

"It gets better. That information was never released to the public. In fact, the whole case kind of—went away. There are no follow-ups in the case file, no paternity tests done on the fetal tissue. Even her car was sent to a scrapyard within a few days of the wreck, where it was crushed and recycled."

"Shit, Asher, someone paid to have the case buried. After they tampered with her car, I'm betting."

"That's my guess. But I don't have any evidence to corroborate that. It's all been lost to time or destroyed. Officially, the local police and the coroner ruled her death as accidental. The file says she lost control at high speeds and hit a tree. She died instantly."

"On a curve?"

"No. A T intersection. She tried to make the turn and went off the far side of the road into a tree."

Ford scoffed. "Close enough. Okay. Um, this is all great information, but it doesn't help us with his current misdeeds."

"No, but it establishes a pattern. And it gives us something to go at Will Cassidy with. I doubt Wendy was calm when she went looking for Johnathan. And from what I've learned so far about the brothers, they're inseparable. Brooke can probably confirm that. In fact, you might want to ask her about it. About Wendy. See what she knows."

"In the morning, I will. Do you have anything more for me?"

"No, that's it for now. I put Dean on a plane this afternoon, armed with what I just told you. He's going to persuade Will to talk. Ezra's not an interrogator, and his friend's hands are tied because of his job."

Ford bit back a groan. "Just tell him to be careful. Bailing him out of jail is not in my budget."

"He'll be fine. It's Dean."

"Yeah." Ford sighed. "That's what worries me." The younger man was a skilled operative, but could be impulsive.

"Don't borrow trouble. Keep your eye on Brooke. I'll keep my eye on the investigation."

Ford let out another long breath. "Yeah. Okay. Fine. Thanks, Asher. I appreciate it."

"You're welcome. Stay safe." The line clicked, then the phone beeped as the call disconnected.

Ford stared at the phone for a long moment before powering it down. If what Asher surmised was true, it made him wonder if there were others in Johnathan's life who had met a similar fate. Who else had paid a price to get Johnathan the life he wanted?

Shaking his head, he put the phone away and stepped out of the pilothouse. He didn't have an answer to that, and he wouldn't get one tonight. It was time for bed.

Moonlight lit the stairs as Ford descended the ladder from the pilothouse. He smothered a yawn. There used to be a time he could run on a few hours of sleep for days straight without a problem. But his beat-up, almost forty-year-old body couldn't do that anymore. Now he dragged if he went more than a day or so with less than eight hours a night.

It wasn't like he hadn't tried to sleep. But every little noise woke him up. Something that wasn't uncommon for him on a mission or a case.

The woman under his protection didn't help, either. Brooke McGinty set him on edge. From the moment he opened his door and saw her standing there with Ezra, something deep inside him stood up and took notice. Every movement she made, he subconsciously tracked. Her smile set off a zing in his gut. And those amber eyes captivated him.

It drove him nuts. He didn't want to be attracted to her. Didn't want to waste brainpower thinking about her on that level. It was pointless. But his body just couldn't seem to get the memo. Even less so when he was tired.

He shook his head. His old age was making him soft. He used to be able to shut things like this down, stuff it in a box, and never think about it again.

Turning to go inside, he stopped short. The woman

haunting his thoughts sat curled up on the bench beside the doorway, covered in a blanket.

She lifted her head. "Hey."

"Hey. What are you doing out here? It's late. You should be asleep."

Brooke lifted a shoulder. "Couldn't sleep. The boat moves too much down below. So I came up here."

"Is your patch not working anymore?" He'd hoped it would last longer. But some people needed more for seasickness than others.

"It's okay. But the rolling was just making things—unsettled. I'm all right out here on the deck."

Ford glanced around. She was protected under the overhang. So long as the wind didn't change direction if it rained. Then she'd get soaked. But there was another problem. "You intend to stay out here all night?"

She nodded.

He sighed and moved to sit down on the bench on the other side of the doorway. So much for sleeping soundly tonight.

"What are you doing?"

"Going to sleep."

"Out here?"

"What? It's not good enough for both of us?"

She let out an inelegant snort. "It's not proper for anyone. But it's the only way I'll sleep. Why are you staying out here?"

"Because you are."

"What? That's ridiculous."

"No, it's not." He swung his legs up and leaned against the wall. "How can I protect you stuck down in my cabin while you're up here?"

She let out a little huff. "What's going to get me in the middle of the ocean?"

"Oh, most likely we'll be fine. But what if Cassidy finds us while we're asleep? At least when we're both on the same level, I have a chance at defending you." The truth was, if Cassidy and his goons boarded their boat, Ford wasn't sure he could take them all on. They'd be armed—and he was too—but one against several were not great odds.

"You know, we can't keep running indefinitely."

"We won't." His conversation with Asher gave him some hope that soon, he and the others could come up with a plan to catch Johnathan Cassidy and get Brooke back to her life.

She gave another snort. "You say that, but I still don't see how your guys are going to pin anything on him when there's no evidence except my short recording."

"Asher uncovered some leverage." He fixed his eyes on her, just making out her face in the low light.

"Leverage? What kind?"

"Did he or Will ever talk about a Wendy Swenson?"

She muttered the name under her breath, glancing away a moment before looking at him. "Not that I recall. Who is she?"

"Johnathan's high school girlfriend. She died in a car accident their senior year."

Brooke's soft gasp echoed off the overhang. "He told me about that, but not her name. Just mentioned it once that his girlfriend in high school died in a crash."

"Did he also tell you she was pregnant at the time?"

"What? No! Seriously?"

Ford nodded.

Brooke looked away, drawing her knees up. She wrapped her arms around them, putting her face in the moonlight. He could see the pensiveness lining her pretty features.

"What are you thinking?"

She continued to stare out at the water. "That I didn't know him at all."

"Tell me what you thought you knew."

She drew in a breath and let it out. A long moment passed. "We met when he took a position with the company a few years ago. At the Christmas party Grandpa throws for the executives and their families every year. He bumped into me, and I spilled red wine on my dress." She lifted a shoulder. "After apologizing profusely and offering to pay for the dry cleaning, he asked me to dance. He was charming, you know? And seemed nice, if not a little awkward."

"So you started dating?"

"Yeah. And things seemed fine. A little boring, maybe, but fine." She shook her head. "I didn't see it. Didn't see the crazy."

"Nothing?"

"Not really, no. He was kind of scary when he got angry, but never violent. It was just a look in his eyes." She gave a little shudder. "I tried not to make him mad."

Ford chewed on a corner of his mouth, digesting her words. "Tell me something? Why did you go for someone like Cassidy? I mean, I get that he was good at hiding his true self, but if the relationship was boring, like you said, why did you let it continue? You don't seem like the boring type."

Brooke's mouth flattened. "Because I wanted the same safe, respectful marriage my parents had. Somewhere along the line, I figured that meant boring. Until my friend Gemma met her husband, I never questioned that."

"I take it they're not boring?"

Brooke chuckled. "Nope. Not even a little."

"Safe doesn't have to mean boring, you know."

"I get that now. And it wasn't all boring. We did things, but it was never spontaneous. And in the romance department, Johnathan was—adequate."

The sudden tightness in her body told Ford she was probably blushing and regretting divulging that information. He regretted it too. It made him want to show her something more than adequate.

"You deserve more than safe and adequate." The words rumbled between them before he could pull them back.

Jesus, Ford. Way to keep your distance. That will not help keep thoughts of her away. He rolled his eyes at himself, glad she couldn't see him well in the dark. The words had just popped out. He must be more tired than he thought.

She raised her head, peering at him through the darkness for a moment before looking away again. "Yes, well, it's not always about what we deserve. I thought what I had was what I wanted."

"And now? What do you want now? Still vanilla? Or do you want some spice?"

Christ. Just shut up, Ford. Why couldn't he stop the tumble of words?

Eighteen

Awash of heat stole over Brooke's body, making her blush from head to toe. She was glad he couldn't see her well. This would be a thoroughly embarrassing conversation in the daylight. It was bad enough in the dark. "I don't think that's any of your business."

"Probably not, but I'm just trying to help you out. I doubt you'd ask yourself such a question."

Indignation rose, replacing the heat. "There you go again, assuming you know me."

"Well, would you?"

She pressed her lips together. "Yes." She pushed the word through clenched teeth.

In the low light, she saw his teeth flash with a quick smile. "Sure you would."

Brooke bit back a growl. He was impossible. "You know what? I think I'll try to sleep downstairs after all." Her feet hit the deck with a thump.

"Stop." He sat up and held out a hand. "I wasn't trying to upset you."

"Well, you did. I don't enjoy being picked on. We all make mistakes. Mine just happened to be a big one."

"You're right, and I'm sorry. Please stay. I don't want you to make yourself uncomfortable by trying to sleep in the cabin. You need to get some rest."

She slowly sat back. "Thank you." She doubted she'd sleep well out here, though. Not with him close by. His mere presence put her body on alert. Especially after that comment about whether she wanted some spice in her life. Boy, did she ever.

Brooke clenched her fists. She did not want spice. Not with Ford. No.

Her eyes traveled the length of his body—well, what she could see of it through the shadows, anyway. Her dream from last night flickered through her mind. She wondered if he'd look the same.

No! She clenched her fists harder, her nails digging into her palms. The pain helped banish thoughts of what he'd look like sans the shirt. She scooted back into her little corner and drew her legs up again. Maybe if she hid in the shadows and pretended he wasn't there, she'd be able to fall asleep.

She shifted, leaning her head against the wall, and closed her eyes, willing sleep to come.

Ford moved; the rustle of his clothing reached her ears. Immediately, an image of him shirtless popped into her brain again. Brooke blew out a breath and curled into a tighter ball. What was wrong with her? She'd never even seen him shirtless. That shouldn't be an image in her mind.

Angry at herself, she pictured a meadow full of sheep and started counting. It wasn't something she typically did, but she was desperate. If she went to sleep thinking about Ford, she'd dream about him again. The last thing she needed was to moan his name in her sleep when he was ten feet away.

She heard him sigh, but kept her eyes closed and tried to

make her breathing slow and even. Maybe he'd go somewhere else for a bit if he thought she was asleep. Then, maybe, she could actually accomplish that feat.

"I know you're pretending."

"So?" She kept her eyes closed. "Stop talking to me."

He chuckled.

Brooke huffed. She opened her eyes. "I want to sleep."

"Hmm, sure."

"I do."

"Brooke, I can hear you thinking from here."

Her cheeks flushed. She was so glad he couldn't actually hear what went on in her head. Or see the blush on her face. "Just because my mind won't shut off doesn't mean I don't want to sleep."

"No, but sometimes we need to purge the thoughts from our minds to make sleep happen."

No way was she telling him the thoughts running through her head. "I'm good."

"You don't have to tell me what you're thinking. How about we just talk?"

"We just did that."

"Let's do it some more."

"Okay." He wanted to talk, she'd make him talk. "Tell me about your wife."

"That's not the kind of talking I meant."

Of course it wasn't. "You didn't specify."

"I'm not talking about my ex."

"Then what do you want to talk about?"

"Yours. Or more accurately, what you know about his family."

A hint of something in his voice stopped her from making a smartass remark about not wanting to talk about her ex, either. There was a level of seriousness there she hadn't heard before. "Like what?"

Ford sat up, shrugging one shoulder. "What was his relationship like with his brother?"

"With Will?" She hugged her knees as she thought. "They're pretty close. They do a lot together."

"Did you spend much time with him?"

"Some. He's a little—strange for my tastes."

Ford's gaze sharpened in the moonlight. "How so?"

"I don't know. He's just—" She swayed side to side as she tried to put into words what Will was like. "Deferential? He always wanted to please Johnathan. And he waited on him. I thought that was weird. Anytime we all went somewhere, Will was always the one to get drinks and things for him. Johnathan never went himself."

Ford hummed. "What about the rest of their family?"

"I only met Johnathan's dad. His mom is dead. She died when they were young. And his dad was between wives when I met him."

"Okay, what's he like?"

"A politician. He's a smooth talker and had a phony smile. I didn't care for him much."

"Is he the only other family member you met?"

"Yeah." She rested her chin on her knees. "Johnathan said he didn't have much family. His dad is an only child, and his mom's family lives out of state."

"Where?"

"Massachusetts."

He hummed again.

"What?" She lifted her head. "Why do you keep doing that?"

"Just thinking."

"Well, enlighten me."

In the low light, he held her gaze for a long moment. "Just making mental notes of things to ask Asher to check into."

"Such as?"

"Like, what happened to Johnathan's mom? And why would Will act more like a servant than a brother?"

"I don't know about that last part, but their mom died in some sort of accident."

"Do you know what kind?"

"He said she fell at home."

"Did he say how?"

"No." Her brows pinched. She couldn't help but wonder now if there was more to that story. So much of what she thought she knew about her fiancé was a lie. How did he pull the wool over her eyes so well? She prided herself on being able to pick up on the crap people told her. It's what made her effective at hiring and firing. But Johnathan flew under her radar, and she'd believed every lie he fed her.

Upset with herself, she sat back and huddled into her little corner. "I think I'm tired enough now. Goodnight, Ford."

She could feel his eyes on her, but refused to talk. If she opened her mouth, she'd start bawling.

"Goodnight, Brooke."

Squeezing her eyes shut, she felt a tear slide down her face. For once, she was thankful he wouldn't leave her alone. His presence held back the sobs.

Nineteen

"It's just a fish, Brooke. You can do this," Brooke muttered to herself. Her face twisted into a disgusted frown as she stared at the deceased fish on the table in front of her. She glanced at the knife in her hand. She couldn't believe Ford was making her do this. He'd been about to gut it when he heard the radio crackle to life with a distress call. As he backed away, he'd handed her the knife and said, "Just do it like I showed you. It's easy."

Whether it was easy or not, wasn't the point. It was gross.

Sucking in a deep breath, she lifted the fish's fin and pressed the knife to the centerline of its belly. The tip pierced the scales. She sliced down, careful not to go too deep. Once she had the belly open, she spread the sides apart and reached in. Warm, wet sliminess met her fingers. She gagged. "Oh, this is so disgusting." Turning her face away, she grasped the innards and pulled. In seconds, she had the fish's guts and spine in her hand. Holding it away from her body, she hurried to the side of the boat, but before she could toss it into the water, a seagull swooped toward her. With a shriek, Brooke ducked, throwing her hands up to protect her head. Fish intestines slapped her in the face.

Shrieking again, this time in utter disgust, she dropped the guts on the deck. The bird snatched them up, its bright white wings flapping hard to lift its heavy load. As it passed over her head, she felt something warm land on her shoulder. Glancing down, her eyes widened. "Oh, yuck!" The damn gull had pooped on her.

"Bleck! Oh, that's just disgusting." Brooke stared at her arm as the runny poop slid down the front of her shoulder and onto her bicep. Face contorted in disgust, she glanced around for something to wipe it off with, but the deck was clear. Where did Ford keep the towels? Or the hose?

The gull swooped overhead again, and this time he had friends. They circled her freshly gutted fish.

Brooke changed direction. "Oh, no you don't." She grabbed the fish by the tail and pulled it off the table. She'd just put it in the cooler until she got cleaned up.

Turning, she took two steps and had to duck as a gull dive-bombed her. "Oh!" She pulled the fish in close and ducked her head. "Fricking bird! Leave me alone!" Hunched over the fish, she headed for the cooler. Throwing open the lid, she tossed the fish inside and slammed it shut. The birds still screamed, circling, but they weren't so close now. She glared up at them. "Ha! Let's see you get it now."

"What are you doing?"

Brooke whirled at the sound of Ford's voice. He stood at the edge of the overhang, a curious dip wrinkling his forehead.

"Protecting our dinner. You left, and the gulls decided I was fair game. Do you have a hose or some towels I can clean up with?" She gestured to the white smear on her arm.

He ignored her and walked to the cooler. "Did you really put a fish in my drink cooler?" He opened the lid. The gulls' cries grew louder.

"Would you rather they took it?" She motioned to the dozen birds now flapping overhead. Poop splatted on the deck, and she sighed.

"No. But we put drinks in this. Now it needs bleached."

"Well, then, maybe you shouldn't have left me down here at their mercy." She eyed the gull that landed on the overhang. It stared at the cooler. She squinted. Was that the one that stole the guts? He couldn't possibly still be hungry.

"We always listen to distress calls. It can be the difference between life and death out here."

Brooke harrumphed. She didn't care that he was right. He'd walked away, and she'd been bombarded. "Whatever. Can you finish the fish so I can clean up? The gulls might leave you alone."

He opened a cupboard, revealing a hose. Uncoiling it, he held out the end. "Here. Don't forget to wash the poop off the deck and bleach the cooler. The bleach is in the galley."

She propped her hands on her hips. "The cooler I get, but you want me to wash the deck? They'll just poop on it again. It's *outside*."

Ford shrugged and hooked the end of the hose over the cupboard door, then walked past her to the drink cooler. "Doesn't mean I want to step in fresh seagull shit." Opening the lid, he removed the fish. The gulls went nuts, but kept their distance.

Brooke let out a soft grunt of anger and tipped her nose up. Was she just too small to be intimidating? She wasn't tiny, but Ford was much larger. He also didn't cower when the birds swooped close. She couldn't help it, though. Birds—especially large ones—freaked her out. Their beaks were just so pointy. All she could see was that dagger coming at her, ready to take out her eye.

Glaring at Ford's broad back, she stepped over to the cupboard and turned on the spigot. She squeezed the nozzle, testing the spray. It hit the deck, bouncing back in fine droplets. The briny scent followed. It was seawater coming out, but that didn't bother her. It would still clean her off.

She eyed the mess on her shoulder and arm, wondering how she could clean it off without soaking herself. She really didn't feel like changing shirts.

Mouth pursed, she set the hose down, then with careful movements, slid her clean arm out of her tank top, holding the other side away from her messy skin, she ducked her head through, then drew it down her other arm. Tossing her top onto the bench seat, she picked up the hose.

A soft, strangled sound behind her made her glance back. Ford stared at her, his eyes round.

Brooke bit her lip, and a red stain bloomed on her face and neck. She hadn't given a second thought to stripping down. When she got up this morning, like every morning, she'd put on a bikini beneath her clothes. It dried faster than her underwear, and she always seemed to end up a little damp when they fished.

As she stared at him, his surprised expression morphed. His light brown eyebrows dipped low and his mint-green eyes took on a steely edge. "Seriously? Trying to butter me up won't get you out of the dirty jobs." His gaze traveled over her exposed skin, then he turned his nose up and went back to cleaning the fish. "Rinse off and put your shirt back on."

Anger burned bright in her gut. Pompous ass! She squeezed the nozzle. A spray of water shot out and hit the deck near his feet.

"Hey! Watch it." He looked over his shoulder and glared.

She blinked innocently at him. "Sorry. There was poop. Didn't want you to step in it."

He narrowed his eyes at her. Brooke just smiled sweetly. She pointed the hose at herself, letting water run down her arm and chest, wetting her blue bikini top. Ford's dark expression disappeared as heat flared in his eyes.

Brooke swallowed hard. He might not be angry anymore, but he was no less scary. He looked like he wanted to eat her up.

She shivered. That could be fun.

No! Don't think like that. She broke eye contact and focused on cleaning up. Ford might be sexy as sin, but she did not need a man complicating her life. She had one of those, thanks.

Through her lashes, she glanced at him. He'd gone back to cleaning the fish. Her gaze strayed to his butt. Those board shorts hugged the firm curve to perfection. Maybe it wouldn't be complicated. Maybe it would just be fun.

A flutter low in her belly sent heat pooling in her core. She looked away from Ford's perfect butt and squeezed her eyes closed for a quick moment. What was wrong with her? It had to be all this forced togetherness. She'd *just* broken off her engagement. Johnathan was a psychopath, but still. A week ago, she'd thought he was normal. And while they'd had a rather bland, though satisfying, sex life, she'd cared for him. She should not be lusting after her bodyguard at this stage.

Her gaze returned to Ford's butt. It was so damn perfect.

Huffing, she turned away, shutting off the water and hanging up the hose. She was clean enough.

"Don't forget the deck."

Biting back a growl, she picked up the hose again. Just for that, she was leaving off her top. He'd just have to deal.

Twenty

Ford eyed Brooke through the windscreen. She lounged on the front deck, stripped down to that damn blue bikini he'd seen the top half of earlier. She'd taken to sunning herself in the afternoons if the weather was good. Today's had been spectacular, so after they ate, she'd grabbed a book and gone up front. Normally, he hid out in the main cabin and looked at charts or cleaned, but they'd been out here long enough he didn't have anything left to clean, and he'd plotted every possible course he could. He thought he could handle sailing them to a fishing spot he wanted to check out. That he could ignore her out there and keep his eyes on the water.

He'd been woefully mistaken. Like a beacon, she drew his gaze. It didn't matter how hard he tried, he couldn't keep his eyes off her long, tanned legs or perky breasts spilling out of her bikini top. He didn't know what was wrong with him. He'd never had a problem ignoring scantily clad women—at least, not since he was a horny teenager. Ogling women while they played on the beach wasn't his thing. Everyone deserved to have fun without being stared at. Plus, it was rude to stare.

But his mind refused to be distracted. She was like a damn magnet.

Angry at himself, he sat down, putting his instrument panel closer up and removing her from view. Part of his problem was the lack of physical exercise. There was only so much he could do on his boat. Push-ups and sit-ups in the main cabin. Pulling up the anchor by hand. Wrestling the fish they caught. None of it was enough to burn off the energy he needed to in order to focus.

He eyed the water. Maybe he should go for a swim. It was shallow here, and there was a decent reef. He could break out the snorkeling gear.

Ford shut down the engine and dropped the anchor, not giving himself a chance to debate the idea. He needed the exercise, or he was going to go nuts.

Leaving the pilothouse, he descended the ladder and opened one of the bench seats in search of his snorkeling gear.

"What are you doing?"

"Going snorkeling."

"Oh, that sounds like fun!"

Ford bit back a groan. He hadn't thought this through. Of course, she would want to go too.

He snagged an extra set of gear. Straightening, he let the seat fall back into place and held the kit out to her. "Here."

She took it, frowning at him. Ford knew he was being curt, but he had to get away from her. He needed to get in the water and lose himself in the ocean before he did something really dumb. Like untie that pretty blue bikini so he could see what was underneath.

Clenching his teeth, he turned away, sitting down to fit the fins to his feet. "Stay within about fifty yards of the boat. The currents can be kind of wacky out here, and I don't know this area all that well." He stood and whipped off his shirt, then turned away, settling his mask over his face and the snorkel into his mouth. Not waiting for her, he penguin-walked his way to the rear exit and jumped into the water.

The warm ocean surrounded him, shutting out the sound of the few gulls that hovered near their boat, hoping for scraps. Beneath the waves, the world above receded and took some of his anxiety with it.

He floated to the surface, keeping his face in the water. Taking as deep of a breath as his damaged lung would allow, he dove, mingling with a school of king angelfish. From the corner of his eye, he saw Brooke, cruising along the bottom after a small ray.

All too soon, his diminished lung capacity forced him back to the surface. But he didn't stay there. Over and over, Ford dove, until the tension in his body ebbed and the agitation gripping his mind disappeared.

Relaxed, he rose to the surface and floated, face down, watching the life teeming below. Even when Brooke swam into his field of vision, his mood stayed serene. *This* was why he moved here. The pristine beauty of the ocean touched his soul and was a balm to the psychological wounds of war. The ocean rejuvenated him. It kept him going. Without it, he wasn't sure where he would be, or if he'd even still be alive. Losing his career had been a blow he wasn't ready for. He'd spent many hours in the water, letting the ocean soothe him as it shut out the world so he could sort through his emotions.

Feeling more like himself, Ford swam back to the boat. He grasped the swim deck and hauled himself out of the water. His legs still dangling, he lifted his mask and looked around for Brooke, but the ocean's surface was smooth.

"I wondered if you were ever going to get out."

Her voice behind him had him turning to glance over his shoulder. She sat on the bench seat along the railing, dressed and dry, watching him.

Ford frowned. "How long have you been back on the boat?"

She shrugged. "Half an hour or so."

He grunted and turned, raising his left leg to take off his fin. Honestly, it didn't surprise him he'd been in the water so long. He'd been in rough shape when he went in. "I guess I got caught up in the wildlife down there." He raised his other leg and removed his other fin, then stood and stepped onto the deck.

"It was pretty, yes."

Ford crossed the deck to stow his gear.

"You know, talking helps."

"Helps what?" He lifted the bench and tossed his gear inside, noting she'd already stowed hers.

"With whatever it was that made you dive over the side in such a hurry."

A quick hitch in his movement as he closed the bench was his only indication that he understood her meaning. Turning, he looked at her. "I'm fine. I just needed the exercise. I don't need to talk."

Brooke unfurled from her curled up position and stood. She crossed the few feet separating them and stopped. "Everyone needs to talk sometimes, Ford. And if you ever want to"—she lifted one shoulder—"well, I'm here."

Before he could respond, she gave his bare shoulder a quick touch, then walked around him and went inside.

Ford looked over his shoulder, catching a glimpse of her as the door swung shut. He sighed and shook his head. He hoped his need to exercise away his feelings hadn't inadvertently made things more complicated. Brooke was far more perceptive than he gave her credit for, and she was figuring him out. He didn't need or want her to get inside his head; Ford doubted she'd like what she found.

TWENTY-ONE

Steady rain pelted the deck. The wide-brimmed hat on Brooke's head kept the water out of her eyes as she fished for dinner. Again. Monotony had set in. Over the last several days, it had been the same thing. Get up, eat, laze around, clean a little, eat, laze around some more, fish, eat, clean, attempt to sleep. Rinse and repeat. She'd learned why the bookshelves in the main cabin were so well-stocked. There wasn't much else to do stuck in the middle of the ocean.

Though, to be honest, they weren't in the middle of the ocean. They were still parked near the rocks off the coast. But Ford wouldn't take her ashore to explore. Said it was too risky. That they could get caught unaware if Johnathan found their boat and they were on shore. It made sense, but it also made for boring days.

The rain didn't help. It had become more frequent and steadier. She was just glad it didn't come with the wind, like the other day. The seasickness patch had helped, but she was afraid of what would happen if things got too rough.

Her line zipped out, snapping her from her thoughts.

"Oh!" Working the reel, she fought the fish on the line. It felt heavier than any of the ones before.

"Do you need help?" Ford's footsteps grew closer as he hurried to her side.

"Maybe." She leaned back, pulling on the rod, then spun the reel. "This is a big one." The fish on her line put on a burst of speed, spinning out line. She thumbed the brake into place, then held on for dear life.

"Here." Ford covered her hand on the pole with his. "Let me take over."

Brooke relinquished the rod. Normally, she'd refuse and do it herself, but whatever was on the other end was strong. She'd either end up overboard or she'd lose the pole. So, she stood back and watched Ford bring in their dinner.

Muscles flexed in his forearms as he worked the rod and reel, drawing in the fish. The fierce concentration on his face gave her a glimpse of the warrior he once was. He looked dangerous and so utterly male.

She turned her gaze to the water as an uncomfortable heat spread through her body. The other disadvantage of being stuck on this boat was it was getting harder and harder to resist Ford's magnetism. Too often, she found herself watching him. Watching the play of muscles beneath his shirt or the flex of his calves as he climbed from one level to the next. Her favorite place to stand was at the bottom of the ladder as he went up. The man had an ass like no other.

A splash made her blink. Her eyes widened as she saw the tailfin. "That's a shark."

"Yep." Ford pulled back and turned the reel. "We're not keeping it, but I still need to get it in to cut the line. I don't want it to have too much hanging from its mouth." He reeled it in more, but the shark fought back. Ford flipped off the brake and let the shark have more line.

"What are you doing?"

He adjusted the line tension. "It needs to tire out a little. If I try to pull it in now, it'll just snap the line." He glanced at her. "Settle in. This might take a while."

"Can I help you somehow?"

"Actually, yes. Get in the bench there and get a pole brace." He nodded to the bench seats flanking the cabin door.

Brooke spun around and opened the closest one.

"Other one."

"Oh." She closed the lid and moved to the other bench. Inside, an array of fishing tackle greeted her. She rummaged through until she found something that looked like it could hold a pole and go around someone's waist. "Is this it?" She held it up.

"Yep."

She closed the lid and wandered over to him. "How do we do this?"

"The hard plastic part goes in front. It buckles in the back."

Brooke bit her lip and eyed him. This would be awkward. "Okay. Don't elbow me in the face."

A corner of his mouth lifted. "I'll try not to."

She stepped up behind him and reached around his waist with the brace. Practically flush against his backside, she reached around his other side and groped for the strap. Her fingers brushed his waistband and the top of his zipper. His muscles jumped at her touch. She clenched her teeth and tried not to think about what was under the fabric. Her fingers skimmed the nylon strap, and she snagged it, pulling it around behind his back. Putting some space between them, she snapped the buckle together. "There."

"Thanks." He put the pole in the brace and attached the thin cables to the reel to hold it in place.

Brooke moved away. "No problem. Is there anything else you need?"

He shook his head. "Not right now."

Leaning against the rail, she tugged her hat a little lower as the rain continued to come down, and settled in to watch him battle the shark. It wasn't a large one, from what she could tell, but every time Ford gained ground, the shark fought back, even trying to go under the boat. More than once, he crossed the deck, until finally, nearly thirty minutes later, the animal's dorsal fin broke the surface.

"Come get the knife out of my pocket." He tipped his head, wiping it on his shoulder, but it did little good. They were both soaked from the rain.

Brooke moved closer, eyeing his shorts. "Where is it?"

"Front right."

She eyed the wet khaki fabric drawn tight over his thigh. Of course it was. That was not a place she wanted to put her hand. Not after the feelings she battled when she strapped that brace around him. But that shark couldn't stay hooked. Swallowing hard, she steeled herself. With her teeth clenched against the onslaught of need about to hit her, she wiggled her fingers into his pocket.

The pole jerked in Ford's hands, and he leaned back, reeling in the line. Brooke lurched away, taking several steps back, as his elbow came toward her.

"I thought we covered this. I don't need a black eye."

"Sorry. Reflex." He didn't look at her, keeping his gaze trained on the water.

Brooke glanced over the rail and saw the shark getting closer to the boat. She looked at Ford's leg and closed her eyes for a long moment, shaking her head. *You can do this. A quick dip in the pocket, grab the knife, and done.* She could ignore the feel of his hard thigh beneath her fingers. Just like she ignored the feel of his hard abs earlier.

Blowing out a breath, she jimmied her hand into his pocket, the fabric stiff and resistant to the intrusion because of the rain. Once inside, his muscles moved under her hand, and she resisted the urge to pause and feel the play of the sinew as he fought the shark. Delving deeper against the wet fabric, her fingers touched the smooth curve of his knife, and she grasped it, pulling it out. "Got it." She held it up, then frowned as she got a good look at it. "This isn't a knife. It's got all kinds of stuff on here."

"It's a multi-tool. Find the clippers."

"Clippers?"

"Yeah," he grunted, reeling in more line. "The hook is on a wire leader. A knife won't cut that. You'll need to clip it."

"Wait. You want *me* to do it?" Her voice ended on a squeak. "Oh, no." She didn't want to be anywhere near the razor blades in that animal's mouth.

"I need both hands to hold the pole. Get ready."

Brooke stood, moving to the rail. She looked over. The shark thrashed as Ford reeled in line. Water sprayed and droplets landed on her face. She ignored them, her eyes widening as the fish fully broke the surface. It was a young hammerhead. "Why did that thing take my bait? I had a tiny chunk of snapper on there." She'd been using small bait. Just enough to catch mahi-mahi. Not a fricking shark.

"Must have looked just right to him. Are you ready?"

"I guess." Her heart thundered in her ears. She couldn't believe she had to get close to that thing. "What's the plan?"

"I'm going to reel it in as close as I can. You're going to lean over the side and cut the line as far down as you can reach. Just don't fall in."

A lump formed in Brooke's throat, and all the moisture drained away. She swallowed hard, her mouth pulling down. "You know how to put in stitches, right? In case it bites me?"

"You won't get bit." He heaved on the pole, then spun the reel. "Okay, lean down."

She took a shaky breath and found the clippers on the

multi-tool. Peering over the rail, she saw the shark flailing just feet from the hull. "Just a little closer." She leaned down, wrapping her left hand around the railing. In her other hand, she clutched the knife. Standing on her toes, she stretched. Her hand slipped, and she let out a yelp.

"Brooke!"

She flailed, throwing her weight back to stay on the boat. A wave helped, tipping the side up. Her feet touched the deck, and she exhaled hard, closing her eyes in relief.

"Are you okay?"

"Yeah." Heart thundering in her ears, she leaned over the side again. The shark thrashed, rearing its head back, mouth open. Brooke swallowed back a surge of unadulterated terror and traced the line down as close to the animal as she dared. "Don't bite me, fish." A wave brought the shark toward her and put the line right between the clipper blades. She squeezed, cutting through the wire leader only inches from its razor-sharp teeth.

Ford shouted in surprise, then she heard a thud. She straightened and turned to see him sprawled on the other side of the deck, still holding the pole.

"Oh my goodness! Are you okay?" She hurried toward him. Halfway across the deck, her foot slipped. At the same time, the boat heaved on a wave, throwing her further off balance. She let out a sharp yelp as she crashed down beside him.

Warm, wet hands circled her arm. "Are you all right?"

She grimaced. "Yeah." Lifting her head, she looked at him through the rain. Water sluiced off his face. His shirt clung to his chest, the damp gray fabric showing off the hard planes of his torso. Her mouth ran dry again, but for a different reason.

Look away, Brooke!

She lifted her gaze, meeting his. His pupils dilated. She bit her lip.

Lightning flashed, closely followed by the roar of thunder. Brooke jumped and hunkered low.

"Come on. We need to get inside." Ford unbuckled the pole brace, then got to his feet and held out a hand.

"Thanks." She took it, and he helped her up.

Another flash of lightning, this one even closer, startled a surprised shout from her. She ducked and ran for the door. Her feet slid again, but Ford was right there to catch her.

"I've got you." He gripped her bicep, then wrapped an arm around her waist, ushering her forward.

Fighting to keep her balance on the slick and shifting deck, she made it to the door with Ford's help and threw it open to go inside. The wind blew, sending a wave of raindrops in with them.

Ford shut the door and followed her into the cabin. "Phew! That was something. Are you okay?" He set the fishing gear on the floor, tucking one end into a corner so it wouldn't roll around.

"Yeah." She pulled the hat off her head and tossed it down. Swiping wet tendrils of hair back from her face, she gathered the hem of her t-shirt in her hands and twisted it. Water ran off in a small stream. "I'm soaked. And cold." She lifted the chilly, clammy shirt away from her body.

"Me too." To punctuate his statement, a small shiver went through him. He motioned to the hall beyond the kitchen. "Let's go change."

He didn't have to tell her twice. She spun on her heel and headed for her room. Inside, she shut the door with a quick flick of her wrist and went to the small dresser bolted to the floor. She'd long ago unpacked, finding it easier to have it all organized than to chase her duffel and suitcase around the room as the boat pitched and rolled. Those were now stored in the bench seats in the main cabin.

Removing a dry set of clothes, she quickly changed. For a

moment, she debated staying put, but her growling stomach made her leave. Without fresh fish, she had to come up with something different to eat. And hopefully soon. She was starving.

Brooke opened the door and came to a halt in the doorway. Once more, her mouth ran dry. Ford stood in the bathroom across from her, shirtless.

Oh, sweet mercy. He looked better than any dream or fantasy she'd ever had. Ripples of muscle moved and bulged beneath his tanned skin. On his belly, the whirl of hair that began on his chest narrowed to a dark gold line, disappearing beneath the waistband of his shorts.

Her core clenched. She wanted to follow it.

"Hey, can you help me?"

Yes! Hot desire flooded her before she realized he meant with something else. Blood welled from his elbow.

"What happened?" She stepped into the hall, frowning, and some of her need to jump his bones faded.

"I skinned it on the deck when I fell. I can't see it to clean it up and bandage it. Could you—?" He raised a brow and tipped his head toward his arm.

"Yeah, sure. Of course." She squeezed into the tiny bathroom with him. His damp, earthy scent filled her nostrils, threatening to derail her thoughts. Clenching her teeth, she picked up the first aid kit he had open on the counter.

"Hold up your arm."

He lifted it, and she dipped her head to get a closer look. He'd lost a chunk of skin, but it wasn't too bad. Rummaging in the kit, she found some antiseptic wipes and a large bandage. With a couple of swipes, she cleaned up the blood, then sealed the wound with the bandage before it could seep much more.

"There." Stepping back, she tossed the trash into the small wastebasket. "That should do it."

"Thanks." He took the first aid kit from her and closed it.

"You're welcome." Without a task to keep her mind occupied, her gaze returned to his naked chest. Scars—ugly ones—crisscrossed his ribs and bisected his pecs. What was left of her ardor died as the reality of what he'd been through slapped her in the face. She looked at him. "You're lucky to be alive, aren't you?"

His expression closed, but he nodded.

Brooke knew she shouldn't pry, but something in his eyes —and his actions the other day when he snorkeled for over two hours—made her wonder something. "Have you ever talked about what happened with anyone?"

"No." The one word was low and held a note of warning for her not to continue.

She ignored it. "Why not?"

"Because it's no one's business. Especially not yours."

"Maybe I'm what you need. Someone impartial, who doesn't know anything about it."

He uttered a soft snort. "Why would that matter?"

"Because I can offer a different perspective." She tipped her head, her brow furrowing. "You beat yourself up over it, don't you? Why?"

Ford set the med kit down and stalked closer, invading her space. "Don't psychoanalyze me. Professionals have tried and failed."

She flashed him a smile, refusing to be intimidated. "Because they were looking at the soldier. I'm looking at the man."

A touch of curiosity entered his eyes before it quickly morphed into something hot. "Yeah, well, the man's got something entirely different on his mind." He raked his gaze up and down her body.

A shiver went up her spine at his blatant appraisal. She

shoved the feeling down, knowing he was trying to change the subject. "Don't." She shook a finger in his face.

He grabbed it, bringing it to his lips to kiss. "Don't what?"

The shiver returned, accompanied by a heavy heat that settled low in her belly. She tugged her hand free. "I know what you're doing. It won't work."

Ford leaned down, his face inches from hers. "What am I doing?" His warm breath washed over her, raising goosebumps on her neck.

"Trying to distract me. Distract yourself. You don't really want to flirt with me. You haven't all week. Even when I stripped down to my bikini top and soaked myself. But suddenly you want to now?" She shook her head. "Running from your feelings doesn't help. They just fester and make the internal wounds bigger."

Instead of the desire in his eyes disappearing, like she expected, the heat flared. Brooke swallowed hard, her own need ratcheting up a notch. She might be in trouble.

He shifted closer. "Just because I haven't flirted doesn't mean I didn't want to." His mint-green gaze met hers. "You're a beautiful woman, Brooke. And an interesting one. But you're also a job."

"Gee, thanks." She rolled her eyes and took a step back.

Ford snaked an arm around her waist and brought her close. "Don't get your panties in a wad, princess. I just meant—"

"I know what you meant. And they're not in a wad." She pushed on his chest, not meeting his eyes. "Let me go."

"Is that really what you want?"

The low tenor of his voice brought her gaze up. The subterfuge was gone. Genuine curiosity burned alongside the desire in his eyes now.

Oh, Lord, help her.

Twenty-Two

Ford had no idea what he was doing. What started as a distraction technique quickly morphed into the thing he'd been trying to avoid. But when he saw that little involuntary shiver she gave, it flipped a switch. He'd spent the last several days avoiding her as best he could. Ever since she exposed that teeny tiny bikini top and drenched herself. Despite his swim, and the others he'd taken since then, she was a temptation—a distraction—he didn't need. So, he'd spent most of his time in the pilothouse and tried to be as stand-offish as he could when he was down on deck. Encouraging any sort of relationship with her would just lead to trouble—this sort of trouble. And now the words were out, and he couldn't seem to make himself take them back.

Her throat worked, and she searched his gaze. Ford held her amber-eyed stare, not backing down. The hooks she had in him now wouldn't let him, even with his subconscious screaming at him that this was a bad, bad idea. She was his protectee. A job. Business and pleasure shouldn't mix.

"It's a good idea, letting me go."

"It is." He really couldn't agree more.

"Then why are you still holding me?"

"Because you haven't said stop."

"Yes, I did."

"Not after I asked you to confirm that's what you wanted. So, yes or no?" Why didn't he just let go? He tried to make his arms loosen, but they refused to listen.

Brooke stayed silent.

"I need an answer, Brooke. Either way." Damn, he really hoped she stayed right where she was. Those rich, honey eyes of hers sucked him in. He basked in their warm depths.

Mentally, he rolled his eyes. He sounded like a damn poet.

Seconds passed. A finger of unease skated through him the longer she hesitated. His hands loosened as he prepared to draw back. The last thing he wanted was to make her uncomfortable.

With an apology forming on his tongue, he moved his hands. Hers shot out and gripped his face, making him freeze. He didn't get more than a quizzical quirk of his eyebrow out before she stood on her toes and kissed him.

Shock quickly gave way to a flood of desire. Days of pretending she wasn't the prettiest woman he'd ever seen had eroded his self-control. When the feel of her mouth on his registered, the reins on his feelings slipped away. His hands returned to her hips and held her close. He took over the kiss, sipping on her plump lips and tasting the inner recesses of her mouth. She was delicious, as sweet as her honeyed eyes.

Her hands slid into his hair, gripping the long strands. Her nails raked his scalp, sending shots of desire straight to his groin. He moaned, deep. Brooke's answering whimper snapped his remaining control. Ford swept her into his arms and carried her through the doorway. He backed straight into her room and toppled them both onto the bed.

Lifting his head, he looked down at her. "Tell me to stop."

"No." She reached for him and drew him back down.

Ford groaned, succumbing to the temptress in his arms.

TWENTY-THREE

What was she doing?

The errant thought ran through her mind, but didn't linger. Other, more intense thoughts—like how amazing Ford's hard body felt under her fingertips—obliterated it. She traced the lines and valleys of his muscled torso, reveling in the feel of the man above her.

Doing this, sleeping with Ford, was not her best idea. But she needed this. Needed the connection. Out here all alone, she'd started to feel isolated. They'd created a cocoon and shut out everyone—everything—else. Even keeping their distance, he'd become her world. And her world needed this. It needed rocked to its core. She wanted him to shatter her and then put the pieces back together.

Brooke tipped her head, her hand sliding through the damp, silky strands of his sun-streaked hair as he kissed and nipped his way down her neck. She had on too many clothes. She needed to feel his skin on hers.

Wriggling, she worked them into a sitting position. Grasping the hem of her shirt, she whipped it over her head.

Ford's mouth left her body as the cotton slid past. Through hooded eyes, he stared at what she uncovered.

"You're so perfect." He extended a hand and cupped her breast. "Just the right size to hold."

Brooke's back arched, her body wanting more. Not one to deny herself such a pleasure, she grabbed the strap of her sports bra and pulled her arm through, slithering out of the stretchy garment. Ford's pupils grew, the blackness edging out the soft green. Fire burned in their depths. He wanted her just as much as she wanted him.

"Touch me, Ford."

"Yes, ma'am." He brushed his fingers over her bare flesh, grazing the sensitive tip of one breast.

Brooke drew in a sharp breath as her core pulsed. Feeling emboldened by her desire, she pushed him back, crawling on top to straddle his hips. Through the fabric of their shorts, she could feel his long, hard length straining to be free. Who was she to deny its release? She snaked a hand between their bodies and found his zipper. The teeth ticked, joining the sound of their harsh breathing in the small room.

"Princess, what are you doing?"

"Nothing."

"Liar."

She grinned and worked her hand through the opening she'd just created. He hissed as her hand closed around his length.

"Careful, babe. Don't end the party before it starts."

"Oh, I won't." She leaned down, putting her mouth next to his ear. "I plan to ride you hard and rocket to the stars." She squeezed him and lightly bit his ear.

He growled, and suddenly Brooke found herself on her back. Ford loomed over her. His hair hung around his face, throwing the hard angles into shadow. But she could see the fierce glitter to his eyes. A warrior come to life. She was his conquest, and he intended to reap the benefits of his victory. She couldn't wait.

His hands attacked the button and zipper on her shorts. In moments, he had them unfastened and down her legs. Her panties quickly followed. The naked desire in his eyes sent a flood of moisture into her core. When he pushed her thighs apart, her body literally wept for him.

With a soft, gentle touch, he skimmed his hands down her inner thighs, then parted her folds. Brooke bit her lip, holding back the urge to beg for more. He didn't make her wait, though.

"Such a luscious treat for me." Edging back on his knees, he pushed hers up, exposing her for his touch. With a single finger, he stroked her center, dipping into her channel to bring moisture from the well and coat the tiny hidden pearl. His firm, but soft touch coaxed it out, and he leaned down, sucking it into his mouth.

Brooke let out a squeak. When he bit down and thrust two fingers into her, the squeak turned into a shout. With just a few strokes and a flick of his tongue, her orgasm broke, sending her soaring. Muscles quivering from the force of it, she tried to close her legs, but he held them open, enhancing the pleasure coursing through her. She rode the waves until they lapped gently at the edges of her mind.

Ford sat back, a cocky smile on his face. "Did you reach the stars?"

"Pretty damn close."

"Hmm. Guess I need to try again."

He got off the bed and shucked his shorts and underwear. Her eyes grew round as she took in his naked form. The man was magnificent. From the top of his rumpled mop of hair, down his muscled chest and chiseled abs, over the fine—and large—specimen he sported between his legs, and to his powerful thighs and sexy toes, he was male perfection. Not even his scars could detract from his maleness. If anything, they added to it.

That cocky smile ticked higher on one side. "See something you like?"

"I'd say yes, but I'm afraid it would go to your head. You already have an ego the size of North America."

He put one knee on the bed, crawling toward her. "Only North America? Wow. I've risen in esteem in your eyes."

She hummed. "Well, you did get me three-quarters of the way to the stars."

"Three-quarters, huh? I guess it's time for the afterburners." Reaching her, he covered her body with his, fusing their mouths together.

Brooke drew her knees up, hugging his hips. His shaft bumped her entrance, making her core clench. She raised her feet, hooking them around his waist. Ripping her mouth from his, she grasped his face. "Now."

A smile flirted with his lips. "No."

She slithered a hand between them, grabbing his swollen length. "Yes." She squeezed.

His eyes rolled back, and he let out a quick pant. Clenching his teeth, he looked at her. Steel met her gaze.

"Patience, princess."

She pouted as he pulled his hips away. "I hate you."

He gave a sharp bark of laughter. "Shall we find out how far I can take that particular feeling?"

"No." Need pumped through her veins. If he didn't finish her soon, she wouldn't be responsible for her actions. "Just continue as you were."

It was his turn to hum. He drew a hand down her side and over her hip, stroking her center again. At the same time, he took the tip of her breast into his mouth and sucked. Hard. Brooke's eyelids fluttered. That felt so, so good. A moment later, something thicker probed her entrance. She opened her eyes to see him leaning over her. He rolled his hips, teasing her with the tip of his shaft.

She growled. "Don't make me take over."

He chuckled. "I'd like to see you try. You like vanilla, remember?"

"Oh, shut up and—oh!" Her words ended on a gasp as he drove into her. Brooke rolled her hips, helping her body accommodate him. It sent fissions of heat shooting through her core and down her limbs.

Slow and steady, he drove her up the cliff. Brooke matched him thrust for thrust, grinding against him in hopes that he'd speed up. But he didn't. He kept the same slow, maddening pace.

She growled in his ear, then nipped at the lobe. He sucked in a breath, and his pace faltered. She moved to his neck, nibbling on the sinewy tendons. With a groan that morphed into a dark growl, he grasped her hips and slammed into her. Brooke's head fell back. "Yes!"

The exquisite friction sent her spiraling higher, and in moments, she broke. Her scream of pleasure bounced off the cabin walls, and she clutched her thighs around his waist, holding on for dear life. Ford stiffened above her, his guttural moan mixing with her cries. After several more grinding thrusts, he collapsed on top of her, then rolled, taking her with him.

More sated than she'd ever been in her life, Brooke laid there, eyes closed, and tried to catch her breath.

"Was that enough spice for you?"

A laugh bubbled up at his low words. She opened her eyes, staring into the languid depths of his green eyes. "It was a good start. I'm sure you can do more, though."

He huffed a laugh. "Damn. Give a girl an inch and she wants a mile."

Oh, he had that right. Now that she'd had a taste of paradise, she wanted more. She had a sneaking suspicion Ford had just ruined her for other men.

TWENTY-FOUR

Ford awoke to the sight of pre-dawn light filling the porthole window. Brooke snored lightly beside him. Shifting to prop himself up on one elbow, he stared down at her. He raised a hand and stroked the soft skin of her arm, brushing her hair back to reveal a creamy shoulder. She didn't even stir at his touch.

He sat up, letting his hand fall away as he watched her sleep. What the hell did he just do? He didn't need this complication. He knew that when he started flirting earlier. But she'd been picking at a part of his memory he wanted to keep locked away. When he felt the door cracking, he did the first thing he could think of that was guaranteed to distract her: flirt. He'd annoyed her enough by ignoring her the past few days, he thought she'd just roll her eyes and stomp off. But no, she'd given an involuntary shiver, and something inside of him woke up and roared.

Ford scrubbed a hand over his face and got out of bed. Still naked, he walked out of the room as quietly as possible to go shower and dress. Lying there, contemplating how much he'd complicated his life last night, wouldn't help anything. And he'd be tempted to repeat the experience. He still was. Brooke's lithe, feminine body fit to his like a glove.

Glove.

He groaned and uttered a soft curse as another thought hit him. He hadn't gloved up. Ford shook his head. *Christ, way to go Wagner.* All he could hope was she was on some sort of birth control or it was the wrong time of the month. And that Cassidy hadn't given her some disease. From what he knew about the man, though, Ford doubted he'd take the chance of getting a communicable disease. Might mess with his lifestyle.

Grabbing some clothes, he ducked into the bathroom and started the shower. After a quick wash, he dressed and went topside. There was just enough light now to see without tripping and breaking his neck.

Waves lapped softly against the hull, the seas calm as the sun flirted with the horizon. Ford loved this time of day. It was so quiet and peaceful. And promising. Every morning, he said a quick prayer of thanks that he got to experience another day on this planet. At one time, he wasn't sure he'd ever see another sunrise, so he took every day for the gift it was.

Climbing the ladder, he went up to the pilothouse and picked up the binoculars. He'd deliberately parked them between some rocks. He had a decent vantage point up here, but they weren't easily seen from a far. He'd also taken the chance and cut their running lights. Out here, they'd shine like a beacon; there were no other boats.

Satisfied they were alone, he started the engine. Without a fish last night, they needed to fish this morning, and the best place for that was further out.

Maneuvering around the rocks, he steered them out into open water. Beyond the protection of the rocky coast, he slowed and scanned the water again. It was still clear. When he was out where he wanted to be, he cut the engine, then went down to the main deck and tied a lure onto his favorite pole.

He'd just cast the line into the water when Brooke exited the cabin.

"Hey." She hesitated in the doorway.

"Hey." He glanced at her over his shoulder. "Did you sleep all right?"

"I did, yes." A pretty blush stole over her cheeks. "I guess my mind shut down after—" She flipped a hand back and forth.

His body tightened at the memory. "Yeah." He turned back to the water. The slow tick of the winding reel filled the silence.

"Um, about that..."

Ford brought the pole back as the lure cleared the water. "You're on the pill, right?"

"Oh." Surprise colored her voice. "I take the shot, actually. Johnathan wasn't ready for kids, and it's more reliable than my ability to remember to take a pill."

"Good." He cast the line out. It hit the water with a plop. "Now that we have that out of the way, what happened, happened. And it can't happen again."

"Now hang on a minute." Her shoes slapped the deck as she walked closer.

He kept his gaze trained on the water as she appeared in his peripheral vision.

"I don't regret what happened. If there's one thing I've learned in the last week, it's that vanilla—while safe—is boring. And I don't want boring anymore. Last night was far from boring."

"Agreed. And I don't regret what happened, either. But we can't do it again. I don't want you getting attached. Once Cassidy's in jail and all of this is behind you, you'll go back to Asheville and I'll stay here." He looked at her then. "There's no future for us, princess." That line played on repeat in his head. She wasn't the only one he was worried about getting attached. She was a job, and he needed to remember that.

"Who says I want a future with you? Maybe I just want a fiery roll in the sack. Did you think of that?"

He froze. Well, hell. He hadn't planned on that response. "No, actually. Is that what you want?"

"Yes! Ford, I just got out of a disastrous relationship. I'm not ready to commit again to anyone. But I am ready to let loose and live a little. I am done"—she sliced her hand through the air—"with vanilla."

Ford swallowed, thinking. Since his marriage ended, his relationships with women had been limited. There were a few women who hung around Sam's bar with whom he'd spend a night when he was in the mood for more than his hand in the shower. But none of them ever left him as satisfied as Brooke. He'd be a fool to turn down a repeat. But could she really keep this casual? Could he?

Maybe the better question was, could they keep their hands to themselves if he said no? Just thinking about watching Brooke roam around his boat for the foreseeable future and knowing now what a tigress hid beneath the surface, he knew the answer to that question was a big fat hell no.

His answer must have been in his eyes, because a slow, sexy smile spread over her face.

He clutched the rod. Oh, he was in trouble.

Twenty-Five

Ford stared up at the trillions of stars in the night sky, half asleep. Water lapped gently against the hull of the boat, and a warm breeze ghosted over his face, echoing the warmth in his limbs. Brooke shifted against him, her smooth, bare leg gliding over his rougher one as she settled closer. They were tucked under a blanket on the chaise loungers he'd lashed together to make a bed. When the sky cleared just after dinner and he looked at the radar and saw a lack of rain anywhere nearby, he'd suggested they sleep outside. After the last couple of days stuck in the cabin, he needed the fresh air; he suspected she did too.

Best decision ever. Making love outside with the waves and stars as background made it feel like they were the only two people in the entire world. And now, after the best sex of his life, he floated in that state in between wakefulness and dreaming. It was a heady feeling.

He ran his fingertips over the sleek, warm skin of Brooke's hip, anchoring himself to reality. He wasn't ready to sink into oblivion just yet. Not until he'd savored every last second of this feeling. When this was over and she left, he was going to miss this. Miss her. The very thing he'd feared had happened; he was getting attached. He knew he shouldn't. But he'd been unable to stop her from getting under his skin. Or from finding his heart and snuggling up close. She was working her way into dangerous territory, but he couldn't bring himself to care enough to stop her. It hadn't taken long, either. Only a few days.

He rolled his eyes at himself. He was such a sap, and that had only set him up for heartache. It would hurt when she left.

Brooke shifted again. Ford tipped his chin down to look at her. Her eyes glittered in the moonlight, making his heart skip a beat. That pull that drew him to her tugged harder. He still couldn't bring himself to resist. Reaching up, he touched her full lip with his thumb. "You okay?"

"Yeah. Just can't sleep."

"Why not?" Given another couple of minutes and he probably would have been out cold.

"My brain won't shut off. I think it's just a lack of activity."

He curved a hand around her butt and squeezed. "You want *more* activity?"

She chuckled. "You know what I mean. I'm used to meetings and emails and walking around the resort property. Not fishing and reading and—other things. I'm just restless." She looked up. "How do you do it?"

"Stay sane in the face of boredom?"

"Yeah."

He shrugged one shoulder. "I've had a lot of practice. When I was active duty, I'd spend a lot of time without much to do when we were out on missions. It was a lot of sitting around, waiting for stuff to happen. Then when I left, I needed the slower pace, both because my body was recovering and because I couldn't handle anything too mentally taxing.

My head just wasn't in a good place. Now, it just doesn't bother me. I prefer it, actually. In case you hadn't noticed, I'm not a people person."

She chuckled again. "Nope. Never occurred to me."

His mouth curved up. "I know you are, though. And I'm sorry we're stuck out here. I know you miss your life."

"It's not even so much my life as my family. And my friends. Every Sunday when we were all in town, I'd meet my mom and dad for coffee at this little shop with tabletop games—chess, checkers, stuff like that. We'd sip our drinks, try to beat each other, and just chat about nonsense. Anything but work. Dad started the tradition when I started working for the resort. Said it keeps us feeling like family and not just work colleagues."

"Smart man." Ford liked that her dad was trying to maintain a relationship with Brooke outside of work. It explained a lot about why she didn't have a stick up her butt like so many rich women he'd met. "So, you're an only child?"

"Not by choice. My parents wanted more, but my mom couldn't stay pregnant for whatever reason. I was born seven weeks premature. And she'd been pregnant three times before me. Are you an only child? You've never mentioned any siblings."

"I don't have any, no. Not that I know of, anyway. My parents actually never married. And I didn't see much of my dad growing up. Then he died while I was overseas. I didn't know him well."

"I can't imagine that. I'm a daddy's girl."

He smiled. "I can see that. And I'll get you back to him soon. Asher gets closer every day to getting what we need to take Cassidy down."

"I'm glad. As nice as the break has been, my life is a hot mess. I'm ready for it to be over." She let out a soft snort. "And you know, if I'd listened to my friends, I wouldn't be in this predicament."

"How so?"

"Things haven't been great between me and Johnathan for a while. He was always blowing me off for something else whenever we made plans with my friends. A couple of them asked me if I was happy. I just shoved it away as a rough patch. If I'd taken the time to think about their question, I probably would have ended things sooner."

"Maybe. But things could have also turned out worse. You didn't know Cassidy was a psycho then. Imagine how he would have reacted if you'd done that?" His guts twisted just thinking about what could have happened to her if she'd dumped Cassidy sooner. "You wouldn't have known to watch your back, because you wouldn't have known what he was capable of."

"I hadn't thought about it like that." Her quiet voice held a hint of fear.

Ford kissed the top of her head. "You might be on the run, but at least you know what you're up against. And you're safe."

She tipped her face up to look at him. "I am. I have you to thank for that. I'm sorry if I've seemed ungrateful. I do appreciate what you've done for me. I'll never forget it."

Uncomfortable with the serious turn the conversation had taken, he waggled his eyebrows, attempting to lighten things up. "It's been a pleasure."

She smacked his chest, a deep frown on her pretty face. "Stop. I'm being serious."

His smile slowly faded. "I know." He studied her for a long moment. His eyes roved over her face, taking in her soft skin turned alabaster by the moonlight. "And you're welcome." Ford put his hand under her chin and leaned down to press a tender kiss to her lips. Warmth unfurled in his chest, bleeding outward to spread down his limbs. It was a foreign feeling, and it took him a second to recognize it as contentment. Until that moment, he thought he'd been content living his life the way he wanted in Costa Rica. But it hadn't been contentment; merely appeasement. He'd needed space when he left the military, and somewhere down the line, he'd mistaken appeasing that desire for being content. It took being here with Brooke for him to understand that.

Ford pulled back, staring down at the lovely woman in his arms. His world shifted, spinning a full one-eighty. How was he ever going to let her go when this was over?

A slight dip marred the space between her eyebrows. She tipped her head. "What? Why are you looking at me like that?"

He forced himself to smile. "No reason. You're just beautiful in the moonlight."

"Oh." Her eyes rounded, and there was enough light for him to see a slight stain on her cheeks.

Needing a distraction—both from the thoughts now running through his mind and to keep her from asking more questions—he kissed her again, harder this time.

Her breathy whimper of need wiped his unsettling thoughts away. He gave in to the need now flooding his veins.

Twenty-Six

The warm sun caressed Brooke's body as she laid on the forward deck. She stretched, knowing she should get up. She needed to use the bathroom. But the weather was just so nice, she couldn't make herself abandon her patch of sun. After all the rain, she wanted to bask in the sunshine and dry out.

Footsteps alerted her to Ford's presence. She glanced over and smiled as he appeared.

"Hey, princess." He stopped beside her, one side of his mouth lifting. A twinkle shimmered in his eyes. "Fancy a swim?"

Brooke looked at the water and bit her lip. In theory, it sounded great. But the memory of that hammerhead she cut loose last week lingered.

"The sharks here are relatively docile."

She sent a sharp glance his way. "How did you know what I was thinking?"

"I could see the worry on your face when you looked at the water." He shrugged. "I took a guess. Come on." He held out a hand.

She only hesitated another moment before she took it. "If I get eaten..."

He chuckled. "You'll be fine. Just punch the shark in the eye if he tries."

Her eyes widened. Knowing her luck, she'd miss and shove her arm right into the shark's mouth.

His chuckle turned into a full-blown laugh. "Stop worrying. Shark attacks are rare. They'll mostly ignore us if we see any."

He whipped his t-shirt over his head, and Brooke lost her train of thought. "I'm sorry, what?"

His gaze heated. He wrapped his arms around her, settling his hands over the curve of her butt, and tugged her close. "Be brave, babe. You can do it."

Brooke was too distracted by the feel of his growing shaft against her belly to pick up on the gleam that entered his eyes. Before she knew it, her feet left the deck and he was on his way to the rail.

"Ford! What are you doing? Put me down." She smacked his back.

"Okay." The gleam intensifying, a wide smile spread over his face. He swung her into his arms and tossed her over the side.

With a shriek, Brooke flailed, taking a breath and closing her eyes a moment before she hit the water. The warm, crisp waters of the Pacific closed over her head. Kicking her feet, she broke the surface as Ford landed beside her with a splash.

"You jerk!" She shoved his shoulder as he came up for air.

He laughed and kicked back to float. "You were perfectly safe. And you were going to jump in, anyway. I just hurried the process along."

She rolled her eyes. It didn't matter that he was right. It was the principal of the thing. "You're still a jerk."

"No argument there, princess."

Huffing, she let go of her anger. "You know, for being on the run, this is pretty nice." When she fled Asheville, she never imagined she'd be cruising around in a boat on the Pacific, feasting on fresh seafood, and swimming in the ocean. She'd imagined a dank, dull room in some roadside motel. Definitely not this. She looked at Ford. And definitely not her companion. Going back to her real life might actually be a letdown.

"So, did you hear anything new from Asher?" She knew he'd been checking in every night, but he hadn't told her what they'd talked about yesterday.

Ford stilled. Brooke frowned and straightened, treading water. "What? What did he say?"

He eyed her for a long moment before speaking. "Asher hacked Johnathan's bank accounts, then traced the money he paid to the people on our tail. It goes to an offshore bank account. He hacked that, too, and found out it's registered to a mercenary group known for their lack of scruples. They go where the money is, and Johnathan Cassidy paid them well."

She frowned. "Where did he get the money? I mean, I know his family is well-connected, and his job pays well, but most of his wealth is tied up in real estate or his trust fund."

Ford's mouth flattened. He glanced away for a long moment before looking back. The reservation on his face made her heart pump faster.

"He's been embezzling from your family's company. Asher found evidence of payments to shell companies. They all lead back to Johnathan or Will. Asher compiled all the information and sent it to the FBI. Will's in custody."

Brooke gasped. "Are you serious?"

Ford nodded.

"How much money are we talking?" While she didn't doubt Johnathan had embezzled, it couldn't be that much. The company was doing well.

"Twenty-two million dollars."

"Holy—" She broke off and looked away for a moment. "I can't believe no one noticed."

"He was the CFO. Who else would be looking?"

That was true. The CFO had a lot of autonomy. The board oversaw Johnathan's office, but they only met quarterly and reviewed reports prepared by the CFO's office, which they compared to tax filings. If nothing seemed strange, they would never notice. However he funneled the money away, he'd done so within the U.S. tax framework.

"How long has this been going on?"

"Two years. He started small. A few thousand here and there. But recently, the payments have been larger. Even if he married you and took over, I'm not sure he wouldn't have skipped town. He was building quite the nest egg. I think you were cover for his operations. No one wanted to look too closely at the boss's granddaughter's fiancé."

Brooke ground her molars. She already knew she'd been used, but it seemed Johnathan's plan was more elaborate than she thought.

"Asher's report also contained proof Johnathan is here. The FBI has issued an arrest warrant and shared it with the Costa Rican authorities. They just need to catch him now."

Her mind whirled. She wasn't sure how she felt about that. She wanted him locked up, but once he was caught, that meant she could go home. And she wasn't sure she wanted to.

"Before long, you'll be back to your old life. Your Costa Rican adventure will be nothing more than a distant memory."

Tears threatened at the cheerfulness in his voice. She sank below the waves to hide them. She knew they'd agreed this was a no strings attached arrangement, but he sounded almost giddy to be getting rid of her. That hurt more than Johnathan's betrayal. Realizing that turned her tears angry.

Why was she crying over a man she just met? One who apparently couldn't wait to get rid of her.

She surfaced, then gasped as she noticed Ford's nearness. He'd come closer while she was underwater and was only inches away.

"You all right?" He cocked his head, staring at her.

"I'm fine." She leaned back, pushing the water to move away and create some space. He followed her.

"You're not fine. You're upset. I thought you'd be happy that the authorities have what they need to arrest your fiancé."

"Ex-fiancé. Why do you keep doing that? You don't need to create imaginary distance between us by linking me to another man. I know what's between us is temporary." Venom dripped off her words. She knew she should reel in her feelings, but dammit, he'd come to mean something to her and it hurt that she meant so little to him.

He blinked, surprise on his face. "Whoa. Hold up, princess. Why are you angry? We agreed to no strings. In fact, you're the one who pressed for it. What happened to 'I'm not ready to commit?'"

"I'm still not. But you could act like it'll bother you to see me go."

A frown formed on his handsome face, scrunching his eyebrows together. "That's why you're mad? Because you think I'm ready to roll you to the airport and say sayonara?"

"Well, aren't you? You sure sounded excited that I'd be going home soon."

"No, Brooke. I'm not."

Her angry, jerking movements to tread water slowed. "You're not?"

He sighed. "No. I still know nothing can come of us, but that doesn't mean I won't miss you. Yes, you drive me crazy, but you're also funny and intelligent. And the sex is nice." A teasing light entered his eyes.

"Yes, it is that." Unbidden, a smile crossed her face. It was more than nice. Mind-blowing, earth-shattering, and world-tipping came to mind. Her core clenched with need.

He swam closer. "So, even though this is still temporary, how about we take advantage of every minute?" The heat in his eyes sent an answering bolt of desire through Brooke.

She erased the distance, looping her arms around his neck and her legs around his waist, need strumming through every cell in her body. "I say yes." Before the smile could fully form on his face, she kissed him.

He wrapped his hands around her hips and deepened the kiss. A moment later, they started to sink. Brooke let go with a soft squawk. "Maybe we shouldn't do that in the water."

Chuckling, he started toward the boat. "Agreed."

Swimming behind him, she lengthened her stroke, eager to get out of the water and into the soft bed downstairs. Eyes fixed on the ladder, she almost ran into him when he stopped abruptly to tread water.

"Ford—"

"Stop." He held up a hand. "Do you hear that?"

Brooke stilled and listened. A low-pitched whine echoed over the water. "Yeah. What is that?"

"It's a boat engine." He turned, swimming again. "Come on!"

TWENTY-SEVEN

Lung's burning, Ford made it to the boat in moments and hauled himself out. With a quick glance to make sure Brooke was close behind, he ran over the deck and up the ladder to the pilothouse. Still dripping, he grabbed the binoculars and trained them on the horizon. He scanned the water as he adjusted the focus. A white blur crossed his vision, and he paused. Spinning the focus wheel, he cursed. A large yacht headed right for them. He couldn't see the name, but he'd bet his boat it was Cassidy.

"What do you see?" Brooke called up to him. He could hear her wet feet slapping the deck as she ran toward the ladder.

Ford started the engine, not answering. They needed cover. Now.

"What is it? Is it them?" Brooke appeared behind him.

"Not sure. Go below deck and put some clothes on. Shoes too."

"What? Are we going ashore?"

"Maybe. We'll see. Go." He glanced at her and jerked his head toward the ladder.

Her gaze connected with his for a split second, and he saw the recognition dawn in her eyes of the seriousness of their situation before she turned away to do as he asked.

Curses flew through his mind as he flipped the switch to retract the anchor. *So stupid*. He never should have dropped it. But they'd been fine for days, and swimming sounded nice. He was used to running or swimming miles every day, and the reduced activity was driving him crazy. He figured a little exercise before he got in a different kind of exercise wouldn't hurt anything.

He shook his head. What had he been thinking?

Ford clenched his teeth. He hadn't. That was the problem. He'd been lulled by the peace of the last few days and the relaxation that came with good sex. Somewhere along the line, he'd let his feelings for Brooke override his duty to protect her. Now they both might pay the price.

"Come on, come on." Ford glanced at the winch gauge. He still needed another ninety seconds before the anchor would be high enough for him to move. The last thing he needed was to get it caught on the hull or a rock he couldn't see. He lifted the binoculars and looked at the other boat again. It was still bearing down on them. They were close enough now he could see a man on the bow with his own set of binoculars. A moment later, another man joined him, this one carrying a rifle.

Screw the anchor. Ford shifted the boat into gear. It was high enough it wouldn't catch on anything below. He hoped. He'd just have to take the chance it wouldn't damage the hull. They couldn't stay here.

He scanned his surroundings, calculating exit strategies and the best place to go. He could stay ahead of that yacht, but only going parallel. At this angle, the yacht would catch up if he went north or south. West would send them directly at the ship. His only option was east, toward shore.

Letting out a frustrated growl, he turned toward land. He should have listened to his gut and stayed out to sea, swells be damned. It was too late now, though, and hindsight was twenty-twenty. He needed to focus on the present and what came next.

Throttle open all the way, he headed for the rocks. His smaller boat could maneuver through them. The yacht would have to stay back and send in smaller zodiac boats to get close. It would give him time to retrieve his weapons and get ready.

Spraying water, he zoomed behind the outcropping they'd anchored behind overnight and cut the throttle to let the engine idle.

"Brooke!" He hurried down the ladder.

"I'm here!" She came through the cabin doorway. "What's the plan?"

"Go up and keep us from hitting the rocks. I need to arm myself."

Her eyes widened slightly at the mention of the guns he brought on board before she nodded and took off.

Ford ran inside and through the living area and kitchen to the short staircase leading to the staterooms. Barely over the threshold to his cabin, he shucked his swim trunks, then flung open the armoire. He grabbed a dry pair of shorts and stepped into them, then removed the duffel he'd packed full of guns and ammo. Metal clinked as he set it on the bed. The zipper rasped as he opened it, then removed his favorite pistol from the bag, along with several magazines preloaded with bullets. His rifle and a tactical vest followed. Ford loaded the vest pockets with the magazines. He slipped a knife into one of the chest pockets and put another in his shorts. For good measure, he took the sat phone from his dresser and stuffed it into another pocket. Fitting the vest to his body, he picked up his guns and ran back upstairs and through the main cabin, exiting onto the deck with a bang of the door as it reached the full swing of its hinges.

Scanning the water, he glimpsed the yacht through the tall rocky outcroppings. It was slowing as it approached. He hurried up to the pilothouse and stopped at the top of the steps.

Brooke glanced at him, her gaze raking over his appearance. The deer-in-headlights look on her face was her only acknowledgment of the armory strapped to his body.

"Are you good up here?"

She nodded. "Is all that really necessary?" She motioned to his vest.

"If I want to defend us against the guy with the rifle, yes."

Her eyes widened. "Crap!"

Indeed. "Stay low and don't sink my boat." Turning, he went back down to the main deck, but instead of staying on the rear deck, he went to the bow. He wished he had another man, so he could cover both sides of the ship. He'd just have to do what he could from here.

Positioning himself in a hollow, he peered through the rock pillars. The yacht had stopped on the other side. He couldn't see enough of the ship to tell what they were doing, but he imagined they were preparing to come after them.

He checked his weapons. His heart thumped, and he closed his eyes, taking several steadying breaths. It might have been years since he saw combat, but it wasn't unfamiliar. He just needed to remember his training.

But this wasn't a typical combat situation. And he didn't have his fellow soldiers to rely on or backup only a radio call away. The stakes were much higher.

Ford drew in another breath, calling on the techniques to quiet his mind he'd learned many years ago. Focusing on what he didn't have wouldn't help. He needed to stay present and stay ahead of whatever Cassidy threw at them.

Lying prone on the bow, he waited and watched. Minutes ticked by until he heard the high-pitched whine of a zodiac engine over the low rumble of his idling engine. In moments, the gray rubber boat zipped around the rock pillars with three men on board. Ford eased his rifle up and took aim.

Twenty-Eight

Eyes like saucers, Brooke peered over the console at the small boat that just flew around the rocks. Three men with guns held onto ropes on the sides of the craft as it bounced over the waves. A week ago, she never would have guessed that Johnathan knew such people.

A shot rang out, the sound echoing off the water, and Brooke jumped, letting out a soft scream. That hadn't come from the dinghy. In fact, the little boat had now stopped, and the sides were deflating. Ford must have shot it.

Noise from behind drew her attention. She turned to see another rubber boat come around from the other side of the rock pillars. It, too, contained three men, but the front man on this boat had his rifle raised. He opened fire. Bullets pinged off the hull of the *Hooker*. Brooke yelped and ducked. She heard more shots, but didn't dare raise her head. The sound of yelling reached her ears, but she couldn't make out any words. One of the voices was Ford's.

Footsteps clamored on the ladder leading up to her. Having no idea if they'd been boarded, she looked around frantically for a weapon; her gaze landed on the binoculars.

She picked them up and cocked her arm, ready to hurl them at whoever appeared.

"Brooke!"

Relief tore through her as Ford's handsome face appeared. His disheveled hair fluttered around his face. She lowered the binoculars. "Ford! What's happening? I heard gunshots."

"I took out their boats." He hurried forward and pushed her to the side. "I think now's our chance to make a run for open ocean. Most of their crew is in the water." He opened the throttle and spun the wheel.

The movement caught her unaware, and she tipped backward, landing on her butt on the floor. Grabbing the arm of the chair, she rose to her knees and held on as he steered them around the rocky outcropping. They cleared the pillars, and she saw the yacht ahead to her right. Someone ran along the side, pointing. She raised the binoculars to look. It was Johnathan.

Brooke clenched her teeth, lowering the binoculars slightly. If she ever got her hands on him, she'd wring his damn neck. Then she'd hand him over to the police and let him rot in prison for the rest of his life.

Raising the binoculars again, she checked the yacht for others. There couldn't be that many more men on board, right?

On the stern, she passed over another man. Pausing, she went back to get a better look, then wished she hadn't. "Oh, no. Ford." She looked up, then pointed. "Look!" She held up the binoculars, gesturing for him to take them.

"What?" He glanced at her with a frown and took the glasses.

"On the stern. Please tell me that's not what it looks like."

Frowning, he lifted the binoculars to his face. His short curse told her all she needed to know. He passed the binoculars back to her.

"Hold on."

The moment Brooke took the glasses, he grasped the wheel with both hands and started to swerve. She yelped and grabbed the chair. "So, I wasn't seeing things?"

"Nope. That's a grenade launcher."

Brooke's heart beat faster as he confirmed what she saw. She closed her eyes and said a quick prayer.

A loud whoosh flew past, and a moment later, a muffled boom sent a spray of water into the air.

"Oh my God! Did they really just shoot that thing at us?"

"Yep." Ford spun the wheel, bringing the boat around ninety degrees.

Brooke clutched the chair. "What are you doing? Where are we going?"

"We need distance." He glanced over his shoulder.

She followed his gaze. The yacht filled her view, but was receding as they raced away from it. The man on the stern hefted the launcher to his shoulder. "I think he's going to fire another one!"

Ford spun the wheel in response, zigzagging over the water. The yacht disappeared from view. Brooke let go of the chair and crawled to ladder opening. The man still stood on the stern, aiming at them. A burst of smoke went out the back of the launcher a moment before a projectile headed toward them. "He fired!"

Heart in her throat, she watched as the grenade closed the distance. She braced herself. The boat jolted and a muffled boom filled her ears. Water sprayed into the air. She covered her head, then peeked up at Ford. "Did we get hit?"

His eyes were on the console. "Not directly, but I think the pressure wave broke open the hull. Controls are sluggish. We're taking on water." He smacked the wheel. "Okay, time to go." Spinning around, he grabbed her arm and hauled her to her feet.

"Go? Go where?" Bile rose in her throat as panic set in. There was nowhere to go. They were on the water. Land was half a mile away, and they had no way to get there.

He pushed her toward the ladder, urging her down. On the deck, he hurried her along the outer walkway to the bow. "We're gonna swim."

"Are you serious? They'll catch us."

"Only if they have another zodiac. Yachts like that—they're large, but they still only have so much space. I doubt there's another one."

"So we just make a run for it?"

"Basically." He pushed her around the corner and toward the end of the bow.

She glanced back, then stumbled as he continued to push her forward. "But how can you be sure?"

"I can't, but we can't stay here. We're sinking."

"What?" Voice breathy, her eyes widened. "Oh, this is not happening." Her jaw worked, anger displacing some of the fear. "I really am going to wring his peckerhead neck," she muttered.

Ford paused for half a second. "Later. Right now, you need to swim." He stopped at the end of the bow. "Climb over the rail."

Heart thumping loud in her ears, she curled her fingers around the chrome rail and stared at the water. Oh, this was such a bad idea.

"We're going to jump and swim for shore." Ford pointed straight ahead to a strip of sand in front of the dense jungle.

Brooke swallowed hard. That was a long way.

"Brooke."

She heard him call her name, but couldn't tear her eyes away from the beach.

"Honey, look at me." He shook her arm.

It was enough to tear her gaze away. "I'm scared."

"Sweetie, I know, but there is no other option. The boat's going down. We're going to end up in the water no matter what. And the longer we stay, the greater the chance someone reaches us."

Or blows us up again. He didn't have to say the words. She could see them in the worry in his eyes.

Gulping a lungful of air, she nodded. "Okay." Grasping the rail, she lifted a foot and climbed over.

"That's good. I'm right behind—"

A whoosh cut off his words. They both glanced back.

"Jump!" Ford's loud shout drowned out the sound of her heartbeat in her ears. She yelped as he put his hand square in the middle of her back and pushed.

Her feet left the boat, and a boom sounded behind her. A pressure waved smacked into her, propelling her further away from the boat. Water loomed, and she held her breath.

The warm ocean closed over her head, muffling the noise, but the sudden silence accentuated the ringing in her ears. For a moment, she floated beneath the surface, wondering what had just happened. When the first piece of debris whizzed past her and the second hit her in the shoulder, she snapped out of her shock and kicked her feet, surfacing a moment later. Swiping wet hair out of her eyes, she spun. "Ford!" Pieces of debris still rained down around her. The grenade had been a direct hit. Fire raged from within the destroyed vessel, and thick smoke billowed, further limiting her vision.

Brooke swam toward the boat, pushing pieces of wood and items from the boat out of her way. "Ford!" Where was he?

Loud voices in the distance caught her attention. Through the smoke, she caught a quick glimpse of men on the stern of the yacht. Indecision churned in her gut. She wanted to stay and continue to look for Ford; he could be hurt. But she needed to get to safety. She couldn't let Johnathan capture her.

She glanced toward shore. Ford said to meet there. If she could get to land, she could hide in the trees until he found her. If she stayed in the water, it was only a matter of time until Johnathan made his way over here and plucked her from the waves. If he didn't just shoot her and let the sharks eat her remains.

Shivering at the thought, Brooke scanned the wreckage one more time. Still no Ford.

Where was he?

She slapped at the water and growled her frustration. With a prayer that he was all right, she turned toward shore. She couldn't stay here.

Twenty-Nine

Blood poured from the wound near Ford's hairline, and his head pounded. Smoke filled his nostrils, the acrid scent making his eyes water. Pain lanced his side and back. Wincing, he rolled to his side, then groaned. *Oh, that hurt.* Sucking in a breath, he held it against the pain as he got to his hands and knees. Water flooded in, covering his hands and rising up his forearms. He needed to move.

Carefully, and with his head still spinning, he crawled through the deepening water in his stateroom toward the light shining in from the hole in the ceiling. The blast had knocked him backward, and he'd fallen through the newly created hole in the bow deck. He had to get out of here before the water rose much more. It wouldn't be long and the boat would sink beneath the waves, taking him with it.

A glance back told him going through the door was out. It was deeper under water than his current spot. He was afraid he'd get stuck in the hall or the main cabin if he went that way. No, the only way out was up.

Crawling up on the bed, he stood on shaky legs and stared up at the hole. He'd fit through it, but it was just getting up there that was the problem. Raising his arms, he reached for the edge, but it was just out of reach. He bounced, testing the flex of the mattress, then jumped. His hands closed over the opening. The splintered wood bit into his palms. Ford ignored the pain and hauled himself up with a grunt. He hooked an arm over the deck and pushed up. His chest and back muscles screamed in protest, but adrenaline kept him going. He had to get out of the hole if he wanted to survive. If he wanted to find Brooke.

He pressed up on his palms and brought his legs through the hole. A quick look around showed him the utter devastation of the grenade. His boat was unrecognizable. The pilot-house was gone and thick black smoke billowed from the rear deck. The fuel was on fire. It was a wonder the explosion wasn't bigger. The tank must have ruptured, but been far enough from the blast it didn't blow. Now the released fuel was burning.

Staying low, he scuttled along what was left of the deck, looking for Brooke. The dense smoke made it hard to see more than a few yards. "Brooke!" He waited several long moments, but got no response. He'd pushed her clear of the bow a split second before the grenade hit. She had to be in the water.

He scanned the waves as he made his way to the bow peak. Pieces of debris littered the water, but no Brooke.

The heavy engine of the yacht rumbled to life behind him. Ford let out a soft curse. He'd lost his guns in the blast. All he had were the knives strapped to his body. They wouldn't do him much good on a sinking vessel. Cassidy and his goons would just wait for the boat to sink, then scoop him out of the water. Or shoot him. He needed to get clear.

Decision made, he jumped into the ocean. Breaking the surface, he whipped his head to the side, shaking his hair out of his eyes, and started for the spot he hoped to find Brooke.

He did a quick three-sixty in the water. "Brooke!" He saw no sign of her, and she still didn't answer.

Where the hell was she? Could she have headed for shore? He'd told her that's where they were headed. Maybe she stuck to the plan.

Without a better idea in mind, he started swimming.

THIRTY

Brooke dragged herself to shore, glancing back as she forced her leaden legs to carry her through the sand. She cast a glance over her shoulder, looking for Ford, but saw only waves and the burning hull of the *Midnight Hooker*. "Ford!" Where was he? The blast knocked her clear of the boat, but she had no idea if he made it off. He could have been knocked unconscious and was now at the bottom of the ocean.

Choking back a sob, she turned away from the water and headed for the trees. She felt too exposed on the beach. Shoes squishing, she ran into the jungle. Leaves slapped her in the face, and she was sure she passed through a spider web, but she didn't care. Her sole focus was getting out of the open. Over the sound of the waves, she heard male voices, shouting.

Where was that coming from? She stopped, listening, then edged toward the beach. Staying low, she peaked through the leaves. "Oh!" She slapped her hands over her mouth. Just down the beach, the six men from the zodiac boats ran through the sand, pointing in her direction.

"Crap!" Brooke pushed off the tree and ran. They must have seen her come ashore.

Hands out in front of her, she darted through the heavy foliage. Branches bent, whipping back as she ran past. She tried to stay parallel to the beach, knowing if she went too deep into the jungle, she'd end up irrevocably lost. Her goal might be to survive, but not at any cost. Getting lost was just as much of a death sentence as getting caught.

Her lungs burned as hot as her thighs. After her half-mile swim, her body screamed that it needed a break. Only the adrenaline coursing through her veins kept her legs pumping.

A branch whacked her in the nose and cheek. She let out a yelp, covering her face, but kept running through her now watering eyes. She didn't dare stop. Not yet.

Brooke glanced back for any sign of her pursuers. Another branch hit her in the face, and she flinched, stumbling. Her foot hit a root, sending her flying. With an oomph, she landed on her hands and knees. "Ow." That was going to leave a mark. Grimacing, she pushed to her feet, her knees aching. They'd be bruised later. They wouldn't be the only place. She was sure she'd look like she went five rounds with a champion boxer. She could already feel her cheek swelling, and her nose throbbed like the dickens.

The rustle of leaves and the crack of branches only feet behind her set her in motion again. The male shout that followed was much too close for comfort. Brooke dug deep, needing a burst of speed.

Glancing back again, she let out a terrified shriek. One man was only feet behind.

"Stop, you little bitch!"

Not on your life, buddy. No way would she make this easy for them. They wanted to kill her? They'd have to work for it.

But she only made it a few more yards before a hand snagged the back of her shirt and pulled. She tumbled to the ground with the man.

"No! Let me go!" She pummeled him with her fists and

scratched at his face. He rolled, pinning her to the ground. She tried to bring a knee up and hit him in the groin, but his size made it nearly impossible for her to move.

"Stop squirming," he growled. "Cassidy told us you were feisty, but he didn't mention you fight like a *gato montés*." He wrangled her arms into one hand and flipped her onto her stomach. "I think he not pay us enough for this." Heavy breathing punctuated his accented English.

"Well, you better demand more money, then, because I'll keep fighting. Worse than a wildcat." She yanked at her arms, getting one free.

He cursed, snagging it again. "*Señorita*, you are lucky Mr. Cassidy wants to take care of you himself." He leaned down, putting his mouth by her ear. "But he did not say you had to be unhurt when we turned you over. Just alive."

Brooke turned her head, glaring, but she stilled.

A wrinkle formed between his eyebrows. "What? No more fighting? Pity." He got to his feet, bringing her up with him, as his colleagues reached them. "Marco, rope."

One of the younger men took a small coil of rope from the cargo pocket on his pants. Brooke yanked on her arms, not wanting to be tied up.

The snick of a knife opening accompanied the appearance of a gleaming silver blade in front of her face. She stilled.

"Uh-uh-uh, *gato montés*."

She resisted the urge to kick him in the shin. "When Ford finds you, he's going to stick that knife straight through your heart."

The man laughed, the sound callous and cold. "*Gato montés*, your bodyguard is dead. He blew up with the boat." He leaned in close again. "No, you are stuck with us." He straightened and took the rope from Marco.

Brooke swallowed around the lump in her throat as he tied her up. No. She refused to believe Ford was dead. She needed to hold on to hope that he was alive. Not just so he could save her. She couldn't imagine living in a world without Ford Wagner.

In rapid-fire Spanish, the man asked Marco if anyone had contacted the yacht. He replied with an affirmative and said that they were to rendezvous with the yacht up the beach in the morning. Another boat that could navigate the shallower water closer to shore was coming in to pick them up.

Brooke bit back a groan. She had to stay out here in the jungle with these men all night? "I hope you stuffed bug spray in one of your pockets," she muttered. At least getting eaten alive by mosquitoes was preferable to being turned over to Johnathan. She doubted he'd keep her alive long.

The man holding her gave her a sharp look. "You understood us?"

"Every damn word, *amigo*." Venom dripped from her words.

He narrowed his eyes, then shoved her forward. "*¡Muévete!*"

Brooke stumbled, but kept her feet under her. Sending a death glare over her shoulder, she let him guide her toward the beach. "So, what's the plan? Sit on the beach until this new boat arrives?"

"None of your business. You will do what we tell you. Now stop talking."

Her mouth flattened. She didn't do well being told what to do. It made her want to do the opposite. An idea hit her. She knew just what to talk about. "So, do you have a family? Is that why you took this job? Whatever Johnathan's paying you, I'll double it. He works for my family. Did he tell you that? We were supposed to get married. I thought he loved me, but he only wanted my family's wealth. You let me go, and you can name your price. Also, what's your name? It's weird thinking about you as the guy with the mean eyes."

He growled and kept walking.

"Seriously? You're not interested in my money? Oh, wait. I get it. You're scared of Johnathan. I admit—"

"I am not afraid of *Señor* Cassidy."

"Really? You should be. He has meaner eyes than you do. Colder too." She pretended to shiver. "So, if you're not afraid of him, why so loyal? I guarantee I'll pay better."

"Because we finish what we're hired to do."

"Ah. A man of integrity. I guess I can respect that." And normally, she truly did. Just not when they wanted to turn her over to the man who wanted her dead. "But don't you have a moral compass? I mean, what would your mother think about you turning an innocent woman over to a psycho so he can murder her?"

That made him stop. He turned cold, hard eyes on her. "My mother was a whore and a drug addict until the day she fell off a boat and drowned. She would think nothing of me murdering you myself, let alone turning you over to your fiancé, because she never bothered to think about anything except her next score."

Brooke gulped. *Well, shit.* That didn't go the way she wanted.

"Now, do you have any other tactics you'd like to employ to make me let you go? Or can we walk in silence?"

She rolled her lips in, deciding to save her breath.

"Good." He yanked on her arm, propelling her forward.

It only took a few minutes for them to reach the shore. Mean eyes pushed her down onto a fallen tree trunk and told her to stay put, posting one of the other men on her. He and the rest of them then went off, gathering firewood and food to get them through the night. She hoped they brought back some water. She'd kill for a drink. The swim and subsequent mad dash through the jungle dehydrated her. And it was hot.

She glanced up at the sun through her lashes. He could

have at least set her down in the shade. Where was the damn rain when she actually wanted it?

Raising a hand, she shaded her eyes and stared out at the smoking wreckage of the *Midnight Hooker*. An ache formed in her chest and moisture gathered in her eyes.

Ford, where are you?

THIRTY-ONE

Staying low, Ford crawled through the shallows. He eyed the men on the beach. And Brooke. She sat on a fallen tree, glaring daggers at one of the men. Ford bit back a smile. Even in mortal peril, his princess had her spunk. He just hoped she didn't take it too far. It could backfire on her.

The water barely rippled as he moved, keeping an eye on the activity on the beach. Minutes after he'd jumped off the boat and started for shore, he'd seen Brooke emerge, then take off for the jungle. A few moments later, he'd seen why. The six men from the zodiac boats ran down the beach after her. By the time he'd been close enough to walk out of the water, they were coming back with Brooke's hands tied in front of her. So, he'd stayed in the shallows and watched to see what they were up to. She'd been spitting mad since the one guy plopped her down on the tree trunk. Now, it looked like they were digging in for the night.

Perfect. That gave him time to plan. And to contact his team.

Pushing back, he maneuvered into deeper water and went under, swimming as far as his damaged lung would allow before breaking the surface to take a breath, then diving under again. Around a bend in the shoreline, he left the water, hurrying ashore and into the trees for cover in case anyone came his way. Sinking to the soft loam of the forest floor, he took some deep breaths, wincing as his ribs protested. They weren't broken, but they still hurt like the devil.

Once he was sure he could string two words together without gasping for air, he took the sat phone from his vest pocket and powered it up. He punched in Max's number, then put it to his ear. Static crackled, but between the bursts he heard the low rumble of Max's concerned voice.

"Max, if you can hear me, I need help on the far side of Osa. Near Punta Salsipuedes. Keep your eyes open when you do. Cassidy found us and is in the area." He waited, hoping for a response, but only more static met his ears. Cursing, he hung up. He'd try again later. Let the phone dry out. It was water resistant, not waterproof. He should have kept it in one of those bags, but it was difficult to use on its own. The thick plastic just made it harder.

He let out a snort. He really was getting soft. In the SEALs, hell, even the first year after he left, he would have sucked it up and put the phone in the bag. Now he was paying for it.

Dwelling on it wouldn't change things. He needed to focus on what he could do right now, and that was gather materials to rescue Brooke and get them to safety.

For the next several hours, he gathered wood and stripped vines from trees. For once, he was grateful for his rural Florida upbringing and for having his grandparents as his babysitters. He'd tied many snares with his grandpa as a kid to catch wild hogs and other wildlife, so making them now was like riding a bike. Once he had several tied into loops and cut to length, he crept into the jungle to set his traps.

Coiling one, he set it on the ground, then removed one of

the small sticks he'd gathered from his pocket. With the knife from his vest, he notched it, then sunk one end into the ground. He notched another stick, then attached it to one end of the coiled vine near the slipknot he'd tied to make a loop. Throwing the other end over a branch above his head, he tugged on both sides, bringing the limb down. He held the vines with one hand while he laid the snare out, then tied the remainder off on the limb. Hooking the notches together, he stepped back, saying a silent prayer that they'd stay together until one of Cassidy's goons walked into it.

Satisfied it was stable, he set several others just like it, then rigged some limbs to drop. By the time he was done, he was tired, dirty, and famished. Food would have to wait, though. Darkness gathered, and he wanted to be in position before his quarry settled in for the night. They'd hear him moving once their camp quieted.

Slipping through the thick foliage, he came up behind their encampment, sinking low beneath some large ferns. He'd just watch and wait.

Thirty-Two

Brooke shifted, her back against the tree, and tried to find a comfortable position in the sand. Juan—she'd learned her captor's name—wouldn't let her sit anywhere else, so here she was, trying to find a suitable way to sleep. It didn't help that she wasn't the least bit tired. Too much adrenaline still coursed through her veins.

The wood dug into her back, and she shifted again. With a sigh, she stared out at the water. The sun had set an hour ago or so, and the last vestiges of light lit the horizon. Stars popped in the inky sky flanking the brilliant cloud of the Milky Way.

In other circumstances, she'd feel like this was the best vacation of her life. Between the view, the warm breeze, and the beautiful symphony of the nighttime jungle, it was what dreams were made of.

A quick shout, then a round of laughter to her right brought her back down to earth. This wasn't a vacation, and the danger was very real.

Shifting again, she brought her knees up and looped her bound hands over them. The zip ties bit into her skin, but she ignored the pain. Her shoulders ached from having her hands locked together for so long, and it felt good to support her arms. She leaned forward and propped her chin on her knees, staring out at the water.

The enormity of her situation hit her. Emotion clogged her throat, making it hard to breathe. She swallowed, trying to get rid of the lump, but it didn't work. Tears pressed against the back of her eyes, and she rolled her lips in, pressing them together, hard, to keep them at bay. She wanted to go home. She wanted a hug from her dad and to hear her mom laugh.

And she wanted Ford. Where was he? She'd still not seen any sign of him, despite staring at the wreck since Juan parked her on the tree trunk. Was he right and Ford died in the explosion? Was he at the bottom of the ocean now with the wreckage?

She shook her head and sniffed. She couldn't think like that. He had to be alive.

Huffing out a breath, she sat back and closed her eyes, saying yet another silent prayer that he was all right.

Darkness gathered as the sun sank further below the horizon. Brooke watched as all but one of the men laid down and went to sleep. He paced, watching the jungle. She wasn't sure what he was looking for. Ford would come from the water.

An inhuman shriek from the trees made her jump. Okay, maybe there were more dangers than just Ford. She drew her knees up higher, tightening herself into a ball, now on high alert for things that went bump in the night.

A twig snapped to her left. She whipped her head to the side, staring into the blackened jungle. What was that?

Another branch cracked and the leaves rustled. Brooke's heart thumped in her ears. Her eyes strained as she stared, but it was no use; it was too dark.

After several moments, the rustling stopped. She kept staring, but the jungle stayed quiet. Still wary, she turned back to the water in time to see her guard pause. He, too, stared at the trees.

Oh, God. Brooke got to her knees, getting ready to get up and run. What if it was a panther? They had those down here, didn't they? What if it saw her as an easy meal? She was vulnerable sitting out in the open with her hands tied. How was she supposed to defend herself if one attacked?

Frantically, she tried to remember those videos she'd seen about how to break out of zip ties. You were supposed to pull your arms back and break them over your stomach, right? She tried it, but the ties dug into her wrists. Maybe if she twisted her hands at the same time, it would work.

She held her arms out, ready to do just that, when the guard walked toward the trees. Frowning, she turned. What did he see?

The man leaned forward and picked up a stick. He poked at the low foliage, then stepped back, glancing around before turning back to the beach.

Brooke let out a breath. It must have been nothing. A lizard or something. Some of them got rather large and could make the leaves shake like that.

She lowered herself to her haunches, her heart returning to a more normal rhythm, only to have it spike again, when a dark shape ran out of the jungle and wrapped the guard in a hold from behind.

Ford! She'd know that long, lean form anywhere. Elation that he was alive sent a lump into her throat and made her eyes water.

The man let out a gasp before Ford choked off his air supply with a hold around his neck. In moments, the guard slumped in his grasp. Quietly, Ford laid the man in the sand. Brooke scrambled to her feet, meeting him halfway. She'd known he wasn't dead. And she'd never been so happy to see anyone.

Ford laid a finger over his lips, then took a knife from his vest and sliced through her bonds. Brooke rubbed her wrists as he put the knife away. She wanted to hug him, but the look on his face was all business. He pointed toward the jungle, then tipped his head. Brooke nodded, understanding his silent direction, and they took off for the trees.

Grateful Juan hadn't taken her shoes, she followed Ford through the near pitch-black jungle, trying not to make too much noise. After several long minutes, Ford stopped. She could just make out his eyes, glittering in the starlight filtering down through the canopy.

"Are you all right?" His low voice washed over her like a warm ocean wave. He grasped her arms.

"I'm fine. Are you? I looked for you after the explosion but—"

"I'm okay. I got knocked into the cabin and had to climb out." He took her hand. "We need to put as much distance between us and them as we can. I set some traps to slow them down, but there's no guarantee they'll trip any of them."

"Okay." She let him tug her along. "What's the plan? How do we get out of here? I overheard them say there's another boat coming in the morning. It was supposed to pick us up and take us back to the yacht."

"That's good to know. I tried to contact Max earlier, but the sat phone had a lot of static." He paused and let go of her hand, removing the phone from his vest. A moment later, light from the screen lit up his face.

Brooke gasped as she got her first good look at him. "You're hurt." She reached out.

He curled his fingers gently around hers. "I'm fine." His gaze met hers, then he frowned. "But you're not. What happened to your face?" A fierce glint turned his eyes stony. "Did they hit you?"

"What?" She touched her cheek, feeling the swelling. "Oh,

no. That's from my mad dash through the jungle. I got slapped by some branches. Is it that bad?"

His fingers skimmed her face. "No. Nothing time won't fix. Are you hurt anywhere else?"

She shook her head. The jungle faded away as she stared into his eyes. "I'm so glad you're all right," she whispered.

He threaded his hand into her hair, then leaned in to press a kiss to her forehead. "Same, honey." Pulling back, she watched him swallow hard before he let her go and raised the phone. "Let's see if this thing works now." He punched in some numbers and put the phone to his ear.

Brooke held her breath. It had to. She didn't know how they'd get out of here without help.

"Max, can you hear me?" Ford paused a beat, then his shoulders slumped. "Oh, thank God. Listen, we're near Punta Salsipuedes. Can you meet us at Playa Madrigal tomorrow morning? Bring reinforcements and watch yourself." He listened again for a moment, nodding.

Brooke leaned in, trying to hear what he said, but could only catch the low murmur of Max's voice.

"Okay. There are six of them on land. At least two more on the yacht, and Brooke said they called in another vessel to pick them up. We're going to stick to the beach road, so if we're not at the rendezvous point—" He broke off, nodding again. "Perfect. Thanks." He hung up.

"What? What did he say?"

"That he already alerted the others and is going to call them again. See who's free to help. Part of my last call made it through, and he could tell something was wrong. They'll meet us at Madrigal in the morning and come looking for us if we're not there."

"How far is that?"

"Four or five miles. We need to move."

Brooke blinked, then forced her feet to move as he tugged

on her hand. They had to walk four or five miles in the dark? "How are we not going to get lost? It's almost pitch-black in here."

"We're going to cut back toward the beach and walk the dirt road. No one else will be on it. Your captors are behind us and the others are out to sea. I know you're probably tired, but we don't have a choice."

She scoffed. "I'm not tired. And I want out of here. Lead the way."

"That's my girl. Come on." He picked up his pace.

Brooke did her best to keep up and to stay on her feet. The jungle was littered with obstacles she couldn't see in the dark. They stumbled their way through the dense foliage until they reemerged on the beach. She inhaled a deep breath of the salty air, grateful for the breeze coming off the water. In the trees, it was humid and warm. Out here, the sea breeze cooled her sweaty body and reinvigorated her. Which was a good thing, because they were far from safe.

Ford led her to a road that was little more than two dirt ruts at the edge of the jungle. But it was enough of a path to keep them from getting lost. And it was also mostly clear of trees and ferns, so they weren't tripping over things every few feet. It gave her a chance to study Ford—what she could see of him in the starlight, anyway. Dirt streaked his arms and dried blood darkened the side of his face. His gold-tipped light brown hair looked like it needed a good wash, but his shoulders were square and his back straight, telling her he wasn't in pain. Or he was at least good at hiding it. She hoped it was the former. Ford didn't need more pain. She'd seen his scars and knew he'd had more than his fair share.

She trudged along beside him, doing her best not to think about what he'd been through, but she couldn't help it. After the day's events and her body dipping into its energy reserves to keep her moving, the filter on her mind had taken a hit. So had the one on her mouth, and she couldn't stop her next words from tumbling out.

"You know, you never did tell me why you're indebted to Ezra. Edie told me it was a rescue mission. That you and your team saved her and Ezra. How does that put you into Ezra's debt? Shouldn't it be the other way around?"

The hitch in Ford's step was the only indication he gave that he heard her. Brooke waited, hoping he'd answer.

After several long moments, he did. "My actions saved Ezra and Edie, yes. But I shouldn't have been there. I disobeyed orders to extract them and almost died in the process."

"You disobeyed orders? Why?"

"Because I couldn't let them die. Not when I knew there was a chance my team and I could get in and out without being seen."

He was just talking in circles. "I don't understand. What happened?"

Ford sighed and stopped walking. "A lot of it's classified, but—" He broke off and shook his head. Biting the corner of his mouth, he looked at the ocean, then turned to her. His eyes shone silver in the starlight. "I was deployed. In the Middle East. We were on base just hanging out after coming back from a training mission when we heard about Ezra's chopper going down ten miles from base. We'd had a lot of insurgent activity around us lately and the base commander told us to hold off on going out to look for them." He paused again and shook his head. "The week before, we heard from one of our interpreters how a woman who'd helped us had been captured, then subsequently raped and tortured. When I learned there'd been a woman on the chopper—Edie—I knew that if the insurgents found her, she'd suffer a similar fate. I couldn't let that happen."

"So you disobeyed orders to go look for them?"

"Sort of. The base commander only asked that we wait for more intelligence, never ordered that we not go, so I argued with my immediate supervisor that we needed to ignore the colonel and go anyway. My commander agreed with the base commander that we needed to wait for more information on the crash and the insurgent activity out that way, but I couldn't sit idle that long. I got a couple of my other teammates together and we left."

He ran a hand through his filthy hair. "We found them fairly easily. They were still at the chopper. Edie's commander died in the crash. She had a broken arm. Ezra broke a leg. We got them splinted up and into our vehicle when the insurgents found us." He sucked in a breath and winced. "I took a shot to the chest. It went in under my arm where my vest didn't cover, bounced off the ceramic plate, then back into my chest and came out near my spine and embedded itself in my vest. Ezra grabbed my gun when I went down and fired back, pulling me to the Humvee while he hopped on his good leg."

Brooke gasped. She knew Ezra was tough—she'd heard the story from his wife Amy about how they met—but she'd never imagined anyone could do something like that.

"Anyway, he's the reason I made it into the Humvee. Why I made it back to base alive and didn't bleed out in the sand. He went to bat for me, too, when the base commander wanted to court martial me. Since a direct order was never given, I wasn't technically in violation. The fact that I brought everyone back alive and that I nearly died helped. The Navy deemed that my injury was punishment enough. It meant I was off the teams." He looked away, his expression tight.

She watched him, processing all he said. "Do you regret what you did?"

"No." His answer was swift, and he looked at her again. "Never. Even if the outcome were different and I died, I still wouldn't regret it. Not so long as Ezra and Edie lived."

Brooke nodded, seeing Ford in a new light. "I think I understand now why so many of your former military friends followed you down here. You're a good man, Ford Wagner."

He barked a harsh laugh. "Hardly. I just have a few principles I won't set aside for anything." He lifted a shoulder. "I guess that appeals to some people."

Her laugh was a little more lighthearted. "I guess it does."

They resumed walking. "So." She looked at him and saw him stiffen, no doubt bracing himself for more questions. She pushed on anyway. "What brought the others down here? Max and Asher. And Sam, was it? Besides your charming personality, I mean?"

"We all have baggage, Brooke. And sometimes, we need space to process it. A safe space. I guess they thought this was it. Edie was the first. Max and Sam followed not long after. Asher and Dean are newer. Dean followed Sam. It's not like I advertised; it just happened."

She hummed. "You didn't need to. Your integrity drew them."

He let out a soft snort. "That's funny. You saying I have integrity. Didn't you want to string me up by my toes a week ago?"

Brooke chuckled. "Maybe. But somewhere along the line, I got to know you."

"Yeah, between the sheets."

She smacked his arms. "Don't be a smart ass. I'm serious. You're a good man, Ford. I'm glad Ezra dumped me here. I'm not glad about the circumstances, but the outcome? I can't be upset about that."

He held up a hand. "We're still just two ships passing. Don't read more into it." Giving her a hard look, he walked away before she could say more.

Clenching her molars, she stared at his broad back. Why

did he have to go and act like an asshole? As a defense mecha-nism, his attitude sucked.

She rolled her eyes and walked after him. She supposed that was the point. Be a jerk and everyone stays at arm's length. One day, though, that wouldn't work. Then what would he do?

Thirty-Three

Waves broke over Ford's feet as he stood in the surf, throwing stones into the water. Brooke was still sleeping, but the moment the first rays of sunlight touched his face, he'd been wide awake. It wasn't like he slept well, anyway. Too much danger and too much on his mind. Luckily, they'd stayed well-ahead of the goon squad.

He'd been unable to do much about his thoughts, though. Every time he tried to think about something else, his mind wandered back to what he said to Brooke. Why did he have to remind her they were temporary? He could have just said thanks and let it go.

He launched another rock into the sea. He meant what he'd said, though. Nothing could come of them. When this was over, she'd go back to her life in North Carolina and he'd go back to his here. That was the end of it. He had no desire to have a long-distance relationship.

The high-pitched buzz of a speedboat engine reached his ears. He froze, scanning the water. What he wouldn't give for his binoculars. Backing up, he turned, hurrying to where

Brooke slept. He dropped to his knees beside her and shook her awake. "Brooke. Honey, wake up. We've got company."

She sucked in a long, slow breath. Ford knew the moment his words penetrated the sleep fog. She stilled, then sat up, wide-eyed. "What? Friend or foe?"

"Not sure. Hopefully, friend. Come on." He took her hand and stood, bringing her to her feet. "We need to get behind cover." He nudged her toward a pile of driftwood.

"Do you see anything?" She peeked over the top.

Ford stared to their left, squinting. "Maybe." He pointed. "There." A white shape, higher than the cresting waves, stayed steady near shore.

"What color is Max's boat?"

"White. But it could be the boat Cassidy called in." It was coming closer, so in a minute they'd know one way or the other who'd reached them first.

The shape grew larger as it approached until Ford could make out the man standing behind the wheel. His shoulders drooped in relief. "It's Max." There was no mistaking the tall man with salt and pepper hair and trim physique. He might be forty-five, but Max Carson could keep up with men half his age with ease.

Ford rounded the driftwood, sticking close just in case someone else showed up. As Max approached, Ford raised his arms and waved. Max waved back and slowed, turning toward shore.

"Let's go." Ford pushed Brooke toward the boat. Together, they splashed into the water and high-stepped toward the speedboat.

"Y'all look like hell." Max reached down to take Brooke's hand and help her aboard.

"Gee, thanks." Ford grabbed the rail and pulled himself up. "It's nice to see you too."

"Just stating facts." A teasing smile flirted with Max's

mouth. "Miss McGinty, I'm Max Carson. And I have to say, you still look beautiful, even through the—" He broke off and swirled a finger in the air, gesturing to her face.

Ford rolled his eyes and shook his head. "Cut the crap, Max."

Brooke groaned. "Is it bad? I can feel the swelling."

"You look fine, princess." They had bigger things to worry about than their assortment of minor injuries. "Max, did you see anyone on your way in?"

He shook his head. "Not a soul."

"Where are the others? I thought you were bringing reinforcements."

"Dean's still out of town. Sam had an emergency crop up at the bar—something about a busted pipe flooding everything. Asher's still digging up more dirt on the Cassidys, and Edie went to the police station to meet the federal police. Asher discovered Cassidy paid off the local cops to get a location on you. I guess one of them in Puerto Jiménez saw you and called him. Asher made some calls and got a unit from San José to fly in." He held up a hand. "Sorry, man. I'm it."

"Okay." Ford propped a hand on his hip and stared out to sea, his mind working a plan.

"What are you thinking, Wags? I can see the wheels spinning."

"If their reinforcements haven't shown up yet, maybe we can get to Johnathan. End this now."

"How so?"

"What?" Brooke spoke over Max. She waved her hands. "No. Leave him to the authorities. You said they're coming, right?" She sent Max a questioning look.

Ford scoffed. "By the time they get out here, he'll be long gone. Do you want to be stuck here even longer? And actually, you'll probably have to go somewhere else since Johnathan knows you're here. Where that will be, I don't know. I'm sure Asher can come up with a place we can stash you, though."

She stared at him with her amber eyes rounded. After several silent moments, she straightened her spine and her expression shifted. "How do you plan to get to him? It's just the two of you. I know you only saw one other person still on the yacht, but there has to be more. Like the captain. And probably other crew."

"I know." Ford looked at Max. "Did you come prepared?"

"That is a stupid question." Max put the boat in reverse, maneuvering them away from shore. "Where's this yacht?"

Ford pointed further up the beach. "That way."

Max gunned the engine.

"Wait," Brooke yelled to be heard over the roar. "How do you plan to sneak up on them? Or don't you?"

"She poses a good question, Wags. What's your plan? I don't relish getting shot at."

"If they're still where we left them, they're tucked into a little cove. We can swim around the point and sneak onboard."

"Swim, really? You were the SEAL, not me." Max leveled a look on him.

"Whatever. You go on an ocean swim almost every day." Ford held his gaze.

"Not loaded with weaponry." After a beat, he blinked and flattened his mouth, rolling his shoulders. "Fine. We swim."

Ford gave a quick nod. "Where did you stash stuff?"

Max pointed to the bench seat where Brooke had taken up residence. She stood, grabbing the rail for stability, and Ford opened the lid.

"Holy crap!"

Ford glanced up at Brooke's exclamation. "What?"

"I thought you brought an arsenal." She shook her head. "This is like a full-on armory."

A sardonic smile lifted his mouth. "Max was a boy scout." He reached in and took out a pistol, much like the one he lost in the blast, along with extra ammo. "Do you want a rifle?" he yelled back to Max.

"No. Give me the pair of M and Ps that are in there. I brought the Colt 1911s for you. I brought some short-range radios too."

"Awesome." He found the Smith and Wessons Max wanted and their ammo and brought them up, then went back to arm himself with some flash bangs. Pocketing some zip ties and grabbing the second Colt, he dug through the bag until he located the radios. Taking out three, as well as waterproof pouches and a dry bag, he moved up next to Max. They were nearing the cove.

"So, where's your boat? You anchor off the beach near the yacht?"

Ford's mouth flattened. "No. They blew it up." He handed Max a radio.

Max's dark eyes rounded as he took it. "What? How?"

"Grenade launcher." Ford opened the dry bag and started putting things in it.

Max sent another wide-eyed glance his way. "You're buying me a new boat if they blow mine up."

"They won't." At least, he hoped. He couldn't afford to replace Max's speedboat. Hell, he wasn't sure he could afford to replace the *Hooker*. It wasn't like his insurance covered explosion by grenade launcher.

Max pulled back on the throttle as they approached the point. He maneuvered them near the bend, putting the engine on idle.

"There's the yacht." Max nodded at the large vessel still anchored where they left it. "How many do you think are onboard?"

Ford shrugged. "Half a dozen, maybe. Probably less.

Cassidy, the other man with the grenade launcher, the captain, and maybe a crew member or two. The rest came onshore after Brooke."

"How many went ashore?"

"Six."

"You guys got away from six armed mercenaries? How?"

"I shot their zodiacs and sunk them. They swam to shore. Then the guy on the yacht blew up my boat. We swam to shore—separately—and they captured her." Ford pointed at Brooke. "They didn't see me, though, so once night fell, I took out the one they left on guard, then we ran."

Max tapped his fingers on the steering wheel. "They no doubt know she's gone. What are the chances they went back to the yacht? It's not that far out."

"It's far enough. Would you want to swim that distance in the dark around here?"

Max scrunched his face. "No. These rocks are deadly, even in the daylight, if you don't know what you're doing."

"Exactly. I think they're all still onshore. Probably trying to track us through the jungle. Brooke said she overheard them say there's another boat coming to pick them up to take them back to the yacht."

"Great. We need to get moving. That's at least a half-mile swim."

"Agreed." Ford cinched the dry bag closed, then turned to Brooke. She'd returned to her seat on the bench. "Brooke. Do you think you can handle this boat? Keep it from hitting the rocks, like you did the *Hooker*?"

"Um, yes. Of course. You want me to stay here?"

"Yes. It's too dangerous for you to come along. Even if you could make the swim, what we'll find onboard—" He shook his head. "You're not prepared for that kind of fight." He handed her a radio. "We'll make this as quick as possible. If someone comes, hit this button." He pointed to a button on the side. "It'll light up a light." Hopefully, he'd see it. "If you're in imminent danger, break radio silence, then haul ass out of here. Don't worry about us. Just get to safety."

She took the radio, staring at it for a long moment before she met his gaze again. Moisture swam in her eyes. "Be careful."

"We will." Unable to stop himself, he leaned in and pressed a hard kiss to her lips, then turned to Max. "Did you bring any snorkeling gear?"

The older man raised an eyebrow, but didn't comment on the kiss. "I have a couple sets of fins and masks that I always keep on the boat." He left the controls to open a compartment near the rear bench.

Ford took a set. "These will do." He sat down and put on the fins, then fit the mask over his face. Max did the same.

"You good?" Ford asked Max.

"Yep." He stepped up on the rail. "Last one there buys the beer." He jumped off.

Ford climbed onto the rail, settling the straps of the dry bag over his shoulders and latching the waist belt. With one last look at Brooke, who watched him with worry in her eyes, he jumped.

Thirty-Four

The current tugged at Ford's body as he swam toward the yacht. He'd easily caught up to Max, despite the man's longer frame, and now kept pace with him for the thirty-minute swim to the yacht. When they were within fifty yards of the rear deck, he motioned for Max to stop.

"We need to go in underwater. I don't see anyone, but those windows are tinted."

Max nodded. "We boarding on the rear ladder?"

"Yes."

"Let's do this."

Both men dove under, only surfacing to breathe. Max gained ground, able to stay under longer, and reached the yacht first.

"You owe me a beer," he whispered with a smile.

"Would you really capitalize on a man's disability?" Ford reached down and removed his fins.

"Disability, nothing. You're the fastest swimmer I've ever met." Max removed his fins. "We both know you could have turned on the jets and left me in the dust until we had to go under." He put his fins on the deck and grabbed the ladder. In a few quick movements, he was on the rear deck, hunched low.

Ford followed suit. On his haunches, he shoved their fins and masks into a corner behind a chair on the deck, then took the dry bag off his shoulders. Digging inside, he removed the M and Ps, ammo, and a radio and handed the stuff to Max. "You go right and up. Find the captain and secure him. I'll check the cabin for Cassidy." That bastard was his.

"Sounds good." Max loaded his pistols and stowed the extra ammo. He hooked the radio to his shorts. "Watch yourself."

"You too." With his own guns loaded and his pockets full, Ford took off down the left side of the yacht toward the cabin entrance. Water dripped off of him as he moved, leaving a steady trail from the stern. Ford took slow, measured breaths, keeping his heart rate under control.

Reaching the door, he cracked it open and peered inside. The room was empty. He swung the door wide and passed through, closing it behind him with a soft snick. Inside, he blinked, letting his eyes adjust, then moved toward the rear of the room. This level contained the kitchen, which was surprisingly quiet for the time of day. Maybe there were fewer people on board than he thought.

He moved past the state-of-the-art appliances to the crew's quarters beyond. They, too, were quiet. With the level clear, he returned to the kitchen and ascended the stairs. His heart thumped as he neared the top. He paused, taking a deep breath and poked his head up. The living space was void of anyone. Climbing the remaining stairs, he entered the well-appointed living area. He doubted Cassidy was on this level, either. From what he'd seen of other yachts this size, the next level contained the master suite. Ford would bet that's where the man was. But the man with the grenade launcher could still be on this level. If not, that meant he was probably up with the captain. He said a quick prayer Max would be okay with both men.

On light feet, Ford walked down the hallway, checking rooms as he went. A soft thump and a quiet rustle in the room to his left made him pause. He stared at the open door, waiting to see if he heard anything more. When it remained silent, he raised his gun and moved forward, sweeping into the doorway.

A woman let out a soft scream and backed against the wall.

"*¡Manos arriba!*" Ford barked.

The woman raised her hands. Wide, frightened eyes met his. "*Por favor. No me mates. Por favor.*"

"*No te voy a matar. ¿Hablas inglés?*" He lowered the tip of his weapon, but kept his hands raised as he tried to reassure the woman he didn't intend to kill her.

"Yes. Please, I don't want to die." Her voice wavered and the first tears fell.

"I'm not going to kill you. I'm looking for Johnathan Cassidy. Do you know where he is?"

"*Sí.* He is upstairs." She pointed to the ceiling. "In the main suite."

"Okay. Sit." He gestured to the bed.

Eyes still wide, she did as he asked. "What are you going to do to me?"

Ford opened a pocket on his vest and took out two of the zip ties. "Tie you up. If you're innocent in all of this, the authorities will release you soon." He holstered his gun and put one of the ties around her wrists. The second, he secured around her ankles. "Do I need to muzzle you?"

She shook her head, the movement frantic. "No. I'll be quiet. Please don't forget about me. I have children."

He patted her shoe. If she was involved, she was a brilliant actress. Her tears and fear seemed genuine. "Someone will come for you soon." Backing away, he left the room, closing the door on her sniffling.

With a quick check of the remaining room in the hallway, he retraced his steps, then went up to the third level. His heart rate kicked up a notch, and this time, he could only slow it marginally. He was walking into danger and his body knew it.

Grateful for his bare feet, he noiselessly ascended the stairs and peered into the room. Cassidy sat on the balcony, sipping a cup of coffee and staring at a tablet as though he hadn't a care in the world. Ford shook his head. *Smug jackass.*

His weapon trained on the back of Cassidy's head, Ford walked into the room and crossed to the man's blindside. He ducked behind a chair and glanced around it. The man had turned his head and now stared into the cabin with a frown. Ford waited several moments, then Cassidy turned back to his tablet. He let a few more beats pass, then moved up, stopping beside the planter near the door. Cassidy still faced the water.

Standing, weapon extended, Ford stepped into the doorway.

"You are one cold sonofabitch, Cassidy."

The man jumped, rising from his chair, and spun around. "Who are you?" He glanced around. "How did you get on this ship?"

"I swam." He took a step closer. "And I'm the man whose boat you blew up yesterday. The one who stole Brooke right out from under your men's noses." He took another step. "The man who knows all your dirty secrets and is here to take you to the police."

Johnathan scoffed and rolled his eyes. "What police? The Costa Rican authorities? They've been paid well to look the other way."

Ford bared his teeth in a "got you" smile. The man's face paled slightly. "Did you pay off the federal police too? We know about the locals."

Cassidy swallowed, his Adam's apple bobbing. He set the tablet on the chair. "You still have to get past my men. They're all down below."

"I was just there. All I found was the maid. Try again." He advanced two more steps. "Turn around and put your hands behind your head."

The man squared his shoulders and puffed out his chest, staring Ford down.

Mister fancy businessman wanted to fight. Well, he was happy to oblige. "You know what?" Ford holstered his gun. "You look like you want to fight. After the way you used Brooke, I'm game for that." He raised his fists. "What do you say?" He motioned the man forward. "Come on."

Cassidy hesitated.

Ford fought not to roll his eyes at his lack of spine. "You have an advantage, you know. I just swam half a mile after hiking all night. And after being blown up." It was true. He wasn't at his best. But he could fight in his sleep.

Ford saw the decision enter Cassidy's eyes a moment before he lunged at Ford, swinging away. In one quick move, Ford side-stepped and landed a blow to Cassidy's stomach. The man let out a grunt and pushed away.

With a grin, Ford motioned him to come at him again. "That all you got?"

Sucking air, Cassidy shifted.

"Don't be a chicken. Come on."

Cassidy's eyes hardened. "Take off your vest. It's hardly fair for me to punch armor."

Ford laughed. "You're not going to touch me." Tired of waiting for Cassidy to attack, Ford lashed out. He hit the man in the nose, feeling the crunch of bone under his fist, then followed the hit with another to his gut. Johnathan doubled over. Ford hit him across the left cheek, knocking him to the ground. "That was pathetically easy." He stood over him and nudged him with his bare foot. "Roll over."

Cassidy moaned, curled up in the fetal position. He cradled his face. "You broke my nose."

"You're lucky that's all I broke." Ford took some zip ties from his vest and knelt beside him. None too gently, he yanked Cassidy's left arm behind his back and rolled him onto his stomach. Grabbing his other arm, he tied his wrists together, then hauled the man to his feet. Blood poured down Johnathan's face from his broken nose, soaking his shirt. Ford shoved him toward the door. "Let's go."

"Who are you? How did she find someone like you?"

"I'm Ezra's friend."

Cassidy glanced at him. "The chopper pilot?"

Ford gave a dark chuckle. "You know, you should get more background info on the people around you when you decide to break the law. Ezra was a Night Stalker. Do you know what that is?"

"No."

"He flew top secret missions with Special Forces. My SEAL team included."

Cassidy groaned, making Ford laugh again. "Yep, you were screwed the moment Brooke asked for a ride out of the country."

They made it to the steps leading to the bridge. He gave Cassidy a quick shake. "Keep your mouth shut. I swear, I will use you as a human shield if your buddies start shooting. Got it?"

The man gave a jerky nod. Ford pushed him up the steps.

"Took you long enough. You only had one man to deal with. I took down two."

Ford heard Max's droll voice before he saw him. He led Cassidy onto the bridge, then looked to his right. Max sat in the captain's chair, holding a gun on the captain and the man

Ford saw with the grenade launcher yesterday. Both were tied up and sitting on the floor.

"Hey, I had to search three levels. You went straight up here. Also, there's a maid on deck two we need to not forget about. I left her tied up in one of the staterooms."

Max's head bobbed. "Good deal." He shifted and took the radio from his pocket. "Guess we should call your pretty lady friend and tell her all is well." Max sent a toothy smile at Cassidy. "She'll be delighted to see you."

Thirty-Five

Wind whipped through Brooke's hair and stinging sea spray pelted her face as she rode back to Golfito on Max's speedboat. She didn't really feel any of it, though. A numbness had settled over her in the last hour. Once they left Puerto Jiménez, where Johnathan was now in the custody of the Costa Rican federal police, her brain just shut down. The ride across the gulf was little more than a blur. She was just happy it was over. She could go home now.

Her gaze went to Ford, who stood beside Max at the boat's helm. A smile curved his lips at something Max said. Her heart clenched. She wasn't so sure she wanted to go home. It meant leaving Ford behind. Somewhere along the line, he'd come to mean something to her. She wished circumstances were different.

The small marina from where they'd left days earlier came into view, and Max slowed the boat. They puttered to the dock, and Ford jumped out, carrying a line. He secured them to the pilings with quick, efficient movements.

"Thank you for riding with Carson Tours. We hoped you

had a pleasant trip." Max swept out an arm and bowed low, a wide smile on his face.

His levity broke through her numbness, and she smiled. "It was a smooth ride, thank you."

He straightened and his smile turned more sincere. "I'm glad." He held out a hand to her, helping her step off the boat.

"Thank you." The dock swayed slightly underfoot as she landed. Brooke gave his hand a squeeze, then let go.

"You ready?" Ford tipped his head toward the parking lot.

"Yes." The thought of a shower and a bed sounded fabulous. And food. The police had fed them some snacks, but she wanted a meal. A big one.

Ford waved at Max, then led her down the dock to the parking lot. Brooke frowned when they stopped next to his truck.

"How are you going to drive it? Weren't your keys on your boat?"

"They were." Ford pulled on the driver's door handle. "But Max had Sam drop off my spare keys while we were giving our statements." He leaned in and took a set of keys from under the floor mat and held them up.

"Oh."

"Get in." He sat down in the driver's seat and closed the door.

Brooke walked around and climbed in the passenger seat as the truck rumbled to life. He pulled out of the lot while she fastened her seatbelt. The landscape whizzed by and the setting sun peeked through the trees on the short ride to his house. Silence reigned in the cab, but it wasn't uncomfortable. They were both tired from their ordeal. Brooke's mind was still mostly numb.

Ford pulled into his driveway and cut the engine. Brooke got out, not waiting for him, and walked to the front door. He let them inside, then locked the door behind them.

"I'm going to make us something to eat. I could eat a horse." Brooked headed for the kitchen. "Do you have a preference for what you want? Keep in mind, my culinary skills are limited."

"No. Whatever you want is fine. So long as it's quick."

She glanced back, hearing the weariness in his voice. For the first time, she saw the chink in his armor. Now that they were safe, he'd let his guard down, and she could see the toll the last thirty-six hours had taken on him. She frowned. "Hey, are you okay?"

He scrubbed his hands over his face. "Yeah. Nothing some painkillers and sleep won't fix."

She eyed him for several moments, then nodded. "Okay. How about peanut butter, then? I'd say lunch meat sandwiches, but we've been gone almost two weeks. I doubt what's in your fridge is any good."

"Probably not. Peanut butter is fine."

Brooke nodded and walked to the pantry. She found an unopened jar of peanut butter, but no bread. Biting her lip, she glanced around, seeing a box of crackers. She grabbed them and turned to set the items on the island. "I guess we get peanut butter crackers instead."

"I think there's some cheese in the fridge that's still good." Ford walked into the kitchen and opened the refrigerator. Brooke heard him rummaging around, and he came back out with a block of cheese and two apples.

Silently, they worked together to prepare the simple meal, then sat down on bar stools and ate it. Ford finished first.

"I'm going to take a shower and head to bed." He got up and set his plate in the sink. "Good night."

"Oh. Um, good night." A wrinkle creased her forehead as she watched him walk away. An ache started in her chest. She hadn't expected any scintillating conversation, but she also hadn't expected the cold shoulder, either. Maybe he was hurting more than he let on.

Worried, she shoved her last few bites of apple into her mouth and cleaned up their mess, then headed down the hall. Outside his room, she hesitated. Would he appreciate her dropping in to check on him?

She rolled her eyes. Probably not. Ford had a soft center, she'd discovered, but he was also intensely private. Whatever he was going through right now, he'd want to do it alone.

Brooke took a step back from the door, ready to head to her room, when she heard a heavy thump from inside. Concern overrode her desire to give him privacy. She reached for the knob and twisted it, stepping inside the room.

It was empty, but the bathroom door was cracked and the light was on. She could hear the shower running.

"Ford? Are you all right?"

When he didn't respond, she crossed the room and nudged the door open. "Ford?" Anything more she might have said died in her throat as she caught sight of him under the spray of water in the glass-enclosed shower.

He tipped his head out of the spray and blinked, wiping water from his eyes. "Brooke? What are you doing in here?"

"Um." She cleared her throat. "I heard a noise. I thought —" She broke off and shook her head. "You were so tired when you left the kitchen. I just wanted to make sure you were all right. Sorry. I'll leave." She backed up.

"Wait." He opened the door.

Brooke sucked in a sharp breath, eyes widening as she got a full view of his naked frame. But it wasn't because of all the gloriousness that was Ford on display. It was the bruises decorating his ribcage that stole her breath. She hurried forward. "Oh my goodness! Ford! That looks terrible." She reached out and skimmed her fingers over the mottled purple bruising.

He glanced down at her hand. "It looks worse than it is."

He covered her hand, threading his fingers through hers. "I'm all right."

Her gaze met his. "Are you sure? I mean—"

He put a wet finger over her lips. "I'm sure, princess."

The conviction in his voice and in his eyes eased her fears. But that had the unfortunate side effect of allowing her to recognize that he was indeed completely naked. And wet. Every well-defined muscle glistened in the light. She swallowed, trying to wet her suddenly parched throat.

His eyes heated. The finger on her lips traced her cheek, then he slid his hand into her hair. Goosebumps erupted down her neck and spread along her arms. He tugged gently, pulling her closer. Holding her gaze, he leaned in. Brooke stared into his eyes, feeling something pass between them. Before she could analyze it, his mouth was on hers. Her body took over for her brain, and she kissed him back.

It only took her moments to discard her clothes and join him under the hot spray. Water sluiced over her head, washing away the salt and dirt. Ford's lips caressed hers, and his hands roamed. He picked up the soap bar, running it over her body and stirring her to a fevered pitch. Before she could explode, she took it from him and returned the favor, paying extra attention to his tender ribs.

Ford backed up, bringing her with him, and sat down on the tile seat in the shower. Water pummeled her back as she straddled his lap. He cupped her hips in his large palms, guiding her down and running the tip of his shaft through her wet folds. Brooke sucked in a sharp breath. Five minutes ago, she'd been exhausted to the point of passing out. But now? She was wide awake and ready for the ride of her life.

He nipped at her lower lip, then skimmed his lips over her chin and down her neck. When he found that spot behind her ear that sent fire racing through her blood, she couldn't wait anymore. She sank onto him, encasing him in her heat. He groaned, burying his face in the crook of her neck. Brooke clutched his shoulders, holding on for dear life. If she didn't, she feared she'd fly away. Together, they rocked, finding a rhythm that carried them up the wave of bliss.

Pleasure broke, cascading over Brooke like a waterfall. She moaned, going limp in Ford's arms. He groaned, digging his fingers into her hips before going slack. His hands feathered up her spine, holding her close. They sat there, still entwined, for several minutes, before some starch returned to her bones. She put her hands on his chest and pushed back to see his face. He looked at her through hooded eyes.

"We probably should have moved to the bed *before* we did that. Now my muscles don't work."

Brooke smiled and shifted slightly, her bruised knees feeling the hardness of the tile beneath. He stirred within her, making her smile widen. "Well, not all of you doesn't work."

He smacked her butt, the sound echoing off the walls. "Yeah, well, parts of me can't resist you. But you're not getting a repeat anytime soon. My body's finally done." The weariness had crept back into his voice.

She was in the same boat. No matter how good he felt inside her, she couldn't muster up the energy to go for round two. She rose up and stood. "Come on." She held out one hand to him and reached back with the other to shut off the water. "Let's get some sleep."

He took her hand and got up with a groan. "I hope you don't plan to leave too early tomorrow. I think I could sleep till noon."

Her smile turned tight at the reminder she had to go home. "Yeah. I haven't even thought about how I'll get home. I figured I'd do that once I could focus again." She wasn't sure whether Ezra would come get her, or if she'd have to take a commercial flight back to the States. It was all too overwhelming to think about right now.

"Perfect." He snagged a towel from the shelf beside the shower and handed it to her, then took another.

Brooke turned away, afraid he'd see the dismay on her face. She lowered her head and ran the towel over her legs. She would not cry. That could happen when she was back home and alone. Then she would lament the loss of whatever this was. Right now, she wanted to enjoy the time they had left.

Inhaling a deep breath, she ran the towel over her hair, then hung it on the bar beside Ford's and followed him into the bedroom. He flipped off the light, then walked around to his side of the bed. Brooke climbed in beside him, snuggling into his chest.

It was the darkness and the comfort of his arms that was her undoing. The sob stuck in her throat since they got out of the shower broke free.

Ford's hold tightened. He smoothed a hand over her hair. "It's okay, honey. It's over."

She knew he meant the ordeal with Johnathan, but it was a reminder that she'd have to leave him behind. And that bothered her far more than anything that had happened in the last two weeks.

Thirty-Six

The slam of a car door alerted Ford to the arrival of Brooke's ride to the airport. He clenched his teeth, then forced himself to relax. He'd known this was coming. It was inevitable. He couldn't let it bother him.

A knock on the door propelled him forward. In just a few strides, he crossed the living room and answered it, blinking in surprise when he saw who was on the other side. "Ezra."

The other man flashed him a quick smile and walked inside when Ford stepped back so he could enter. Two other men followed. Ford frowned and directed a questioning look at Ezra.

"This is Cyrus and Elliott McGinty. Brooke's grandpa and dad." Ezra gestured to the men.

"Oh." Ford held out a hand. "Nice to meet you."

The other two men offered him smiles and returned his greeting.

"Where's my daughter?" Elliott glanced past Ford.

"She's down at the beach. Said she wanted a few moments to herself." When he told her that Ezra had landed and a car was on its way to collect her, she'd closed up, then said she wanted to take a quick walk. "She should be back any minute." He turned to Ezra. "I thought you were sending a car to get her."

"I did too. But these two couldn't wait to see her." He motioned to the two older gentlemen.

"And yet it seems she's making us wait." Elliott sighed.

"I'm sure it's not intentional, Elliott. She's been through a lot and probably just needed to clear her head." Ezra sent a glance at Ford, his expression telling him he'd surmised there was more going on. The man had an uncanny ability to read the room. Ford thought he'd pulled off the nonchalant thing well, but Ezra saw something to clue him in.

"Of course. It's been a wild couple of weeks. I'll go get her." He backed toward the patio door, but it slid open as he turned.

Brooke froze in the doorway. "Dad. Grandpa." Her gaze flitted to Ezra, then settled on her family.

"Oh, honey!" Elliott hurried forward and pulled her into the house, enveloping her in a fierce hug. Cyrus came up behind him and gave her one when Elliott let her go.

"We were so worried when Ezra told us what was going on. Are you all right?" Cyrus asked.

"I'm fine. Ford kept me safe."

Elliott directed a soft frown at Ford. "I heard his boat blew up. With you on it."

The pit in Ford's stomach took on a sour note. He didn't need the reminder that he'd almost gotten Brooke killed because he let himself get distracted.

"Dad, he pushed me to safety. It could have been much worse." Her amber eyes met his for a brief moment. "And anyway, it's over." She ducked her head and walked around him. "You guys didn't have to come here. I mean, I'm grateful you wanted to come down and fly back with me, but I'm fine." She reached for her purse, the one thing that hadn't been destroyed in the explosion because Ford had asked Edie to lock it and Brooke's cellphone up in her safe. For that, he was grateful. It had her passport in it. Trying to get her a replacement would have been a nightmare since she'd come in under the radar. He knew Ezra paid a guy to put her in the system, but if anyone looked too closely, they might discover the deception.

"So, are we ready to go?" She gave Ezra an expectant look.

Elliott and Cyrus glanced at each other, then looked at Ezra as well.

"Yes, I guess so. Do you have everything?" Ezra glanced around, a furrow between his eyebrows.

She held up her purse. "This is it."

"Okay, then." Ezra held out a hand to Ford. "Thank you for all you did. Keeping her safe."

Ford shook the man's hand and forced a smile onto his face. "Not a problem. Glad I could help."

Elliott cleared his throat. "Yes, thank you."

"You're welcome." Ford gave him a short nod. He wasn't interested in anyone's thanks. He might have started out doing this as a favor to Ezra, but it hadn't ended that way. He looked at Brooke. She stared at her hands wrapped around the handles of her purse. Her fingers worked the leather.

She must have felt his eyes on her, because she glanced up. That amber gaze bewitched him and made him forget the three sets of eyes watching them until Cyrus cleared his throat.

"Shall we be going?"

"Yes." Brooke looked away, smiling at her grandfather. It didn't reach her eyes. She started toward the door, her expression closed off. "Ford, thank you for saving my life. I'll make sure your boat gets replaced."

Anger churned in his gut. She was walking out of his life,

leaving a giant hole behind, and she was worried about his damn boat? Did the last two weeks not even happen for her? Or last night? "Don't worry about it," he growled through clenched teeth. "Have a good life, princess."

Her step faltered, but then she lifted her chin and breezed through the door. Elliott and Cyrus followed. Ezra brought up the rear, pausing with a hand on the doorknob.

"You okay?"

"I'm fine. Have a safe flight." He gave the man a tight smile, then shoved his hands in his back pockets and glanced out the window.

Another beat passed. Ford could feel Ezra's gaze probing the depths of his soul. He threw up all the barriers he could.

Finally, the man nodded. "I'll let you know when we make it back."

Ford didn't respond. A moment later, the door closed, leaving him alone.

The box of emotions in his chest cracked open, making him ache. He sucked in a breath and slapped a board over the crack. Those feelings could stay locked up. He didn't want to look at them or examine them. There was no point. She was gone. Out of his life and never coming back. He'd known this would happen from the start. Even cautioned himself not to get too close. That it would hurt when she left. Well, he'd been right. His heart hurt with every beat. But what could he do? She had a life to get back to thousands of miles away.

And what did he need a woman for, anyway? He was content with his life. Plus, he had a business to rebuild. A new boat to buy. He didn't have time for a relationship, even if she was sticking around.

Angry at himself for even entertaining thoughts of a life with Brooke in it, he spun around and walked out his back door. What he needed was to get back to work. He'd start by cleaning up his house. Some of the storms that blew through while he was away downed some leaves. The patio was a mess.

Finding a trash can and a broom, he got to work. He had plenty to do. More than enough. Definitely no time for a woman. Nope.

THIRTY-SEVEN

It took everything Brooke had to drag herself into the office Monday morning. She'd spent the weekend at home, wallowing in self-pity over what she'd left behind in Costa Rica. She could have stayed in bed again today and done the same thing, but she knew she needed to get back to her life. To her routine. Lamenting what she could never have wouldn't do her any good. Or help her move on.

"Well, hi there, pumpkin." Elliott paused in the doorway to his office as Brooke came down the hall. "I didn't expect to see you in today. I figured you'd take some time off to recover from your ordeal."

She waved a hand and kept walking. He followed her. "I'm fine, Dad. The best thing I can do is get back to my life. Besides, we need to start the search for a new CFO. I don't want to install anyone from Johnathan's office. In fact, we should probably open internal investigations into them all. I can't believe none of them knew what he was doing."

"Actually, I had your assistant already start both those things. Right after Ezra informed us what happened. I have a list of candidates for the job on my desk. As for the internal investigation, only Johnathan's assistant seems to have known what he was up to. Everyone else has checked out so far."

"Oh." She paused at the corner of her desk. "Great." She pasted a smile on her face and set her purse down. "Well, then, I guess I'll just start with my email. I'm sure it's overflowing."

Elliott stood in the doorway and stared at her. The wrinkles in his forehead told Brooke he had something on his mind. She sat down and glanced at him as she logged into her computer. "What is it, Dad? I can see you thinking. Just spit it out."

He opened his mouth and closed it, then wandered into her office and sat down across from her. Brooke let out a tiny sigh and sat back. So much for diving back into her routine.

"Are you sure you're okay to be here?"

"I'm fine."

"You say that, but there's a tightness about your shoulders and to your face. My happy-go-lucky daughter is nowhere to be seen."

"What are you talking about? She's right here." She forced herself to smile and hoped it met her eyes.

He rolled his eyes. "Try again, pumpkin."

She let her smile fall, and her shoulders slumped. "I'm really okay. Mostly. I just need some time."

Elliott let a beat pass. "Have you talked to anyone about what happened? And not just about the part when Cassidy caught up to you."

She stiffened, wondering if he'd caught the undercurrent of something else running between her and Ford the day they left Costa Rica.

"I mean, your fiancé wanted to murder members of your family. Take over this company. Murder you. Doesn't that bother you?"

"Of course it bothers me." The words were out—and

harsher than she thought they'd be—before she could stop them. She huffed and glanced away, picking up a pen to twirl through her fingers. "I was a horrible judge of character. I let my desire for a stable, reliable marriage override my common sense and the little voice niggling at the back of my head that something wasn't right. You and Grandpa almost paid the price for that." She pushed away from her desk and got up, going to the window to stare out at the trees. "It hurts to know it was my fault."

"Honey, none of this was your fault. Johnathan fooled us all. But he's going to pay for what he did, and we're going to get back to our lives." He smacked his thighs and stood. "However, you do not need to do that today."

She turned, frowning at him. "What do you mean?"

"I mean, young lady, you are to take the week off."

"Dad—"

He held up a hand. "It's not a request. I don't want to see you in this office until next week. Go home. Relax. Hang out with your friends. Just decompress. You're still so tightly wound, it's a wonder you aren't powering all the lights in the facility." He smiled, softening his words, and walked closer, taking her face in his hands. "Give yourself a chance to process what happened. Hmm?"

Brooke slouched and blinked furiously, his tenderness bringing up emotions she thought she'd buried. She wanted to protest, but could see on his face he didn't intend to back down. Her shoulders sagged. "Fine."

"That's my girl." He patted her cheek. "Why don't you go up to the lodge? Maybe the solitude and scenery will do you some good. It always was your favorite place."

"Yeah." Escaping to the lodge did hold an appeal. And if she was going to be forced to take time off, she couldn't think of a better place to spend it. She picked up her purse. "Okay. I guess I'll see you next week."

He tipped his head in acknowledgment. "Call if you need something."

She nodded. "I will. Thanks, Dad."

"Anytime, pumpkin." He shooed her toward the door. "Go. Relax. Get your head on straight. When you come back next week, you can help me conduct interviews for our new CFO."

A frown creased her forehead. "Oh. I should probably take the files with me, so I can acquaint myself with the candidates."

"No." Elliott waved his hands. "Forget I said anything."

"But—"

"No. No work. Just relaxation." He ushered her toward the door, pulling it closed behind them.

"Dad."

"Humor me? Please?"

Brooke sighed. "Fine. No work."

"Good. Now shoo."

She chuckled at the pretend stern look on his face. "Yes, sir." Smiling, she waggled her fingers at him and walked away. A week of nothing. She'd either come back in a better frame of mind or go stir crazy. The jury was out on which.

Thirty-Eight

Brooke startled awake at the peal of the doorbell through the lodge. She blinked, then sat up from her spot on the couch. She'd sat down to read and must have fallen asleep.

Yawning, she set her book on the coffee table and got up. The muscles in her neck protested the sudden change in position. She was still sore from her ordeal last week.

The doorbell chimed again.

"I'm coming. Hold your horses," she muttered. Reaching the door, she twisted the lock and pulled it open.

"Hi!" Gemma beamed at her from the doorstep, a bottle of wine in her hands. Mara waved beside her.

"What are you guys doing here?" A faint smile formed on her face at the sight of her two best friends.

"We stopped by your house." Gemma waltzed inside. "You weren't home or answering your phone, so I called Ezra. Got your dad's number. He told me you'd come out here."

"Oh." Brooke offered Mara a quick smile as the other woman trailed her friend inside. She shut the door. "You guys didn't need to come all the way out here. I've just been hanging out. Reading. Sleeping. Must be why I missed your calls." Or it could be the fact that she'd shut her phone off and buried it in her suitcase. When she caught herself looking at work emails for the third time, she knew she needed to do something if she wanted to keep her promise to her dad. Luckily, the lodge had a landline, so she wasn't completely cut off.

"Mmm-hmm." Gemma gave her a dry look and took off her coat.

"I have." Brooke returned her look and crossed her arms.

"Well, whatever you've been doing, we're here to interrupt. Mara and I decided we needed a girls' night."

"That's right." Mara smiled and removed her jacket. "It's been far too long. Besides, you need to fill us in on what happened. All we know is what we learned from Finn when he talked to his friend at the FBI."

Brooke blinked. "What? How did Finn get involved?"

"You suddenly cut off all contact and don't call me back? You don't think I won't ask Ben to look into things?" Gemma scoffed and waved a hand. "I was worried about you. When even he couldn't find you, he called Finn, who put out some feelers at the federal building. Johnathan's name popped up." She shrugged. "That's all we know. Finn wouldn't tell us more, except you were off the map for a bit."

Brooke sighed. "Quite literally." She tipped her head toward the great room. "Come on. Let's crack open that bottle of wine and I'll fill you in." She frowned, looking at the single bottle of white wine in Gemma's hands. "Is that all you brought?"

"Uh-oh." Gemma glanced at the bottle. "This is some tale, isn't it?"

"Yep." Truthfully, she didn't want to get drunk. But comfort food? That she could do, and there was a pint of double chocolate fudge in the freezer with her name on it.

She led them to the kitchen, where Gemma opened the wine while Brooke and Mara located the ice cream and dished up three generous bowls. They took their treats to the big fluffy couches and sat down.

"Okay. We have everything we need for a nice, long chat." Mara tucked her legs underneath herself. "Spill."

Brooke shoved a bite of ice cream into her mouth as she thought about where to start. "A couple weeks ago, I went to Johnathan's after work. We were supposed to go to some charity dinner. I was a little early and Will was still there. They were in Johnathan's office. Anyway, I didn't mean to, but I overheard them talking. About murdering my dad and grandpa so Johnathan could take over the company."

Gemma shook her head and stabbed her ice cream with her spoon. "Low-life piece of crap. I always knew there was something off about that man."

Brooke had come to realize the same thing. She just wished she'd listened to that voice sooner. "Long story short, they caught me eavesdropping, and I ran. I wanted to go to the police, but I didn't think the evidence I had was enough to convince his cop buddies to do anything, so I decided to leave the country. Go somewhere Johnathan couldn't find me until I figured out what to do."

"So, you went to Costa Rica?" Mara asked.

"Well, originally I thought about somewhere in the South Pacific, but Ezra told me he had a friend who could help." Ford's face floated through her mind, and an ache formed in her chest. She missed him.

"Oh, oh, I know that look." Gemma pointed at her.

Brooke frowned. "What look?"

"The one that says you fell in love with this friend."

"What? No. Definitely not." She held up a hand, warding off the idea. It had been a fling, nothing more.

"You can't deny it. We both know that look." Gemma gestured to herself and Mara, who nodded.

"It's true," Mara said. "That's the same look Gemma had

before she and Ben got together. It's the one that said she couldn't get the man off her mind."

"So? Just because I think about him doesn't mean I'm in love with him. He saved my life. More than once. Why wouldn't I think about him?"

"There's thinking about him in a 'I'll never forget him because he saved me' sort of way, and then there's thinking about him in a 'I can't get him off my mind because I miss him with every fiber of my being' sort of way. And I'm betting it's the latter. Am I right?"

Brooke frowned and took a sip of her wine.

"Ha!" Gemma stabbed the air with her spoon. "I knew it! Tell us about him."

"Yes. What's he like? Was it love at first sight?" Mara speared her with an eager look as she lifted another bite of ice cream to her mouth.

Brooke couldn't help the laugh that bubbled free. "You two are like teenagers grilling their friend about her date with some guy she met at summer camp."

The two women laughed.

"Answer the questions," Gemma said, still smiling.

With a sigh, Brooke settled deeper into the cushions. "It was not love at first sight. More like loathing. I did not want to be there, doubly so when I found out Ezra was just going to dump me on the guy. He was surly and bossy. All I wanted was a chance to process what I'd heard, but he made me color my hair"—she held up a hank of her still blonde locks—"and work on his boat. That's actually how we got caught. It was some corporate retreat thing. One of the men ran in Johnathan's circle and recognized me, even with the blonde hair."

"You had to work on his boat? Like, fishing?" Gemma raised an eyebrow.

"No, it was a sunset charter thing. He put me in charge of the food."

Mara's eyes widened. "Did you tell him you only know how to roast sausage and vegetables in the oven and use the microwave?"

Brooke laughed. "I tried, but he wouldn't listen." Her face colored. "I ruined dinner." She laughed. "Well, sort of. We salvaged most of it, but it was a mess."

"So, what happened after that guy recognized you?" Gemma asked.

"Ford went into bodyguard mode. He made some calls, setting up a surveillance net of sorts, then packed us up. We went out on the water, hoping to stay away from everyone until his team could dig up enough evidence on Johnathan to get him arrested. Except he found me first."

"How did that happen, anyway?" Mara lowered her wine glass after taking a drink. "I mean, I get that his friend probably tipped him off that he'd seen you, but once you were on the water, how did they find you?"

"Someone saw us, I guess, when we stopped for supplies. They must have been nearby, and they trailed us out of port. After that, I think it was just dumb luck. Ford's plan had been to go anchor out at sea, but the water was too rough from the weather, so we stayed closer to shore. It kept us safe from the ocean, but made us easier to find."

"So." Gemma waggled her eyebrows and gave Brooke a naughty smile. "What happened while you two were stuck together on that boat?"

Brooke felt her face heat and knew she was beet-red. She cleared her throat. "Um, things. Things happened."

"Good things?" Mara asked.

"God, yes." Need curled low in her belly at the memory of what happened on the boat. And in the shower before she left.

Gemma hummed. "See? I told you we could tell you were in love."

"Good sex does not equal love, Gems."

"No, but it's a start. Tell us about him. Not the sex part, but what he's like. Was he still surly and bossy after you got to know him?"

Brooke lifted a shoulder. "Sometimes. But not really. He's nice. And funny. Smart. So, so smart." She shrugged again and looked down at her bowl. "He's just Ford." She looked up to see Gemma and Mara share a look. "What?"

Her friends smiled at her.

"You're totally in love," Mara said.

Brooke rolled her eyes and shoved a bite of ice cream in her mouth so she wouldn't say something snarky. Didn't they see she wasn't in love? Didn't want to be in love.

But if you aren't in love, what's this ache deep inside that never goes away?

She shoved the voice away and scowled. "It doesn't matter," she told them and herself. "He's thousands of miles away. We lead completely separate lives in different countries."

"What if you didn't, though?" Gemma tipped her head, giving her a speculative look.

Brooke frowned. "What do you mean?"

"Your family owns a resort chain. What's stopping you from opening a resort in Costa Rica?"

"That's ridiculous." Brooke waved her spoon. "It's called Appalachia Resorts for a reason."

Gemma shrugged. "So? Start a spin-off company."

"I can't—that's—" She broke off and frowned. A seed of an idea emerged.

"Brilliant?" Mara finished for her.

Brooke grunted, the idea spinning out in her mind like a spiderweb. Plans and ideas swirled, erupting so fast she couldn't latch on to much of anything.

Gemma patted Brooke's knee and grinned. "You're welcome. Invite us to the wedding. Costa Rica sounds awesome."

With a huff, Brooke lifted her wineglass to her mouth. Dammit. This was not how this week was supposed to go. How was she supposed to get her head on straight and be ready to go back to work when Gemma planted ideas like that in her head?

THIRTY-NINE

Loud music smacked Ford in the face as he walked into Sam's bar, Tripwire. He swore, the only reason Sam kept the music so loud was because he was partially deaf. That, and it discouraged patrons from talking to him. He was the most anti-social bartender Ford had ever met.

Moving through the small crowd, Ford caught the eye of the young man behind the bar, a local named Santiago. The man tipped his chin in acknowledgment. In response, Ford mouthed, "Sam?" Santiago pointed toward the door leading to the back. Ford waved in thanks and pushed through the swinging panel.

The decibel level immediately dropped as the door swung closed behind him. He passed through the kitchen to the office down the hall and rapped his knuckles on the doorframe.

Sam looked up. "Hey."

"Hey. What's up? I got your message."

Sam snorted. "Took you long enough."

Ford shrugged. "You know I don't—"

"Like talking on the phone. Yeah, yeah." He picked up his cell and sent a text.

Ford frowned. "Everything okay?"

"It's fine." He stood up. "Come on." He pushed past Ford and headed for the back door.

"Where are we going? What's going on?"

Sam held the door opened and motioned for Ford to precede him. "An intervention."

"What?" Ford halted abruptly. "What are you talking about?"

"Don't be dense, Commander." Sam rolled his eyes, then pointed to his truck. "Get in."

"I do not need an intervention." Ford crossed his arms and planted his feet.

Sam looked at him over the top of his car. "Seriously? You've been a churlish asshole since Brooke left. Get in the truck." Not waiting for a response, Sam got into the driver's seat and started the engine.

Ford huffed. So he'd been a little short with people. He wouldn't say he'd been an asshole.

The passenger side window rolled down. "Get in, Ford." There was an edge to Sam's voice Ford hadn't heard before. His old friend meant business.

Letting out a low growl, Ford dropped his arms and stalked toward the car. "Fine. But I'm not talking about my *feelings.*" He yanked on the door handle and sank into the seat. Sam pealed out of the parking lot in a cloud of dust as Ford fastened his seatbelt. "Where are we going?"

"Max's."

Not needing more information than that, Ford stared out the window in silence on the short trip through town to Max's house on the hill. Sam turned into the drive and punched in the gate code to let them in. The iron bars swung inward, and he drove through, steering the car up the jungle-lined driveway.

The foliage parted, revealing Max's house—a mansion, really. The cream stucco house with its terra cotta roof screamed, "I'm rich," but if he hadn't seen the way Max lived for himself, Ford never would have guessed Max had money. He was as down-to-earth as they came.

Sam rounded the fountain in the center of the driveway and parked near the front door. He cut the engine and got out. Ford followed him up the steps and they let themselves inside.

"Max?" Sam's voice echoed off the tiled entryway. "I got him. He's not happy about it, so you should probably start pouring the libations."

Ford rolled his eyes. Alcohol wouldn't help. He'd already tried that. All he'd managed to do was to give himself a hangover. The feelings were still there and compounded by the throbbing in his skull the next morning.

Max appeared on the balcony above. "Hey, guys." He rounded the banister and loped down the stairs. "Let's go out by the pool." He led them through the house and out the French doors to the oasis in his backyard. "Have a seat." He motioned to the table set up with drinks and a meal.

Ford's stomach growled. He'd been about to make himself something to eat when he listened to Sam's message and decided to see what his friend wanted first. He was starving.

But this meal came with strings. Suspicious about what their plan was, Ford sat down and eyed his friends. "Say your piece."

Sam and Max shared a look. Max picked up his water glass and took a drink before leaning back to pin Ford with a stare.

"I don't have time for this." Ford pushed his chair back.

"Oh, sit down, Wags. We're not here to lambast you about your attitude. We just want to help."

Hands on the armrests, Ford's gaze bounced between his friends. They both seemed determined, but not angry. "Fine." He scooted his chair back in and picked up his fork. "But I'm eating while you talk. It's been a long time since lunch." And it would help him hide whatever emotions crossed his face while they did so.

The two men shared a look again before Max spoke. "It's been a month now since Brooke left. We were hoping with time you'd process what happened, but if anything, you've just gotten surlier. Enough that your customers have noticed."

Ford stilled for a moment, then scooped up a bite of the paella on his plate. "If you're talking about that group of eco-tourists, the one guy was a total jerk. I fish responsibly, and as yet, there's no alternative to plastic fishing line."

"I'm not talking about him. I'm talking about that young couple here on their honeymoon. The one with the wife who was about Brooke's age? Blonde?"

"And? I never took them out. What did she have to complain about?" He'd talked to them when they came in to the office only long enough to know they wanted to take a half-day fishing trip before Max took over. "You made their reservation."

"Yes, and after you left, the husband commented on your churlishness. Asked if you were okay. I saw the look you gave the wife. She made you think of Brooke, so you reverted to the cloak of anger you've had around yourself since she left."

"I'm not angry."

"Oh, bullshit," Sam said. "You are too. And you need to deal with it. Because right now, you suck, Ford."

Blowing out a long breath, Ford laid his fork down and sat back. He turned his head, staring at the glassy water in the pool. So he'd been a little—off.

"It might help to talk about it," Max said.

Ford looked at him. "I already told Sam I wasn't going to

talk about my feelings. I'll deal with things and be fine soon enough."

"Really?" Max arched an eyebrow. "Because it's been a month, and you're worse now than when we came back." He leaned forward on his forearms. "Just admit you miss her and you made a mistake letting her leave."

Ford's eyebrows dipped in a fierce frown. "What was I supposed to do? Tie her to my boat? Oh, wait. I couldn't, *because it blew up.*"

Max heaved a sigh. "Ford, you're not mad about the boat."

"Of course I'm mad about the boat. The *Hooker* was the real moneymaker of my little fleet."

"Right, but Brooke replaced it. I saw the new one when it arrived a couple weeks ago. Why haven't you used it?" Sam asked.

Ford's mouth flattened as he thought about the gleaming white, deep-sea fishing boat in his slip at the marina. He hadn't even been onboard yet. He couldn't bring himself to step foot onto it.

"We think it's because it reminds you of her." Max lifted his water glass and took a drink, arching a dark eyebrow over the rim.

They weren't wrong.

"So, the question is, what are you going to do about that? That's a mighty fine boat she sent you. Have you thanked her?" Max asked.

"No. Why should I? It's her fault the first one blew up." He crossed his arms and looked at the pool again. He knew he sounded like a child, but he didn't want to think about Brooke.

"Again, bullshit." Sam slapped the table, making the place settings jump.

"Sam's right. You're just sore she's gone. I think you fell for her and it hurts too much for you to think about her."

Everything Ford had locked away the moment Brooke walked out of his house rose to the surface. "Of course it hurts!" He pushed away from the table and stood up, pacing toward the pool. He whirled to glare at his friends. "That little minx took her pretty little hands and"—he lifted his hands and tangled his fingers together wildly—"to my heart. It's so jumbled up, I don't know how I feel. Except I know there's a hole that wasn't there before. It's like the light went out on the world." Everything just felt—dull.

Sam and Max shared another look. A sly smile spread over Max's face. "You know how you fix that, right? You go after her."

Ford scoffed. "To what end, Max? Tell me how we mesh our lives when hers is there and mine is here? Are we just supposed to be satisfied with phone calls and short visits a few times a year? That's not any way to have a relationship."

"You're right, it's not. But denying yourself—and her—the chance at real happiness isn't right, either."

"I am happy," Ford growled.

The two men laughed.

"No," Sam said. "You're not."

Ford glared. "So, what should I do? Give up everything I've built here? Move to Asheville? And do what? River fishing charters? Work as a security guard? I'm happy here."

"We get that," Max said. "But things have changed. You have changed. And you need to reconcile your feelings for her with your life. Because right now, they're at odds and eating away at you. It's not healthy."

"Yeah," Sam muttered. "For any of us."

Some of the fight left Ford at Sam's quiet words. "I'm sorry. I know I've been a bit of a bear."

Max tipped his head. "Mildly, yes."

Ford ran a hand over his jaw, feeling the rasp of his short

beard. "I'll think about what you said, okay? And I promise to not be so…" He flipped a hand back and forth.

"Asshole-ish?" Sam said.

Ford chuckled. "Yes. That."

"Good." Max gave a short nod. "Now sit down and eat. Did you see the playoff game between the Reds and Diamondbacks last night? I was on the edge of my seat the entire time."

"That was a hell of a catch by the Reds' centerfielder, right?" Sam said.

Ford sat down and picked up his fork again, listening to his friends discuss baseball while his mind mulled over what they'd said. What *did* he want?

He didn't have an answer yet, but Max and Sam were right. He needed to figure that out. This state of flux would eat him alive if he didn't.

FORTY

Brooke curled deeper into the blanket she'd wrapped herself in to ward off the chilly, early November wind. She took a sip of the hot chocolate in the slate-blue mug she held, and a soft smile spread over her face as she watched the sunset. This was the most content she'd been since she returned from Costa Rica. The ache of leaving Ford behind was still there, but with the help of her friends and family, and lots of days and nights at the lodge, she was on the mend.

She took another sip of her cocoa, letting the steam warm her chilled nose. She'd probably have to go in soon, but not yet. Everything but her nose was toasty warm.

"You know, after everything you went through, I'd have thought you'd be more careful about your security."

Brooke jumped at the sound of the voice coming up the stairs to her right. Hot chocolate sloshed over the rim of her cup, and she shook her hand. The pain didn't register, though, because the owner of the voice captivated all her senses. She blinked twice, thinking she was seeing things. "Ford?"

"Hi, princess." He stopped at the top of the stairs, looking just like she remembered, just more covered up in deference to the colder weather.

"What are you doing here? How did you know where to find me?"

"Ezra." He walked closer.

"Of course," she muttered. That man would make a better chief of security than chief pilot. He had his thumb on the pulse of everything.

"As to why I'm here, well, that's a little more complicated."

She frowned, not tracking. Then a thought occurred to her. "Is there something wrong with the boat I had delivered to you? If it's got a problem—"

He held up a hand. "It's not the boat." He gestured to the chair next to her. "May I sit?"

"Um, sure." She eyed him warily as he sat down, wondering what was going on.

"This is nice. Quiet. It's a little cold, though." He sent a half-smile her way.

His attempt at levity slid right past her. She was too confused. "Why are you here?"

He puffed out his cheeks and ran his hands over his jean-clad thighs. Brooke's frown deepened. He seemed nervous.

"Ford, is everything okay?" Her eyes widened. "One of your team. Are they—"

Again, he held up a hand. "Everyone's fine. Peeved at me because I've been a bit of a jerk the last few weeks, but fine."

"You've been a jerk to your friends? Why?"

He let out a low laugh. "Because I missed you." He didn't look at her when he said it. Just stared out at the sunset.

Her eyes grew round, and her heart skipped, then raced. "What?" He couldn't be here because he missed her. Could he?

"Max and Sam—they cooked up a plan and got me alone. Told me in no uncertain terms I needed to deal with my shit and figure out how I felt about you. And then do something about it." He looked at her then. "So, here I am. Doing something about it."

Brooke blinked, her mouth agape. She knew she looked like some sort of fish statue that spewed water from its mouth, but she couldn't help it. It was like someone pressed pause on her brain. Her mind refused to process anything he just said.

"Brooke?"

She snapped her mouth shut and looked away, raising her mug to her lips. She took a drink, her mind now spinning. From the side of her eyes, she perused him. He looked good. Nervous, but well. The exhaustion that had been in every line of his body the last time she saw him was gone. The broad-shouldered man who looked like he could take on all her demons was back. And looked damn sexy in that gray wool peacoat. She took another drink of her cocoa.

"You're going to make me spell this out, aren't you?"

"Yep. Because I'm confused."

"It's actually not that complicated. I miss you, so here I am."

Her stupid heart galloped at his words. They didn't mean anything. They couldn't. "I've missed you, too, but Ford—" She stopped, shaking her head. She didn't know how to put it into words without sounding dismissive.

He sat up and reached for her hands, folding his larger ones around hers and her mug. "I know we lead different lives in different parts of the world. But Brooke, my life in Costa Rica... it's nothing without you. It's dull and has no joy. You took that and the light with you when you left. It just took me a bit to realize I need it. And you." He shook his head. "I live in the most beautiful place in the world, but it's nothing without you there."

"Oh, Ford." Her voice came out thick with emotion.

Heart hammering in her chest with a hope she didn't want to believe, she blinked, then sniffed, looking away.

"Princess, I know what you're going to say. Your life is here. And that's fine. I wouldn't come here asking you to give everything up for me."

That brought her eyes around to his again. "What? Wait. Are you saying you—you want to move here? Ford! No. You love Costa Rica."

"I do. But I love you more."

All the air left Brooke's lungs and her mind returned to freeze-frame mode.

He smiled. "I see I've shocked you. Who knew a declaration of love was what it took to make Brooke McGinty speechless?" His expression sobered and turned earnest. He reached out and fingered a lock of her now brown hair. "But it's true. After Sam hauled me to Max's and they laid into me about my attitude, I went home that night and laid awake, thinking. About what happened. My past. My life in Golfito. You. And once I sorted through all the noise, there you were. Everything pointed me back to you. And nothing else made any sense without you there to share it with. I don't want it if you're not there."

She clutched her mug, the tips of her fingers turning white. Ford took the cup from her hands and set it on the table, then threaded their fingers together. The light over the back door blinked on as the sun descended behind the trees, bathing his face in a golden glow. It bounced off the highlights in his wavy brown hair. Her heart clenched as a wash of emotion flooded her. "You'd really do that? Give up everything to come here?"

"To be with you, yes."

"I can't ask you to do that." Especially not when there was another way. That plan that had been percolating in her mind since Gemma and Mara's visit a week ago surged forward to stand front and center.

"You're not." Some of the earnestness left his expression. "I—"

Brooke laid a finger over his firm lips, wanting to cut off his line of thinking. She wasn't rejecting him, and she could see that's where his mind was going from the wariness that had crept into his eyes. "I love you, too, Ford."

He stilled, and she dropped her hand.

"I'm thrilled that you want us to be together. But I don't want you to give up your life for me."

"But—"

"Let me finish?"

Curiosity swirled in his light eyes, and he nodded.

"My friend Gemma said something to me last week, and it got me thinking. I probably would be on a plane to you soon if you hadn't beaten me to it."

"Oh?"

She nodded. "She and my friend Mara—like your friends —badgered me until I admitted how I felt about you, then they reminded me that my family owns a resort chain."

His brows knit together. "I researched your family while you and Edie went shopping. Aren't most of the resorts in the eastern U.S.?"

"They are, but we have a few holdings elsewhere in the world. But none in Costa Rica. Yet."

Recognition dawned in his eyes, along with a glimmer of hope. She let a slow, happy smile bloom over her face.

"You want to open a resort in Golfito?"

"I do. Do you think the local government would be amenable to that?"

"Actually, yes. So long as it's eco-friendly to support the sort of tourism they want there. We've seen more and more visitors the last several years. An eco-lodge resort would be welcome, I think."

"Good. Because I already put the legal team on it. They're researching regulations and properties as we speak."

The hope in his eyes blossomed and a wide smile spread over his face. "Seriously?"

She nodded. "Yep." She leaned into him, looping her arms around his neck. "You know, this endeavor of mine is going to mean I'll be spending a lot of time down there. I'll need a place to stay."

He hummed, dipping his head. "Really? I can think of a spot for you."

"Yeah? I hope it comes with a super comfy king-size bed and a sexy, naked man who loves me."

"Oh, it does."

Brooke's happy laugh died in her throat as he swooped in and kissed her. But it couldn't stop the elation filling her heart. She pushed back and stood. "In the meantime, there's one of those super comfy king-size beds inside. I think we should get a head start."

"That's a wonderful plan, princess." In one smooth, swift movement, he stood and scooped her into his arms, blanket and all.

Brooke let out a surprised shriek, then laughed as he hurried into the house.

Thank you for reading Ford's Fight. Do you want to read Ezra's story for FREE? Join my mailing list! His story, Stranded with Ezra, is EXCLUSIVE to my subscribers! You can find the sign-up form on my website, ashleyaquinn.com. My list also receives sneak peeks of my latest work and access to exclusive giveaways. Also, please consider leaving a rating or review on Amazon and or Goodreads for Ford's Fight. It would be greatly appreciated!

Thanks again for reading!
    - Ashley

~

Keep reading for a sneak peek at Dean's Dilemma in the Wagner Brigade Series.

Dean's Dilemma

Wagner Brigade
Book 2

PROLOGUE

FIFTEEN YEARS AGO...

"Wendy, please. Don't go. You're too upset." Annabeth Swenson held her older sister's hands as she pleaded with her to stay. "You can talk to him tomorrow. I think you should just try to get some sleep."

Wendy shook free of Annabeth's hold. "Like I'll really be able to sleep. I'll just lie awake, thinking about—" She stopped and shook her head. "No. He can't use me all year, then dump me like a piece of garbage because I don't fit into his plan. Not now."

"What do you mean? I don't understand. You were ready to dump him just last week!"

"That was then." Wendy picked up her jacket and put it on. "Things have changed."

Annabeth frowned. "They have? How?"

"I can't say. Not yet. But trust me, they have." She pulled her long, toffee-colored locks free of her jacket collar. "I need to find him. Make him see reason."

"Wendy, no." Annabeth blocked the door. "Please stay

here. I'll stay too. We can have a sleepover and just talk. I can get my roommate to cover for me. The dorm monitors will never know." Which was true. It wouldn't be the first time Annabeth had spent the night in her sister's dorm without them knowing. Sneaking things past the women who were supposed to enforce the dormitory rules was ridiculously easy.

"Not tonight, Annie. I really need to talk to Johnathan. It's important. Now, move, please?" Wendy softened her tone and gave Annabeth a sad puppy look with her bright blue-gray eyes.

But Annabeth wouldn't be swayed. "No. I just have a bad feeling about you going out. You're too worked up. I don't want you to do something you'll regret." She loved her sister, but Wendy could have a temper.

Wendy huffed and cocked out a hip, propping one hand on it. "I'm fine. Yes, I'm angry. Seething, in fact. But really, what am I going to do to him besides yell? Stab him?" She rolled her eyes. "Get real. Now, move." Her voice had a harder edge to it, the attempt at charm now long forgotten.

Annabeth crossed her arms. "No."

Wendy's eyes took on a glint Annabeth hadn't seen before. A shiver of unease went down her spine.

"Listen, you little brat. I don't need you to look out for me. I'm a grown-up, and in a week, I'll be completely on my own. Out of this damn school and in a place of my own. With Johnathan. He is my future. Nothing you or he says will change that. Now either you move or I'll move you."

Wendy and Johnathan were moving in together? Annabeth stared at her sister in shock. That was news to her.

"Annie," Wendy growled.

Annabeth searched her sister's eyes, but all she saw was steadfast determination. She would indeed move Annabeth out of her way to get what she wanted.

"Fine." Annabeth stepped to the side, getting angry now.

She hated it when Wendy treated her like a little kid. She might be three years younger, but she wasn't as naïve as Wendy thought. "But please don't do anything stupid."

Wendy gave a mirthless laugh as she opened the door. "Too late, little sister. Much, much too late." She closed the door.

Frowning, Annabeth stared at the wooden door. What did she mean by that? What had she done?

With a sigh, Annabeth tipped her head back and stared at the ceiling for a long moment, then shook her head. Whatever it was, Wendy would tell her when she was ready. Letting out a soft, frustrated growl, Annabeth grabbed her backpack off the floor by the desk and shoved her books inside. One thing was for sure—she wasn't going to sit here and wait for her to come back. Or make excuses with the dorm monitor about where she was. Wendy could explain that when she got back. She might have a week until she graduated, but until then, she still had to abide by the school's rules or face the consequences. And considering how much of a bitch she'd just been, Annabeth hoped she did get in trouble.

Slamming the door behind her, she strode down the hall and outside, crossing the courtyard to her own dorm. She swiped her key card through the reader and yanked the door open, then ran upstairs, using her card again to get into her room.

Her roommate, Olivia, looked up as she entered. "Hey— whoa. What happened?"

"My sister's bitch and an idiot, that's what." Annabeth threw her bookbag down, then sank onto her bed with a huff. "She's off chasing after Johnathan. Says she won't let him dump her."

Olivia frowned. "Didn't she hate his guts last week because she thought he was cheating on her and wanted to dump him?"

"Yep." She flopped back on her mattress and sighed. "I'm done trying to figure it out, though. If she wants to screw up her life and stay with that cheating asshole, then fine. But I'm not wasting anymore breath trying to convince her not to." She sat up. Her feet hit the floor, and she stood, moving to her armoire. "I'm going to take a shower and go to bed."

"You sure? We can stay up and talk if you want?"

"No. It'll just make me angrier. I don't want to put anymore energy into it. I'm going to shower, put my head-phones on and just"—she fluttered a hand—"try to think about something else." She grabbed clean clothes and shut the door.

"If you're sure..." Olivia's voice trailed off.

"I am." Annabeth offered her a soft smile. "Thanks, though."

"Of course. You're my friend. I don't like seeing you upset."

"You're the best, Liv."

Olivia grinned. "Don't forget it."

Chuckling, and feeling a little less angry, Annabeth grabbed her shower caddy, then left the room and went down the hall to their shared bathroom. She picked her favorite shower room and shut the door, then drew back the curtain and turned the water on to boiling. She'd let the water erase the rest of her anger. Stripping out of her clothes, she stepped into the spray and shut the curtain.

Twenty minutes later, feeling like a boiled lobster, she figured she should leave some water for the others and shut off the tap. Drying off, she put her pajamas on and went back to her room.

"Feel better?" Olivia asked. She got up and picked up her shower things.

"I do."

"Good."

Annabeth offered her a smile and picked up her headphones as her roommate left. She scrolled through her iPod and found the playlist she wanted, then scooted under her covers and turned off the lights. Liv had left on her small bedside lamp, so Annabeth didn't feel bad about plunging the room into darkness. She wouldn't kick any furniture coming in with that little light on.

Yanking her comforter up, Annabeth buried herself and closed her eyes. Wendy's face popped into her head. With a growl, she snuggled deeper and focused on the music.

Think about something else. Like your finals tomorrow. She had to get through the next couple of days, Wendy's graduation, then she could go back to the Vineyard with her parents and spend the summer on the beach.

But no matter what she did, her mind kept going back to Wendy, and it wasn't until well after midnight that she drifted off.

The next morning, one glance out the window was all it took to bring last night's argument back. Her sister's dorm was right across the courtyard. Grimacing, Annabeth moved away from the window and got ready for the day. She had a few minutes before she needed to head to breakfast, so she'd go check on Wendy. See if she was doing all right.

God, she was so stupid. Why was she even bothering? Wendy hadn't cared that she was upset last night. Why should Annabeth care if she was okay this morning?

But her feet still carried her across the courtyard and into Wendy's building. She hurried down the hall to her sister's room and knocked. No one answered, so she knocked again. "Wendy, it's me."

"She's not there."

Annabeth glanced back and saw Wendy's roommate, Stella, coming out of the bathroom. "Oh. I guess I'll wait until she's done." She nodded toward the door from which Stella emerged.

"She's not there, either."

"What? Did she leave already?"

Stella walked closer. "I haven't seen her. She was gone when I got in last night and still gone—or gone again—when I got up."

Annabeth frowned. "Okay. I guess I'll check the mess hall. If you see her, tell her to find me?"

"Sure." Stella swiped her key card and entered her room, leaving Annabeth standing in the hall.

Turning, she headed for the door. She had to eat anyway, so hopefully, she could kill two birds with one stone. As she neared the exit, the dorm monitor's door opened and a police officer emerged. Annabeth slowed and moved closer to the wall to edge past.

"Oh! Annabeth! There, officer, that's her sister." The dorm monitor's voice carried through the doorway.

Dread punched Annabeth in the stomach. She stopped and looked at the policeman.

"You're Wendy Swenson's sister?"

Annabeth licked her lips and nodded. "Yes. What's this about?"

"Oh, honey." The matronly woman the school employed for Wendy's dorm, Miss Blumenthal, pushed past the officer and came toward Annabeth with her arms outstretched. "I'm so sorry." Her red-rimmed eyes registered in Annabeth's mind a moment before the woman enveloped her in a hug.

"Miss, I'm sorry to inform you; your sister's been killed in a car accident."

The man's words echoed through her brain like a shout in an empty hall. It bounced off every corner of her mind and made her ears ring. "Wendy's dead?"

Miss Blumenthal nodded and hugged her tighter.

No. It couldn't be. She sucked in a sharp breath. "You're sure it was Wendy?"

"Yes." The officer nodded. "The woman in the car matches the driver's license we found with her. I'm sorry."

Pressure mounted in her face, and tears welled in her eyes. "No," she whispered. Annabeth sniffed hard. She couldn't lose it. Not here. "Um, was she alone?"

The officer's gaze sharpened. "Was she supposed to be?"

"Maybe. She left here looking for her boyfriend, Johnathan Cassidy."

Miss Blumenthal straightened and wiped her face. "I knew that boy was a good for nothing waste of her time."

The officer cast a glance at her, then looked at Annabeth again. "She was alone, yes. Whether she talked to him, we don't know, but we'll track him down. Maybe he can give us some insight into her mental state. We're not sure how the accident happened. Hers was the only car involved."

The need to cry hit Annabeth with renewed vigor. She choked back a sob and pushed away from Miss Blumenthal. "Excuse me." Pressing the back of her hand to her mouth, she dashed out of the building. One thought played on repeat in her mind: she should have tried harder to stop Wendy from leaving.

ONE

Dean Adler shoved the laptop away and stood. Walking to the window in his hotel room, he nudged the curtain aside with one finger and looked out. Cars whizzed by on the highway just beyond the parking lot, the noise muffled by the thick glass and brick building.

Pensive, he glanced back at his computer. He'd just gone over everything he'd forwarded to Asher about what he learned about Johnathan and Will Cassidy. It was enough to give the police leverage in their investigation into the brothers, but something still bugged him.

When Asher sent him back to the States to dig up dirt on the man terrorizing the woman Ezra Chastain brought down to Costa Rica for Ford to protect, Dean figured he'd find a history of cheating. Maybe some palm greasing to encourage the authorities to look the other way here and there. And he'd found both those things. But Johnathan Cassidy's misdeeds went back much further than just the last couple of years; and they involved his younger brother, Will.

He moved away from the window and back to the desk, staring down at the laptop screen. Smiling gray-blue eyes stared back at him from the grainy online newspaper photo. The young woman, Wendy Swenson, had been Johnathan's high school girlfriend. She'd died in a car accident a week before they graduated. And she'd been pregnant. After what Dean had learned about the Cassidy's, he had his suspicions about what happened. At first glance, it sounded like what it was—a tragic accident. But something about it didn't sit right with him. How did a young woman lose control of her car on a clear night on a road she'd traveled many times before? He supposed the police's theory that she was angry and distracted was plausible, but Dean just didn't buy it.

Glancing away, he drummed his fingers on the desk. He had a decision to make. Go home or stay and dig into Wendy Swenson's death. His head told him to go home. It had been a week since he sent the information to Asher, and his investigation here had stalled. Remaining in the States and looking into Wendy's accident would lead him on a path to nowhere, he had a feeling. But still, his gut told him to stay.

Dean sighed and scrubbed a hand over his face. If he went home, this case would haunt him, and he'd regret not pursuing it. "Dammit." He reached for his phone. His boss, Sam Brackley, wouldn't like that he'd be down a bartender longer than expected, but he'd understand. He dialed Sam's number.

The thump of a heavy beat came over the line, almost drowning out Sam's voice. "Brackley."

"Sam, it's Dean. Listen. You know all that information I sent to Asher on Cassidy?"

"Yeah?"

"Something I uncovered—it just doesn't sit right. I'm staying here a little while longer to look into it."

"What? Hang on." The noise receded to a dull roar.

"Okay, that's better. What are you talking about? What did you find?"

"Cassidy's high school girlfriend died in a car accident right before they graduated. Autopsy said she was pregnant. Something doesn't feel right."

"You thinking it wasn't an accident?"

"Maybe. On paper it looks like one, but after what I've learned about Johnathan Cassidy, I'm not so sure. The man's a real piece of work. I want to stay a little longer. See what I can find out."

"After all this time? Dean, there can't be any evidence left."

"Probably not, but I need to try."

Sam let out a long sigh. "All right, fine. Martina was asking if she could work some extra shifts, anyway."

"Good. I'm glad it'll work out."

Sam scoffed. "Yeah. Just don't stay too long. I don't think she meant indefinitely."

"Copy that. Thanks, Sam."

"Yep."

"How are things down there with Ford?" The pseudo-boss of their unofficial protection agency was out on a boat with Johnathan Cassidy's fiancé, keeping her safe after she overheard him planning to murder members of her family.

"Fine for now. I haven't talked to him, but he calls Asher every night. They're out on the far side of the Osa Peninsula, just waiting. Hopefully, the information you said you sent will be enough to end things."

"I hope so too. Okay. I'll stay in touch. Let you know what I find out."

"Sounds good. Be careful, Dean. The Cassidys have a lot of money. They might not like you digging around in their son's life."

Probably not. "Will do. Talk to you soon."

"Bye."

The line clicked in Dean's ear, and he lowered the phone. His gaze went to Wendy Swenson again. It didn't matter whether the Cassidys would like his actions. Or what they tried to do to stop him. He couldn't let her death go unpunished if she was murdered. Dean tapped the computer screen. "I will find out what he did to you. I promise."

About the Author

Ashley started writing in her teens and never stopped. Her first novel, Smoky Mountain Murder, came out in 2016, and she has since published two more series and has plans for more. When not writing, you can find her with her nose stuck in a book or watching some terrible disaster movie on SyFy. An avid baseball fan, she also enjoys crafting and cooking. She lives in Ohio with her husband, two kids, three cats, and one very wild shepherd mix.

Website: https://ashleyaquinn.com

goodreads.com/ashleyaquinn

amazon.com/Ashley-A-Quinn/e/B07HCT4QST

Ford's Fight

Dean's Dilemma

www.ingramcontent.com/pod-product-compliance
Lightning Source LLC
Chambersburg PA
CBHW021308190726
48288CB00003B/739